Twisted Sisters

Other Titles by *New York Times*
Bestselling Author Jen Lancaster

JEN
LANCASTER

Twisted
Sisters

New American Library

New American Library
Published by the Penguin Group
Penguin Group (USA) LLC, 375 Hudson Street,
New York, New York 10014

USA | Canada | UK | Ireland | Australia | New Zealand | India | South Africa | China
penguin.com
A Penguin Random House Company

First published by New American Library,
a division of Penguin Group (USA) LLC

First Printing, February 2014

 REGISTERED TRADEMARK—MARCA REGISTRADA

LIBRARY OF CONGRESS CATALOGING-IN-PUBLICATION DATA:
Lancaster, Jen, 1967–
Twisted sisters/Jen Lancaster.
    p. cm.
ISBN 978-0-451-23965-5 (hardback)
1. Sisters—Fiction. 2. Families—Fiction. 3. Success—Fiction. I. Title.
PS3612.A54748T95 2014
813'.6—dc23   2013033481

Printed in the United States of America
10 9 8 7 6 5 4 3 2 1

Set in Sabon
Designed by Spring Hoteling

For JSS and JPK, my sisters by choice

I don't believe an accident of birth makes people sisters or brothers. It makes them siblings, gives them mutuality of parentage. Sisterhood and brotherhood is a condition people have to work at.

—*Maya Angelou*

Big sisters are the crabgrass in the lawn of life.

—*Charles M. Schulz*

Me and my sisters all have such different body types.

—*Kim Kardashian*

Twisted
Sisters

Prologue

"Do I know you?"

The well-appointed woman peers at me over her Whole Foods shopping cart, brimming with free-range chicken, organic fruit, and glass-bottled Kombucha.

I'm not surprised she's finally asking. She *seems* like someone who'd recognize me, clad in the unofficial Lincoln Park Trader's Wife uniform of perfectly buttery-blond ponytail, high-speed sneakers, Lululemon, and more ice than you'd find in your garden-variety cocktail. I noticed her watching me while I debated between frisée and spring-mix greens and then later when I perused wild-caught salmon. (Naturally, I buy only seafood approved by the Monterey Bay Aquarium's Seafood Watch Program. And who wouldn't? Sustainability *matters*.)

She continues, "I'm so sorry—this is weird, right? But I feel like I know you somehow." She taps a couple of expertly manicured fingers on her artificially enhanced lips as she tries to piece together our connection.

I smile beatifically, as this sort of thing happens to me *all the time*; it's one of the complications of being a local celebrity. I find that people have a lot more fun when they finally determine who I am on their own, so I opt not to offer any clues.

"Did you graduate from Maine South High School?"

Public school? Oh, honey. No. But bless your heart for marrying up.

I shake my head. "I attended Taylor Park Academy." I don't mention that this is Chicago's most infamous Ivy League feeder school, as anyone who cares is already familiar with their commitment to academics.

She furrows her brow and searches my face. "Hmm . . . did you go to Northern?"

Again, a great big *no* here. I attended the University of Chicago for undergrad and master's, even though I was accepted to Yale and Stanford, too. Clearly, Taylor Park Academy is no joke. Had Obama not been elected for a second term, this is where his kids would matriculate. However, I'm a public figure, so I'm loath to make this potential fan feel bad about her subpar education.

"No, I'm afraid not."

It's irrelevant to mention that my older sister, Mary Magdalene, attended Northern. Of course, she was there for only a year before she dropped out to marry her high school boyfriend.

(Ahem, *shotgun wedding*, ahem.)

Presently, Mary Mac—that's what we call her for short—has churned out more kids than I can count. It's like she's a hoarder, only for children. In terms of personal achievement, she's pretty much the patron saint of minivans and stretch marks. What is that meme I've seen about the prolific *19 Kids and Counting* mother? Ah, yes, "It's a vagina, not a clown car." Add one persecution complex, stir, and, boom! Meet my older sister.

Among numerous others, Mary Mac and her contractor husband, Mickey, have a couple of identical ginger daughters named Kacey Irelyn and Kiley. I can't tell them apart for the life of me, so I generally just refer to both of them as Kiley Irelyn. Perhaps if the little ingrates sent thank-you notes when I gave them birthday presents, I'd be better able to determine who's who. But apparently American Girl dolls grow on trees in that house, so my efforts are thus unrecognized.

Anyway.

I still have to pick up pasture-raised eggs and a probiotic supplement, then bring everything home to refrigerate before my call time, so I need to move this along. I volunteer, "Perhaps we met at Pepperdine?"

Before I can even mention their doctorate program, I see a flash of recognition in her face and I steel myself for the inevitable, ready to tell her, no, I did *not* major in *Battle of the Network Stars*. Because that joke wasn't already old the second my younger sister, Geri, first uttered it a decade ago.

Let me ask you: how is it a negative that my college campus, situated on a Malibu bluff overlooking the Pacific, was so bucolic that ABC simply had to film their campy television battles there in the seventies and eighties? I chose Pepperdine *not* because Scott Baio ever pitched a javelin there, but because they have one of the top psychology programs in the country.

I mean, there I was, paying for my PsyD with grants and loans I'd garnered on my own, on my way to becoming Dr.

Reagan Bishop, and did anyone in my family give me the credit I deserved? No! Instead, they all brayed like jackasses, congratulating bratty teenaged Geri on her hilarious quips.

Bah-ha-ha! Battle of the Network Stars! *Hey, Reagan, will you take Greg Evigan's classes on potato-sack races or will it be obstacle courses with William Shatner?*

Seriously?

I'm a licensed psychologist; Geri's a licensed *cosmetologist.*

I deal with what's inside the human head; she concentrates on what's on top of it.

Plus, Geri was barely three years old when the iconic TV battles ended back in 1988. In theory, she's not capable of discerning a Charlene Tilton from a Tina Yothers. I suspect long-suffering Mary Mac fed her that line. Mary Mac and Geri are a decade apart and haven't a thing in common, save for a love of pop culture, a lack of ambition . . . and a grudge against me.

I've counseled my fair share of families in which the siblings' alliances are constantly realigning. Most often, this is due to the perception of the parents' having picked a favorite, regardless of how inadvertent the choice may be. The other siblings get caught up in the injustice of not being in the spotlight. As the spotlight shifts, so do alliances.

Of course, this has never been the case with the Bishop girls. Those two have been Team NotReagan since day one. From choosing what TV show to watch to deciding what color to paint our bedroom, Geri and Mary Mac have always cast their votes together, neatly eclipsing any opinion I might have had. Of course, I'd get them back come birthday time, requesting mile-high peanut butter pie for my dessert because of Geri's nut allergy. Ha! No pie for you!

(Side note? It's my professional opinion that Geri's been faking her supposed nut sensitivity ever since there were fixings enough for only one ham sandwich for our packed school lunches.)

Anyway, since my family never seems to appreciate what I've accomplished, please allow me to blow my own horn for a minute. (I try to practice self-validation whenever possible because it's an important ingredient in cultivating positive self-esteem.) Not only did I skip a grade in elementary school, graduate from Taylor Park, and garner two degrees at U of C in four and a half years, but I also received my PsyD with highest honors. While my classmates were still muddling through their clinical training, I was already in private practice, being named one of Chicago's Top Doctors by *Chicago* magazine. And that's how Wendy Winsberg found me.

Yes, *that* Wendy Winsberg, grande dame of daytime talk television for almost three decades and, according to *Forbes*, the number one entry on their 100 Most Powerful Women list. When she finally burned out on hosting a daily show herself, she formed the WeWIN cable network with a plethora of what she calls "fempowering" television for women.

The crown jewel in her lineup is the breakout show *I Need a Push*, in which participants learn to become their best selves by overcoming obstacles and changing behaviors. They also receive sassy haircuts and wardrobe makeovers, but that's really not my department.

As for my role?

To quote Tina Fey, I'm a pusher, meaning I'm the one who manifests the push.

Two and a half years ago, I put my practice on hold and became one of the show's lead psychologists. Although I miss taking private patients, I excel equally at working in depth with the participants. In my old practice, I spent an hour a week with my clients. That's barely enough time to scratch the surface on someone's latent daddy issues, let alone his or her present-day problems with work, finances, relationships, et cetera.

But with *I Need a Push*, I have the luxury of almost unlimited time. In some cases, I'm able to spend up to two months administering daily one-on-one cognitive therapy, so by the time pushees have their tips frosted (or whatever it is *Push*'s hairdressers do), they're returning to their lives able to face challenges with a new and improved set of behaviors.

I'd like to see you fix someone's life armed with nothing but a flatiron, *Geri*.

I glance down at my watch as an indication that we need to wrap this whole how-do-I-know-you business soon. Things to do, groceries to shelve, lives to touch, et cetera.

The shopper gives a self-conscious laugh. "I'm keeping you—I apologize. But this'll drive me crazy until I figure out our connection, and then in the middle of the night, I'll wake my husband up by shouting, *'Spin class!'* or something. Wait, are you in my spin class?"

I shrug. "I'm more of a runner than a spinner." Time at last year's Chicago Marathon? Four hours, twenty-nine minutes. Personal best, thank you very much. Working to get my pace down to less than ten minutes per mile, though. (I *believe* in me; I can do it!)

Of course, Geri's decided she's an athlete now, too, having just walked a 5K. Not ran, *walked*. Took her over an hour and required the whole damn family waiting for her at the finish line holding banners and balloons. From the way everyone was celebrating, I thought they were going to carry her off on their shoulders Cleopatra-style, chanting, *Hail the conquering hero!*

Yes, Geri, hurrah for the bare minimum!

Yet when I crossed the finish line at my first *marathon* after having run 26.2 miles? My family members were all whooping it up in the beer tent and they missed *everything.* Where were my banners? What of my balloons? Who was carrying me off on their shoulders? (Trust me? I'm a lot lighter.) There I was, wrapped up in the Mylar blanket, all alone searching for my missing cheering section. Typical. Later, Geri admitted, "We didn't figure you'd be done so soon. Hell, it takes me that long to drive 26.2 miles!" I scowl, remembering the incident.

The shopper becomes apologetic. "You know what? I'm being a pest. I guess I'll just wake my husband when I figure it out. Thanks for indulging me." She gives me an awkward little bow and begins to circle her cart over to the cheese counter.

Okay, game's over. Feeling magnanimous (largely because I am magnanimous), I draw a breath to tell her that, yes, *I'm* the one she saw in all the magazines, and in the *Tribune,* and on WeWIN. I've lectured at colleges across the country and I've been on morning shows, on all the cable news networks, and one week last fall, I cohosted with Dr. Drew. And once in a while, the paparazzi publish a shot of me with my überfamous mentor, Wendy.

But before I can share the highlights of my CV, she spins back around and snaps her fingers, face wreathed in a smile. "Oh, my God!"

I know what's coming next and I can't help but swell with

pride. Indeed, I've accomplished so much already in my career and my life.

"You're Geri's sister!"

Of course I'm the hairdresser's sister.

Of course I am.

CHAPTER ONE

Jersey Girl

"Are you still in love with Lorenzo?" I ask.

Dina's kohl-lined eyes are rimmed with tears as she contemplates her answer. With dozens of sessions under our belts over the past month, we've come so far. She's finally let down her guard and lately her insights have been coming rapid-fire. I'm so proud of her progress and I'm confident Wendy Winsberg will be thrilled with this episode. This is the exact kind of positive change we want *I Need a Push* to manifest.

And if highlighting positive change wins us a Daytime Emmy?

All the better.

Dina unfastens the white plastic claw-clip holding back torrents of black hair and rakes inch-long French-manicured tips through her mane. Somewhere, underneath the spandex leggings, the bronzer, and all the bravado, lives a wounded little girl . . . with a serious penchant for leopard print.

But my job is not to judge.

Although as I'm an expert in human behavior, I'd be particularly adept at doing so.

Take Dina, for example. Here she is, a bright, attractive—albeit somewhat flashy—girl with her entire future ahead of her. Maybe she won't become secretary of state with her liberal arts degree from Rutgers, but still. Her life is rife with possibility. (Again, save for cabinet-level work.) But surely there are accounts she can manage, minor projects she can spearhead, cell phones she can market, or memos she can draft to other entry-level managers. I fail to understand why she's willing to jeopardize her potential for some oily Pauly D wannabe club DJ/bouncer. *Push* intervened at the insistence of both her parents and the family court judge. If she can't curb her behavior and ends up saddled with a restraining order, she may as well buy some clear heels and prepare for her debut on the main stage.

I take in her artfully shredded racer-back tank and visible bra and realize it's possible she already owns stripper shoes.

"I am, but I'm trying so hard not to be. Oh, Dr. Reagan, it's like, whenever I think about him I feel so frigging . . ." She scans the horizon, where a few brave boaters are navigating the sun-dappled water, taking their first sail of the season.

In therapy, deliberate silences are as important as actual conversation. I nod encouragingly as she chooses her words. Sometimes when they take too long to find the words, I use the opportunity to jot down my shopping list.

What? It's called "time management" and that's why I'm a pro.

Dina and I are discussing her abandonment issues while we stroll the path by Lake Michigan. With blue skies and balmy breezes, summer's come particularly early to Chicago, so Craig, our nebbishy director, wanted to provide a more visually stimulating backdrop than the studio. Mind you, the presence of two cameramen, a couple of sound and lighting guys, Craig, a hair and makeup stylist, and one hapless production assistant who keeps spilling my tea isn't exactly conducive to unfettered communication at first, but after a while, even the most self-conscious forget we're rolling.

Earlier, I noticed a couple of college girls wearing bikini tops paired with their shorty-shorts as our broadcast team made our way past Oak Street Beach. Our secondary cameraman noticed the coeds, too. After enough time passed that his filming the nubile sorority girls morphed from "collecting B-roll" to "peeping Tom," I had to remind him that *I Need a Push* is not about titillation, okay?

Again, unless titillation wins us an Emmy; I can't stress that enough.

Although, technically, I imagine Wendy would be the one who kept the Emmy, but surely I'd have a chance to pose for photographs with it, as I would have done the lion's share of earning it. Without me, and to a lesser extent Dr. Karen, there is no show. What separates us from makeover programs like *What Not to Wear* is the psychotherapeutic element. At least once an episode, I will bring viewers to tears with my innate understanding and ability to facilitate change. Bank on that.

Regardless, after filming for three hours today, we may end up with two minutes of usable footage, so I don't come down too hard on the second cameraman for his lasciviousness. Everything's digital, so he's not exactly wasting tape.

Currently, we're heading down the path to where the volleyball nets have been set up on North Avenue Beach. I've spent a lot of time in this spot over the years, so I'm familiar with many of the league players here. The idea was mine to come this way; I figured if it's imperative we have eye candy on-screen, we may as well include some cute guys in the shots as well. Worked in the movie *Top Gun*, yes?

(Related note: What exactly happened to Val Kilmer? He used to be Channing Tatum levels of attractive. From Batman to fat man he went. Mark my words: He's an emotional eater.)

Of course, my focus ought to be on Dina, so I circle around and stand in front of her. I maintain intense face-to-face contact so she understands that I'm really hearing her.

Also, my left side is more photogenic. Ask anyone.

"Dina, I understand you want to be strong, yet I'm hearing there's more. What aren't you telling me? When you say 'I'm so frigging . . .' and then trail off, I'm sensing something unsaid."

Spill it, Jersey. I need my aha moment.

She bows her head in shame. "I . . . Dr. Reagan, I went to his frigging Facebook page."

Damn it, I thought we were past this behavior. I can't let her witness my aggravation, because this is not about me. Instead I calmly ask, "Dina, what did I tell you about Facebook?"

(Seriously? Sometimes I'm overwhelmed at my level of competency.)

She sighs and bats her false eyelashes as she repeats my sage advice. "Facebook is the devil's playground."

"And what do I mean by that?"

"You mean that I'm never going to get over him if I keep spying on his activities."

"Consider this: A scab can't heal if one keeps picking at it and reinjuring the wound." I place a hand on my hip and cheat my face toward the camera, as there's nothing inherently unethical about capturing my best angle while doling out life-altering advice. "I have to be firm here, starting with the advice I've given you. Are those the exact words I chose? To 'not spy on his activities'?"

She shrugs her delicate shoulders. "Basically."

"Dina, tell me what I say."

Sotto voce she says, "Don't stalk your ex."

Boom. There we go. That's the moment we'll use in the show's promo. The whole crew smiles and the secondary cameraman tries to hide his smirk, but I ignore them, this being a therapeutic milieu and all.

"Thank you. Sounds like a brief refresher course is in order, so let's discuss Dr. Reagan's Rules again." At some point I'd like to write a book, possibly called *Dr. Reagan's Rules*, so it doesn't hurt to start branding early and often.

Dina stops walking and slouches onto one of the hard wooden benches across from the volleyball nets. Craig motions for her to face me so she catches the light and then he films us from the back side in order to frame the players in the distance. She fiddles with a neon zebra-stripe bra strap (oh, honey) and stares down at her lap.

"Dr. Reagan's Rules, please, Dina."

With much hesitation, she finally begins to recount my rules. "Um . . . don't check in on Lorenzo's Facebook. Ignore his Twitter feed. Stop texting him at all hours. No more following his Instagram account. Don't drive by his house. Don't drive by his brother's house. Don't drive by his mother's house. Don't steal the trash from the frigging cans outside his house. Don't go to the club on the nights he works there. Stop asking his friends about him. Throw away stuff that reminds me of him." She sighs wearily. "Did I name 'em all, Dr. Reagan? Or was there one more?"

I hold my hand to my ear, middle fingers cupped with my thumb and pinkie extended. Sometimes I use gestures to emphasize my point, and also to remind the camera that I'm still here.

"Oh, yeah, don't call his cell phone no more just to listen to his outgoing message. But I haven't done that in a long time, I swear to God."

We're both aware that "a long time" means "a week" but it's a far sight better than the thirty times a day she'd been doing it. Why Lorenzo didn't just change his phone number after the first hundred hang-ups, I don't know, but he's not my patient/not my problem. I strongly suspect some narcissistic tendencies on his part, though. Who tattoos *his own name* on himself? Also, I had no idea Chevrolet was still making Camaros. I figured they disappeared around the time that *Saved by the Bell*'s Zack Morris finally had his testicles drop.

I smile encouragingly at Dina. "Excellent."

She nods and attempts to put on a happy face, but it's clear there's more troubling her.

"It's just on Facebook—," she begins.

I'm resolute here. "Devil's playground."

She exhales so hard that she appears completely deflated. "Believe me, I get it. I've seen frigging Lucifer on the jungle gym and I wish I hadn't, you know? But I noticed he has a new girlfriend and she's not even cute."

I start to say, *They never are,* but I catch myself. I'm careful not to insert any personal commentary into our sessions because it's not appropriate.

Besides, this is not *my* time to complain.

But believe me, I could complain about plenty.

Plenty.

Just this morning I had a voice mail from my mother telling me how Geri placed third in some White Sox bar's karaoke contest. Which . . . whatever. Perhaps once she dusts all the stray hairs off herself at the end of the day, she needs an alternative creative outlet.

However, today's about Dina, not me.

". . . and the more I flipped through his photos . . ."

Ultimately, though, I don't care how Geri occupies her free time. Although I'm surprised she has any, what with her busy sponging-off-my-parents schedule.

And I need to be present here because Dina's so close to another breakthrough.

". . . like I'm standing all by myself on a desert island, without makeup or nothing and . . ."

Yet all I'm saying is maybe it would have been nice for my mother to express this kind of maternal pride when I was on *Good Morning America* last week. Of course, she didn't even watch the episode—she said she'd forgotten to program her DVR. Way to demonstrate familial pride, Ma, especially since on this particular visit? George Stephanopoulos was flirting with me.

Well, I can't say he was flirting for sure, but what heterosexual male wouldn't with my co-commitments to diet, exercise, and clean living?

I heard from all the interns afterward about how fantastic I looked. "Oh, Dr. Reagan, you should always wear emerald green! What was that, a Diane von Furstenberg wrap dress? Amazeballs!"

And yet when Geri does the most innocuous thing, like sing in a karaoke contest, my parents reach Amber-alert levels of word spreading. One time in fourth grade, Geri earned an A for some stupid poem she'd written about a bird who flew through the air like he just didn't care. You'd have thought Ma and Dad were going to contact the Globe Theatre, as clearly she was Shakespeare reincarnate.

Do I even need to mention that I skipped the fourth grade entirely? Their response? "Nice job, but that doesn't get you out of doing the dishes."

". . . the same thing happened with my dad . . ."

Focus, self. Focus. Dina needs you. The *show* needs you.

Was the bar even crowded the night Geri won her Major Award? Or were there only, say, three people performing? What, she came in third? What if third means last? The people who graduated last in my program at Pepperdine are still technically doctors of psychology. Terrible doctors, no doubt, but doctors nonetheless. And are any of them on television? I think not.

". . . what if this is it for me? What if I never find happiness? How will I . . ."

Sure, sure, you're a national hero, singing "Total Eclipse of the Heart" like you meant it, Geri. You're a champion. Someone should pin a damn medal on your chest. And then maybe our parents could put your medal on the mantel, right next to the photo of me with my Emmy. You know, the one that I *actually will have earned someday very soon.*

That's when I notice that Dina and the entire crew are staring at me, waiting for me to comment. Crap, I must have really drifted off there. But let's tell the truth here: Sometimes therapy can be boring. It's all "me, me, me." Well, what about *my* thoughts and dreams for once?

I have all kinds of issues and dilemmas right now, largely due to Sebastian. We're technically on a break, but then he'll still come over. Yet afterward, he's hesitant to call me his girlfriend (not that I need labels) and he doesn't invite me to his work gatherings. It's confusing and distracting. My romantic life was decidedly easier when I was with Boyd back in California, but what was I going to do? Follow Geri's advice to drop out of my doctoral program and marry an amateur surfer? Not in this lifetime.

So while everyone awaits my input, I pull out the ultimate old chestnut, the one that every mental health professional relies on when she's grown bored/distracted or plain old fell asleep. (Listen, it happens.)

"How does that make you feel?"

Actually, this is a phrase that's much more in line with Freudian psychoanalysis, where a patient's drives are largely unconscious and rooted in childhood. Seriously, Sigmund? Give me a break. If my psyche were truly formed in my childhood, then I'd be a hypercontrolling, tightly wound, empathy-lacking basket case from everyone ganging up on me and being jealous all the time. I'd say I turned out pretty damn well, if for no reason other than I don't have to shake strangers' hair out of my underpants every night, *Geri*.

Anyway, I practice cognitive-behavior-based therapy, which is more about how patients' actions influence the way they see themselves, rather than how they feel. Regardless, my red-herring question puts us back on track.

Dina surreptitiously adjusts her silicone parts while she ponders her reply. I'm on the fence in terms of surgical enhancement. On the one hand, I'd look fantastic if I went up a cup size (especially according to Sebastian). On the other, gravity's been kind and I can't say I'm a fan of elective surgery and the resulting onslaught of pharmaceuticals.

I tune back in when Dina says, "I feel like . . . I need to understand what he sees in her. I wanna hear what he says to her. Like, how is it different with her than it was with me? So I didn't only visit his page—I went to hers, too."

I grimace. "Devil's. Playground."

I wonder if Geri actually received, what? A certificate of merit? Did the audience clap? Did she have all her south side cohorts there to lull her into a false sense of security? I'm sure Céline Dion need not watch her back.

Then I feel a flash of guilt for not giving Dina my undivided attention.

All right, I'm listening now.

"This is dumb, but I wish . . ." Dina tends to trail off a lot. When I'm quiet (and actually paying attention), I draw more out of her. People are generally far too reticent to allow prolonged gaps of stillness, rushing to fill the awkward silences with nervous, self-revelatory chatter.

But if Geri did receive a tangible artifact of some sort, I guarantee my parents will put the damn thing on display with all her old soccer participation trophies on the shelves next to the fireplace.

This? Right here?

Is why *Push* needs to win that Emmy.

I slap my thighs a couple of times to refocus. I'm not letting the world's lamest little sister throw me off my game. Dina interprets this gesture as a demand that she start getting real.

". . . I wish that I could, like, insert myself into her body." Suddenly, the whole crew snaps to attention, particularly the second cameraman. He's fresh off a stint filming MTV's *The Real World: Logan Square* and he's desperately disappointed that no one's having threesomes in hot tubs on this show. Of course, he won't catch hepatitis C on this particular job, so I guess that's the trade-off.

Whoa, I just had a brainstorm! Seven strangers and one shrink (read: PsyD) picked to live in a loft and have their lives taped to find out what happens when people stop being polite . . . and start getting therapy! I make a mental note to run this idea past Wendy later.

I would kill it in my own spin-off.

Kill. It.

I notice Dina blinking at me again and it's on me to pick up the conversational thread. "So I understand what you're communicating. Do you mean you want to insert yourself *biblically?*" I query. Funny, but on the spectrum between heterosexuality and homosexuality, I'd have placed her firmly on the Team Nope, Not Once, Not Even at Camp That Summer end of the continuum.

Dina's immediately flustered. "God, no, I'm not attracted to her, nothing like that. Alls I'm saying is I wish I could trade places with her for a day. You know, ride around in her head or something. Or swap bodies to see how Lorenzo reacts to me as her. Like in the movie *Freaky Friday.*"

Unfortunately—or not—I spent most of Lindsay Lohan's career in Drescher Library and I'm largely unfamiliar with her oeuvre. Although, frankly, I'd welcome the opportunity to sit that child down with the DSM-IV. So troubled. Her neuroses are buying someone a beach house—I guarantee that. And if I could get my hands on Charlie Sheen? Hello, early retirement!

"Are you referring to astral projection?" I ask. Dina blinks three times in rapid succession and the entire crew seems confused, so I'm obligated to explain the concept. "Astral projection is a kind of out-of-body experience. Your mind separates from your physical body and your consciousness is able to travel outside of your corporeal self."

"Yes! Like, body swapping and stuff! That! I want to do that."

I give Dina a wry smile. "I'm afraid that's a little outside of my area of expertise."

Also?

The concept of astral projection is utter and complete horseshit, but I dare not say this out loud at work. Wendy Winsberg has a huge mystical/spiritual bent, so much so that last season she hired a ridiculous new age healer named Deva for the show. I avoid her whenever possible. I guarantee whatever ails my patients can't be cured with some gewgaw or artifact from Deva's oddball little boutique, even if it is across the street from Prada.

But, if it were possible to astral project, particularly if I were to be able to swap bodies and not just rattle around a different dimension, I know exactly where I'd go. I'd head straight for Geri's meatball-shaped vessel because I'm desperate to understand why everyone falls all over her. She's not particularly smart or terribly driven or even that cute, yet you'd think she hung the moon. There's a reason she has a Svengali-like hold on the rest of the world, and I'd make it my job to discover what it is.

I'd also prove she's not allergic to nuts. (That was *my* ham sandwich, damn it!)

I stand and gesture toward the walking path, largely because it's the golden hour, which is the most flattering lighting of the day. I make sure I'm on the left side for maximum sunset benefit.

"Dina, why don't we address the issues within our locus of control before branching into metaphysics?" She quickly falls into step next to me, the crew clattering along in front of us. When we're on the move, they have to walk backward in order to film our faces.

Here we go, money shot! Clear a space on the mantel, Ma!

"Dina, take out your phone."

She blanches beneath all her bronzer and blush. "No, Dr. R, please. Not that."

"It's time," I say in my most authoritative voice. The primary cameraman circles behind us and pans in over Dina's shoulder. "Strong, Dina. You can do it." With a hand trembling so profoundly that her bracelets clatter, Dina extends a shaky finger and pulls up her Facebook account. I instruct her, "On the count of five, Dina. This is what we've been working toward. Let's go. Five . . . four . . . three . . . two . . . one."

Everyone gathers around to watch Dina finally, blessedly, delete her (frigging) Facebook account. The crew can't help but let out a rousing cheer.

"You did it, Dina!"

I'm so overcome with pride that I hug her to me. Wow. Those are like a couple of kettlebells in there. So not a surgical selling point. Is that what happens when you cheap out on the augmentation? They get hard? Wouldn't they hurt? Like, all the time? Would I even be able to sleep on my stomach? And how would I run any kind of distance with them? I'd need three bras! Plus, for all of Sebastian's enthusiasm, I can't imagine he'd appreciate a handful of concrete. Besides, what I have going on is far better than Geri and her ridiculous rack. She claims they're homegrown, but she was flat when I left for my doctorate and stacked when I came home. And everyone else in the family is small to mid-busted, save for Great-Aunt Helen and her uniboob. I mean, Geri's already proved herself a liar with the nut business and—ahem, Dina.

Focus, self, focus.

I ask, "Tell me what feeling you have now that you're rid of that temptation."

Dina lifts her head, and it's almost like she's taking in the scenery for the first time. The sun, the lake, the after-work crowd, released from long days in the office and confining business garb, filtering onto the walking path. Then she shows me the brightest smile in all of New Jersey.

"I feel . . . free. I feel like I can breathe again for the first time in a very long while."

Damn, it feels good to be a gangsta.

A few more days like this and I'll have the confidence to turn her over to the makeover team. I find once I figure out our pushee's insides, working on the outside is pure gravy.

Before Dina can further express her joy, a Lycra-clad biker whizzes perilously close to us, causing the production assistant to drop my beverage, which splashes all over Dina's leggings.

"Yo! *Yo!* Yeah, I'm talking to you, you frigging Lance Armstrong wannabe. *This* is the walking path." She gestures with talon-tipped fingers. "*That* is the bike path. Follow me here—walkers go on walking path, bikers go on bike path. But maybe they need to post a big, frigging sign that says 'Bikes *and* Douche Bags,' so you understand that this means you ride there. Oh, you're riding away from me? Really? Big man! Get your narrow ass back here, ya frigging pussy!"

Two points to make here:

This is likely not the episode to earn me a spot on my parents' mantel.

Also, I may need to touch upon anger-management skills before sending Dina back to Perth Amboy.

CHAPTER TWO

Boat Drinks

"Is this seat taken, Reagan Bishop?"

A figure hovers over me. I can't see her face because the sun's to her back, but I can easily discern her voice, especially because of her bizarre penchant for saying my first and last name together all the time. Who does that?

I crane my head around, as though to indicate the plethora of empty chairs on this side of the pool that she may not have noticed. Since we're here in Hawaii, the majority of people at the resort prefer to catch rays rather than huddle on the side of the pool in shadows. But I pride myself on never once having had a sunburn, which is why my skin's still the color of freshly poured cream. (Or, if Geri's to be believed—which she is not—Elmer's Glue.) Even when I was at the beach all the time with Boyd years ago, I was careful. With my umbrella and sun hats and towel fortresses, Boyd would laugh about how no one would ever guess I lived in Malibu.

I glance uneasily at the chair next to me. Ugh, why does she have to sit with me? It's aggravating enough that I'm compelled to deal with her antics at work. Like the time she insisted we swish our tongues into a cup of water and scrub our eyes with the backwash because it was supposed to cure us of our allergies? Hello, *conjunctivitis*! Or how about the time she made us lie down and covered us with stones for a purpose I've yet to understand? Utter nonsense. I'm willing to put up with that foolishness at work, but here? On our fantastic thanks-for-a-second-great-season trip to Maui from our benevolent benefactor, Wendy Winsberg? Patently unfair.

Plus, I'm very busy waiting for a text. Sebastian's been doing that I'll-come-see-you-but-then-I'll-ignore-you business again that's been going on ever since he insisted we take our break last month.

He told me to text when I got here, and I did, and he's yet to respond. So frustrating, and yet I figure if I provide him with ample time and space, he'll realize I'm exactly what he needs, largely because he's exactly what I need.

I love that Sebastian's as focused on his career as I am. He won me over when he shared his ten-year plan. Sure, Boyd was fun back in the day, but he had no tangible goals (save for competing in the Billabong Pro) and his ten-year plan was basically to not be eaten by a shark. Boyd was like ice cream for dinner: delicious in the moment, but ultimately a poor lifestyle choice.

Without benefit of an official invitation, Deva settles in next to me. I pretend to be immersed in the awful book I grabbed in the airport bookstore. How do I inevitably wind up with memoirs penned by hacks? I hate when writers try to pass off their clear and present neuroses as humor. The author claims to be "bitter," but anyone with credentials would assess her as "borderline."

Camille said you stole a bag from a homeless guy.

Insufferable.

I could write circles around this moron.

I snap shut the book because even a conversation with Deva would be less painful than this dreck. I quickly calculate how long I might have to chat with her before I can feign sleepiness. Given the angle of the sun, fullness from brunch, and how late the luau ran last night, I estimate fifteen minutes.

Deva makes short work of slathering herself in sunscreen, due to the fact that her hands are the size of catchers' mitts. I offer a tight smile and she grins back. Perhaps this won't be so bad.

"Tell me everything about you, Reagan Bishop."

Ugh.

"A lifetime is a lot of ground to traverse," I reply lightly, glancing down at my phone. Why am I not hearing back from him? The trading desks have been closed for hours. What's he busy doing?

She shakes a massive finger at me. "Ah, Reagan Bishop, as Creighton Abrams says, when eating an elephant, take one bite at a time."

I try not to grit my teeth. "Yes, but the problem there is that I'm a pescatarian." True story. I haven't touched any live protein source other than fish in years, unlike Geri, who I'd wager hits the Golden Arches every single day. My body's a temple and I'm not about to worship with a Big Mac. I believe you are what you eat, which makes Geri a basket of cheese curds and a mountain of buffalo wings. I'm a proponent of clean, organic eating, which means I have to be constantly vigilant. You should have seen me last week when a new barista at the indie coffee shop by the office tried to slip non-organic white milk into my latte instead of almond. I had to ask her, "I'm sorry, are you trying to kill me?"

Deva laughs. "That was a metaphor, Reagan Bishop. No one's asking you to dine on pachyderm. Although once while traveling in Mongolia with descendants of Kerait tribesmen, I ate boodog. Let me assure you, marmot does *not* taste like chicken. I'd say it's more of a—"

In order to stop her from whatever comes next, I rattle off my bio. "Let's see, born and raised in Chicago, attended Taylor Park Academy, then U of C, then Pepperdine, and I did my clinical internship at Northwestern Hospital. Had my own practice for a while, but now I work for *Push*." Then I give her another polite smile and start to reach for my sunscreen, which is underneath my phone.

I'm tempted to ask her where one receives a new age education but suspect it's from the University of I Don't Care.

Deva stops me from grabbing my bottle of 100 SPF Neutrogena by laying a massive mitt on my arm. "You've told me what you do, Reagan Bishop. Now tell me who you are."

Damn it, why couldn't anyone in my social circle join me on this stupid vacation so I wouldn't be subjected to this nonsense? Wendy sprang for two plane tickets per employee, plus meals, lodging, and spa treatments, but no one could make it. I tell you what, if someone were to offer *me* an all-expenses-paid trip to Maui, you can be very sure I'd rearrange my schedule accordingly. But no. I heard an endless chorus of, *Aw, Reagan, it's my busy season,* from Rhonda, Bethany, and Caroline.

As for Sebastian, he said he didn't want to give me the wrong idea about us if he came with me, which might have been easier to swallow were he not in my bed at the time.

Like I said, the business with Sebastian is confusing.

So now I'm forced to make banal chitchat with someone who sells dream catchers for a living. Yes, *this* is why I earned a doctorate.

I reply, "I feel like I just told you everything about me."

Deva folds her legs underneath her and assumes a Buddha pose, her billowy caftan belying her slight figure. "Not even remotely."

I stall for time by grabbing the foo-foo cocktail served in the pineapple rind sitting next to me. Wendy's arranged for a different tropical libation to be sent out to each of us every hour on the hour. I finally took one so the perky pool waitress would stop incessantly bothering me.

I normally eschew alcohol as I don't enjoy losing track of my faculties (unlike *some* people), but clearly these are extraordinary circumstances. I take the smallest of sips and the flavor is not wholly unpleasant.

But before I put any more of this concoction into my body, I'll need the 411. I flag the server.

The college-aged girl in a powder blue polo and a white tennis skort trots over. According to her tag, she's named Hope.

"Hi, I'm Hope. How may I be of service?"

"What's in this?"

She peers at my pineapple. "Let's see . . . there's an orchid, cherry, and pineapple garnish—got it! This is our pool bartender's take on a Hurricane. They're only available when Troy's on shift. Delicious, right?"

"That depends on what's in it."

"Sure, totally understand. Okay, first Troy uses 10 Cane Rum, which is an artisanal, gold-medal-winning varietal from Trinidad. The name's derived from their harvesting cane in bundles of ten. What's unique is this rum boasts notes of pear and vanilla, so it doesn't have the heft and the mouthfeel of lesser rums. Because this 10 Cane is crafted from sugarcane and not molasses, it's most similar to Brazil's famous cachaça liquor. You may notice some commonality to that of a caipirinha?"

I shake my head.

"No? Alrighty. Then we blend in fresh lime juice, passion fruit juice, pineapple juice, a hand-macerated papaya puree, and house-made simple syrup."

"Which means no high-fructose corn syrup?"

"Never!"

"All ingredients locally sourced and organic, I hope?"

"Of course!"

"Even the papaya?"

Hope smiles politely. "I assure you, ma'am, not only is the papaya local, but it came from certified, nematode-free rootstock. We pride ourselves on serving our guests nothing but the finest! In fact, even the cane sugar was grown right here on Maui."

"And would you happen to know the farm's policy on pesticide use?"

I appear to have stumped her.

"Do you mind if I check on that and get back to you?"

I hesitate, finally saying, "No . . . I'm sure it will do. Thank you, Hope." As she skulks away, I quietly note how much I hate when the servers can't answer a simple question about the items they serve. This is probably why she carries trays for a living.

I'm in the middle of a second, grudging sip when Deva asks, "Have you a lover, Reagan Bishop?" which propels an inadvertent spray of slushy rum and local juice out my nose.

I'm loath to answer her for a variety of reasons, ranging from this being a gross violation of the social norm to my being genuinely puzzled about my own status. See: *Beeswax, None of Your.* How do I explain the break we're on, when I'm not sure I understand it myself? And why did he request the break in the first place? I respond, "At the moment, no."

She tents her hands and rests her chin on her fingertips. "I could sense that your aura regarding love was out of balance."

Drink.

"Have you read Pamala Oslie's seminal work on auras? Specifically *Life Colors* and *Love Colors?*"

I take another sip. "I'm waiting for the movie."

Deva's face lights up and she claps together her great paws. "Oh, sweet Goddess, there's a film? I'm so— Ah. Ha-ha! You *got* me, Reagan Bishop. Under that dour exterior, you're actually quite funny."

I immediately bristle; I'm not dour.

Am I dour?

No, I am *not* dour.

Maybe I'm not as lighthearted as, say, Geri, but few people are without the use of drugs, and everyone knows my stance on Big Pharma. I mean, anyone can pop a Dr. Feelgood, but true change is manifested only through an active commitment to cognitive therapy.

Was I dour when Boyd and I drove the entire length of the Pacific Coast Highway naked that night? I think not. Then again, fooling around with him when I should have been focused on my dissertation almost cost me my doctoral program.

I remember how my academic adviser screamed at me in her office about how I was throwing away what would be a brilliant career. So, much to my entire family's chagrin, I broke up with Boyd because it was for the best. He didn't understand why we couldn't find a balance, maybe meet halfway. But what's halfway between a doctor and a surfer/bartender?

Yet my point remains that I'm not dour.

To punctuate this point, I drink.

And then I drink some more. Because I'm not dour.

I decide to change my tactics and I start asking Deva some questions. "Is this your first time visiting Hawaii?"

"Goddess, no. I'm here whenever I can get away. I own a beach home up the coast."

Huh. Even shacks in Maui start at a cool million. I'm suddenly intrigued. Perhaps I should revise my view on her. Here I thought she was just the weirdo who insisted on smudging the studio with burning sage before our broadcasts.

"You're kidding," I reply. "I was under the impression you sold kachinas and hand-carved bongs for a living. No offense, of course." There's no way she could afford a beach house on her salary. Despite the ample perks Wendy provides, we're still on a cable network, so I actually earn *less* than when I was in private practice. But if we ever make it to network, that will all change. That's what I'm banking on, anyway.

"I take no offense. I sell many things, Reagan Bishop. My business interests are varied," Deva explains with some vagueness. "Also, in terms of P and L, you'd be surprised at the markup on tribal art. I carry artifacts from a Maori chief who's such a savvy entrepreneur he could run Morgan Stanley." She stops to reflect on her statement. "I mean, if he ever put on pants."

"Noted." I believe my requisite fifteen minutes are up. Ultimately, a weirdo with a beach house is still a weirdo. I begin to close my eyes and lean back in my lounger.

"Why are you out of harmony with your family?"

I sit straight up. "Excuse me?"

"I'm noticing discord in your second chakra."

Of course you are.

Deva continues, "The Sanskrit translation for the second chakra is 'the dwelling place for the self.' The second chakra is most closely linked with sexuality and creativity. However, because this chakra also has six petals, that portion relates to the numerology of six, which pertains to nurturing and links back to family and community."

"Like you do," I quip.

She blithely continues, "My concern, Reagan Bishop, is I'm seeing signs your second chakra is weak, which can manifest itself in any number of problems, most likely in your sense of self-worth."

Drink.

"I assure you my self-worth is *not* an issue," I state. I mean, Taylor Park and U of C and Pepperdine? Accelerated career path? Lead psychologist on *Push*? Years of self-validation? "I'm fine, thank you. More than fine. I'm borderline magnificent." And I will be fully so once Sebastian and I figure out how to navigate this minor blip in our relationship. Hello! Text me back now, please.

Until then, I shall enjoy another sip of this delicious tropical beverage. And I will say this: the cane sugar doesn't possess a pesticide-y aftertaste.

Why would anyone question my self-worth, especially when doing the whole apples-to-organic-apples comparison with my family? What the hell has Mary Mac or Geri ever achieved, other than robbing me of a peaceful childhood?

"According to John E. Groberg, a weak second chakra can lead to your feeling like a martyr."

At the moment, I'm feeling annoyed, not persecuted. "Deva, I'm telling you that all is well." I take another pull on my pineapple. This concoction has to be full of vitamin C. Really, I'm consuming it for nutritional purposes. But Troy should consider blending in some wild blueberries for the antioxidants.

Deva studies my face before tracing the outline of my body with her eyes.

It's disconcerting.

Finally she says, "Your second chakra indicates you're easily offended and prone to being upset. Couple that with the six numerology and all signs point to disharmony in the family."

Okay, now I'm angry and somewhat emboldened by the liquor. "Deva, that is *enough*. Why don't you go back to whatever planet you're from, or maybe your beach house, and stop peddling your new age nonsense in my direction. The fact is that I'm a mental health professional—I have a damned *doctorate*—so I suspect I have a better handle on what I perceive to be my issues than you do."

Deva smiles beatifically. "I'm not from another planet, Reagan Bishop. I'm from La Grange, Illinois."

I wave my pineapple at Hope. "I'm going to need another one of these."

Three hours/multiple pineapples later, I wake in my lounge chair. I immediately check my phone. No texts. I remind myself to have a chat with the front desk because clearly there's an issue with the wireless service here.

That's when I notice the sun's low in the sky and Deva's gone, leaving nothing behind save for my bottle of Neutrogena sitting with a note penned on Ritz-Carlton, Kapalua's stationery reading *You might want to use me, Reagan Bishop. See you at dinner!*

I glance down at my formerly milky epidermis, which is now not only fire-hydrant red, but also throbbing.

Fantastic. I guess I can cross "burn self to a crisp" off the old bucket list.

As I wend my way around the lushly landscaped pool and back to my room, flashes of our conversation come back to me and I'm mortified all over again. Perhaps I should be grateful that I'm already the color of a candy apple, thus no one can see me blush.

"I'm curious about your name, Reagan Bishop," Deva prodded somewhere around third-pineapple o'clock. "Were your parents fans of the Gipper and his Star Wars defense system?"

I recall laughing into my cocktail, which, in retrospect, was less of a "frosty drink" and more of a "tasty truth serum."

This? Right here?

Is why I never drink, at least since my days with Boyd. And look where that almost got me.

Yet something deep inside of me must have felt the need to

unload, so I shared. "Not at all. My parents are lifelong Dems. Hard-core. In fact, my mother started working for the Daley administration when he was elected. They grew up on the same block, so he trusted her. She started off in the secretarial pool, but eventually she became Richard M. Daley's personal assistant. She was his right hand. For a solid decade, my mother was unofficially the second most powerful person in the city of Chicago. You wanted to talk to 'da mare'? You had to get through Maggie Bishop first. She retired when the new guy was elected, though, because she despises him almost as much as the Olympic selection committee. Profound loathing. Refuses to use Rahm's real name and will only refer to him as Tiny Dancer."

It's common knowledge in Chicago that Mayor Emanuel is both short of stature and a classically trained danseur, hence Ma's moniker. He's also close friends with Wendy Winsberg, so I've met him a few times at her parties. He smells like pine trees and power.

Of course, since the family despises him, I automatically add him to the buddy list.

I continued, "I thought my mother was going to excommunicate me last week after our photo appeared in *Chicago Nouveau* magazine when we chatted briefly at a fund-raiser for the Joffrey Ballet. I'm guessing this is why you believe my chakras or colors or whatever are askew."

Of course, it was Geri who ratted me out, as my mother would never touch that magazine because she believes it fosters the whole idea of a "new" Chicago. In her purview, the Chicago she loves ends at the border of the Bridgeport neighborhood where her family's lived for three generations. We butt heads because they're patently old-fashioned; Chicago's no longer a Carl Sandburg poem. I'm sorry, Ma, but the new

Chicago is more than just hog butcher for the world or stacker of wheat. (And who eats wheat anymore? Read *Wheat Belly*—it'll transform your way of looking at grain.) Point? We've progressed past our roots as a sheltered midwestern burg where we all know one another—we're now a metropolitan destination with world-class dining, lodging, and entertainment.

This is why we clash, my family and me.

Whereas I'm urbane and cosmopolitan, they'll lose their minds if someone dare serve ketchup with their hot dogs.

Anyway, one of Geri's clients must have been thumbing through the issue while under the dryer or something and she pointed out the photo to Geri, who couldn't even wait for her shift to end to squeal on me.

It's called *a life*, Geri. Perhaps you should get you one.

"Meaning there are indeed issues in the family, Reagan Bishop."

"Wait, did I say the stuff about Geri out loud?"

Deva nodded.

Damn you, vile, delicious, vile pineapple!

That's when I began to drink in earnest, and I'm not sure what flew out of my mouth next. Hopefully with a couple of gallons of Fiji water and a rigorous barefoot beach run in the morning, I can exercise/exorcise today's mental and physical transgressions.

I make my way through the lobby, my besmirched skin glowing like a halogen bulb. I can actually feel waves of heat radiating off me. When I pass a family standing at the registration desk, I distinctly hear a mother tell her child, "I'm so glad we packed your sun shirt." Argh.

I enter the elevator and press the button for the club floor. Although I'm not a producer or director, my room is up here with all the show's brass. I have no issue with receiving most favored treatment. Consider this—participants can't change without my expert guidance. A sassy haircut won't fill a hole in the soul. Really? I'm the axis on which the whole operation spins, hence the ocean view.

As I retrieve my key card, I notice Patty, the show's executive producer, leaving her suite next door. I adore Patty—in so many ways, she's the parent I wish I had. Whereas Ma can be rigid and brusque, Patty's a true earth mother, relaxed and accepting and brimming with understanding. She's caring and compassionate and open, and no matter what stress the show brings, the whole *Push* crew is encouraged to seek solace and comfort in Patty's tapestry-covered, pillow-strewn, candlelit office.

"Good afternoon, Patty."

She's so distracted that I have to greet her again before I catch her attention. Maybe I wasn't the only one lured onto the rocks by the siren song of Troy's pineapple drinks today.

She digs in her satchel while she speaks. "Reagan, my dear, how are you?"

I glance down at my lobster-red limbs and quote that old commercial. "I got a sunburn and I feel like a French fry."

Patty glances up and then shoots me a withering look. "I don't understand why you girls today aren't more careful. Haven't you learned the dangers of excessive tanning by now? Melanoma is the silent killer! How many more of your sisters must die from entirely preventable deaths?"

Whoa, what? But I don't . . . I never . . .

Before I can even begin to verbalize a protest, Patty says, "I have to go—I'll see you at the dinner tonight."

I wince as I shift my bag, the straps digging into my inflamed skin. "No, I'll probably just order room service and—"

"Wendy has an announcement and *you will be there to hear it.*"

And with that, she flounces off, her long skirt and Stevie Nicks sleeves flapping in the breeze behind her.

What was that about?

CHAPTER THREE

Trading Up

"What's everyone doing during hiatus?" chirps Mindy, the sprightly, albeit butterfingered production assistant who's perpetually fumbling my hot beverages. I barely recognized her outside of her usual cargo shorts and U of A sweatshirt. Somehow in the past three days, she's turned as brown as a native in the Hawaiian sun, with nary an extra freckle, whereas I'm practically fluorescent except for the large white circles around my eyes from my sunglasses. Shameful.

As for our upcoming hiatus, we wrapped the second season late last week and we're not due to start shooting again until after Labor Day. As previously mentioned, I might not earn quite what I did in private practice, but I didn't have summers off, either. During the break, I plan to accommodate a few of my favorite private patients while I allocate the bulk of my time to training for the October marathon and snapping up continuing education credits. I'm agog with anticipation over my upcoming course on Exposure and Response Prevention in Practice!

Everyone even tangentially related to *I Need a Push* (and their guests) is sitting in the Anuenue Room at the Ritz, waiting for Wendy Winsberg to arrive and deliver the keynote speech. Actually, our jobs entail a whole lot of waiting for Wendy to announce something or other, so this is pretty much business as usual. If she had a million bucks for every speech she gave us, then . . . well, you do the math. That's why I find it so curious that Patty was acting oddly about this particular invocation.

I specifically opted to sit at a table close to the bar, as I want ready access to ice to soothe my ravaged skin. Unfortunately, the younger staffers chose this table for its drinks-adjacency, so they've been swilling free liquor and yammering away for what feels like an eternity.

I just lost twenty minutes of my life to an in-depth rehash of every time Taylor Swift's been dumped in the past five years. I figured I could listen, or I could poke out my eardrums with a shrimp fork. As I eye my utensils, I'm not confident I made the right choice.

Anyway, apparently the girls are still Team Jacob, despite their never, ever, ever getting back together. But after listening to my tablemates deconstruct failure after perpetual failure, I'm half tempted to get ahold of her manager and suggest we work one on one. With her pattern of consecutive, terrible breakups, it sounds like she may be the author of her own misfortune. I can help her.

(A giver, that's what I am.)

Two seats over, Dr. Karen draws a breath, as clearly she's ready to pontificate. Are the tsunami-warning bells chiming?

Because we're about to be swept out to sea on a tidal wave of bullshit! Quick! Run for higher ground! Grab a palm tree!

I'm hesitant to say I have a nemesis, because I'm a mental health professional who's adept at processing and compartmentalizing negative feelings.

But if I did have a nemesis, it would be Dr. Karen.

She's the polar opposite of me in everything from philosophy to looks. I'm in my early(ish) thirties, whereas she clearly crawled out of the primordial ooze. I'm selfless and humble; she's practically tattooed her CV on her forehead. Like anyone cares she went to Harvard. Look at her all ropy and gnarled in her vintage pastel suit—and why is she wearing a hat? What is she, the Queen Mum?

"Well, *I'm* writing a book," Dr. Karen declares. "I have the top literary agent and he's desperate for me to finish my manuscript. He's already calling my work the Next Big Thing."

Ugh. I wonder if she had to buy an extra seat on the airplane to accommodate all of her carry-on smug-gage? Even though Deva advocates junk science like astrology and numerology, I have more respect for her than I do for Dr. Karen. And why is her book already being called the Next Big Thing? I'm sure I could write a book if I had even a moment of free time. Mine would absolutely be better than hers.

Dr. Karen's the show's other mental health professional, only she's a licensed psychiatrist, meaning she can prescribe meds. And prescribe she does! Are you momentarily sad? Here's an antidepressant! Are you the slightest bit unhappy with the numbers on the scale? Well, a shot of HCG is exactly the jump start you need! Have you ever so briefly lost your ability to focus? Amphetamines to the rescue! She pays no attention to behavior cues and heads straight for a chemical solution; it's so counterintuitive to all that I practice.

"Ooh, exciting!" Mindy shrieks. Mindy shrieks a lot. You've never seen anyone so enthusiastic about minutiae. She's only now finally shut up about the bagged nuts, dried fruit, and bottled water waiting for each of us in our hotel rooms. I can't even fathom her reaction to the gratis minibottles of shampoo and mouthwash, but I suspect her Facebook followers have been briefed ad nauseam. "What's your book about?"

Oh, sweetie—let's not pretend you read.

Dr. Karen glances conspiratorially around the table. "It's a collection of stories from my patients who've experienced side effects when taking a certain benzodiazepine."

No one seems to understand what this means, so I offer, "It's a sedative/hypnotic, like you'd find in your garden-variety sleeping pill."

Which I would never advocate, even if I were able to write scripts. When *my* patients can't sleep, *I* help them resolve the issues keeping them up at night. The last thing I'd do would be to substitute a little tablet for talk therapy.

Mind you, I'm well aware that prescription drugs have their place and serve important purposes. Certain pharmaceuticals are mission critical and no one's going to cognitively process away their cancer or diabetes. But personally, I take umbrage at handing out psychotropic drugs like Halloween candy, especially in lieu of exploring other avenues of behavior modification.

"Yes, exactly, Reagan," Dr. Karen says, surprised that I'm actually familiar with what she's saying.

This is exasperating, as Pepperdine isn't exactly clown college. (And it's not like they hosted *Circus of the Stars* there, either.) "Naturally I'm familiar, what with being a doctor and all," I reply curtly.

Then Dr. Karen literally pats my hand in an infuriatingly

condescending manner. The way she reaches for me instantly reminds me of a praying mantis grabbing at a leaf. Why did it take me until now to make the comparison? Put that bug in vintage Dior, apply too much rouge, and I swear I couldn't tell the difference between them.

"Of course you are, my dear," she says. "Anyway, the book's called *The Thanwell Diaries* and it recounts the bizarre behavior I've documented from patients taking that drug."

"What's Thanwell? Like Ambien?" Mindy's equally bronzed buddy asks. What's her name? Crystal? Jewel? Amber? Something gemstone inspired and vaguely white trash—that much I remember.

"Thanwell is like Ambien on crack," I interject. "The drug is absorbed ten times more quickly and is prone to cause delusions and hallucinations. I'm at a loss to understand why the FDA hasn't pulled this dreadful product. Those who take it report a high frequency of episodes where they engage in all kinds of risky behavior, like sleep driving, sleep eating, sleep shopping, etcetera. I worked with one gentleman who after ingesting Thanwell—which he took against my counsel— serenaded his entire condo complex. This incident was troubling for a number of reasons, namely because he can't sing, it was four a.m. on a Tuesday, and *he was completely nude*, save for a pair of cowboy boots. He was so humiliated afterward that he put his place on the market, sold it at a loss, and moved out of town. He was almost ruined financially."

Dr. Karen snorts in a most unbecoming fashion and slaps the table. "That's *hilarious*! Give me his e-mail address! I'd love to include his story in my book. Oh, wait until you hear what this one lady did . . ."

Before Dr. Karen can launch into her story, I slip away

from the table. Technically, she's not violating patient confidentiality, yet I've no desire to encourage her spilling salacious details.

Besides, that story's for *my* book someday.

Of course, if I'd listened to Boyd, I'd have dropped out to write and follow him on the thus-far-unpaid surfing circuit. He said with the way I devoured books and observed human behavior, he was sure I'd produce something amazing. Let's see . . . a doctorate and guaranteed professional success, or one enormous crapshoot of which I'd never hear the end if I were to fail? No contest there.

I step out onto the lanai for a quick breath of air before the evening's programming begins.

From behind me I hear, "Reagan Bishop, tear down this wall!"

I whip around to see Deva, grinning like the Cheshire cat. Instead of her usual dashiki or ikat caftan, today she's all wrapped up in the traditional garb of boldly printed Hawaiian kapa cloth. Does she even own a pair of jeans? And what does laundry day look like at her house? I have to wonder. She's also opted for a haku lei floral headpiece woven with orchids and banana leaves. She's quite the contrast to me in my white J.Crew sundress with a dove gray cardigan and hair pulled up in a high bun.

Deva explains, "You said when growing up, people would always quote Ronald Reagan because of your first name. I thought 'tear down this wall' could be our thing."

"Deva, this is *not* going to be our thing. Do you not recall the part earlier where I told you how much I hated that?"

Undaunted, Deva reaches up to scratch under the back of her headpiece. "Well, you were slurring pretty badly by that point, Reagan Bishop. My apologies for misunderstanding."

To this day, I'm aggravated that my parents saddled me with this unfortunate moniker. For God's sake, Geri was named after my mother's idol, Geraldine Ferraro, the first woman to run for vice president. "Reagan" is a true anomaly, particularly given my parents' political bent. Granted, I was born on the day Reagan took office in 1981, and while he was being sworn in, the Iranian hostages were released after 444 grueling days of captivity. The only explanation offered is that Ma was so overcome with hormones and morphine—mostly morphine—that naming me Reagan was a fait accompli. By the time she came to her senses, the birth certificate was a matter of public record.

I suspect this is the exact moment when I adopted my Just Say No view on prescription drugs.

Before I can elaborate, we notice Wendy entering the ball-room. Rather, we're alerted to her entrance when the entire ballroom lets out a collective gasp. Twenty-five years in the business and she still has that impact on people. Deva and I quickly slip in at the back of the room and plant ourselves in the first open seats we can find.

I'll admit it—I sometimes experience *cutis anserina* (goose bumps) when Wendy speaks, such is her charisma. As she steps onto the dais, the crowd switches from reverent silence to a cacophony of cheers that take three whole minutes to quell. Her presence is legendary, although not necessarily because Wendy's considered beautiful. I'm not being snarky here—as she herself says, she's a little too short, a little too lumpy, and a little too ethnic (read: Jewish) to be a cover girl, which is so ironic considering all the magazines she's graced in the past three decades.

Wendy leans up to the microphone. "Hello, gorgeous people! How are you enjoying Mauiiiiiiiiii?" She draws out the word "Maui" for a good five beats.

The crowd bursts into prolonged applause, which dies down once only everyone's hands begin to ache.

"I want to thank you all for joining me on this journey."

More applause.

"Not just to Maui, but in this journey we call life."

Would it be ungrateful to point out that sometimes Wendy speaks in phrases most commonly found cross-stitched on pillows?

"And life is a journey, not a destination."

So much applause.

(So much cliché.)

"This trip is my way of saying thank you for all your efforts, especially those of you who've been here from the beginning. Like you, Patty. You're more than my executive producer—you're my soul mate and my sister. Where would I be without you? Wait, don't answer that," she laughs. "Without you, I'd be back in Providence, covering city council meetings."

The crowd continues to go wild, save for Patty. Seems like Patty should be basking in Wendy's reflected light most of all, as they've been best friends ever since they met as cub reporters for the *Providence Journal* thirty years ago. Yet the look on Patty's face is decidedly unreadable.

She's probably just overwhelmed. Wendy has that effect on people. I'm glad she uses her power for good; otherwise she could be a Bond-level supervillain.

"And we're doing fine work, necessary work, all of us, from assistants to producers. Every one of you is an equally vital member of the Wendy Winsberg family."

I shift a bit when she says this. Is Mindy really as vital as I am? Look at her sitting there with her mouth all agape, lapping up every word Wendy says like it's the gospel. Don't get me wrong, I'm a huge fan, and Wendy's helped orchestrate an awful lot of positive change. But she's not the Second Coming.

As for Mindy's worth being equal to mine, at least in an employment situation? She spills drinks; I change lives. On the continuum of what makes a difference, I suspect Mindy and I are on opposite ends of the bell curve. Sure, she serves a purpose and I'm grateful for all the coffee-shop runs, but let's be real here.

"In fact, we're all doing God's work."

Except probably Mindy.

Come on, it's an almond milk latte and not the Miracle of Lourdes.

Perfect example of what I'm talking about with this one? A couple of weeks ago, I was finishing up with our last pushee. We were outlining a list of coping strategies she could employ when her mother started to overstep her boundaries. Craft services had just put out lunch and the studio crew was about to descend on the buffet like locusts. We'd worked through breakfast and I knew my pushee was hungry, so I asked Mindy to bring her a plate. What does she do? She literally brings an empty plate!

I just can't with this one. I really just can't.

Wendy then recaps our show's success stories, with the aid of a massive video screen behind her, playing a montage of everyone from the bulimic teen ballerina to the families in crisis to the hoarding grandmother. She points proudly to the screen behind her. "This is what happens when we push."

As she speaks, all the guests we've helped file out onstage, healthy, happy, and whole, and we all take to our feet. This is such a surprise! We didn't expect to see these pushees again. Almost every face in the crowd is wet with tears, and I realize I've inadvertently reached for Deva's hand.

What can I say? I'm not immune to having a moment.

Wendy's voice is powerful and her words fill the room. "I sought the Lord's guidance on how we can continue our important business. After much prayer, He showed me the solution."

The audience begins to raise their arms in the air, as though to testify.

"He speaks through me!"

Okay, I *was* having a moment, but suddenly this is getting a little too cult-y for my liking. I feel like any minute now the waitstaff will roll in carts of Kool-Aid and tracksuits. Deva and I unclasp hands.

"*I Need a Push* has enriched my life, more so than all those years of hosting my own program. So I want you to hear this directly from me."

Everyone continues to hoot, holler, and carry on, save for Patty, Deva and me. Deva and I catch each other's eye. She mouths, *What's happening here, Reagan Bishop?* and I raise my shoulders. Deva may be on an entirely different astral plane sometimes, but she's astute enough to understand that joyous news is almost never uttered after the phrase "I want you to hear this directly from me."

Consider: It's rare that anyone will tell you, *I want you to hear this directly from me. I love you and insist on making you my wife.* Or *I want you to hear this directly from me. Here's a check for a gorillian dollars and you can retire!*

The "hear it from me" is generally employed when trying to make the unpalatable more appetizing. It's meant to cushion a blow, and said blow is generally delivered by whoever is instructing you to hear it from them in the first place. "Hear it from me" is far more likely to be followed by *Your mother and I are separating,* or *My test came back positive.*

Mind you, this isn't always the case, but it is often enough that I'm a bit wary.

"*I Need a Push* is too important for a nascent cable network."

This?

I can agree with this.

The crowd goes batshit crazy.

Wendy milks the following words for all they've got. "So . . . Weeee . . . Arrrrre . . . Headeeeeed . . . Toooooo . . . *Networrrrrrrrrrrrrrrrrrk!*"

Oh, Wendy—you got me! I really didn't expect you to deliver this kind of news! This is simply fantastic. Instead of languishing on some cable network no one's even heard of, we're headed to the major leagues! *In your face, Geri!*

The crowd is in such a frenzy that no one even notices when Patty stalks out of the room, except for Deva.

Deva leans in to say, "We should follow her, Reagan Bishop."

So we do.

We're able to track Patty because she's left a bread-crumb trail for us. And by "bread crumb" I mean "a string of profanity so vivid and profound that the words hang in the air behind her." Also, there's a swath of tipped-over lounge chairs and side tables. We catch up with her out on the beach.

"I sense you're troubled, Patty," Deva begins.

"No shit, Sherlock," she replies.

"Help me understand the source of your irritation," I add.

"At the moment? *You*." Patty stabs her pointer finger at me and then at Deva.

I tell Deva, "Classic transference." Then I say to Patty, "Clearly you're redirecting your negative feelings at us, instead of the source of your frustration. We're here to facilitate. Please, allow us to do our jobs."

Patty spits, "I thought her job was selling bongs."

Burn! I can't stop myself from snickering.

But Deva's unfazed. "It's true; I carry water pipes hand hewn by Nepalese craftsmen. In their culture, ganja has been used for centuries in religious festivals. Actually, one can find cannabis prevalent in almost all ancient cultures. The Chinese have been using it in their medicine for almost two millennia. In Africa, the Bashilenge used to greet one another by saying '*Moio!*' which loosely interprets to mean 'hemp.'"

"What you're telling me is that your bong customers are all ancient Bashilenge and not, say, garden-variety frat boys," Patty hisses.

"Should the men of Theta Chi be denied the pleasure of finding Nirvana simply due to having been born of privilege?" Deva counters.

I try another tack. "Patty, please, we've never seen you like this and we're concerned."

Also? Superinterested.

"Well, that's ironic," she says. "You should be worried about *you*."

"I don't follow," I admit. Why would anyone worry about me? I'm outstanding, which is one of the affirmations I give myself every day.

Patty flops down on the sand, having run out of steam after toppling all the pool furniture Godzilla-style. Deva and I settle in on either side of her. She stares out at the horizon before finally saying, "We had a good thing going on *Push*. The best, really. We had the ability to be nimble—we could take the time we needed. We were accountable only to ourselves. Everything will change with the network in charge. *Everything*."

I completely disagree. "By 'everything' don't you mean we'll finally be paid a competitive wage? Rumor has it I'll be adding a zero to my paycheck! And we'll have access to resources we've never had. Plus, we'll reach an entirely new audience. What's the downside?"

I mentally tally the upside—with more money, I could turn my building into a single-family and I wouldn't have to lease the other apartments out to unenlightened frat boys. I could travel more. I could fork out enough cash to get a natural-looking/feeling boob job, and not just one of the quickie discount ones that are like two grapefruit halves under the epidermis. (Yes, Posh Spice, I mean you.)

Sure, I was worried for a minute when Wendy started with the hear-it-from-me business, but this is a huge opportunity. This change will absolutely raise my individual profile. Maybe *I'll* finally write a book. Wouldn't Geri love that? And if we're headed to network TV, I presume this means we'll be on at night instead of our current weekly midafternoon time slot, ergo we'd be eligible for a *Primetime* Emmy, which is far more impressive than sitting around at a banquet full of aging soap stars. Oh, the spackle on those women (*and* men!).

"Granted, there will be perks in terms of budgetary concerns, like, you and Deva will finally have a wardrobe allowance," Patty admits.

Ha! Screw you, Ann Taylor Loft! Neiman Marcus, here I come! I start to give Deva a high five, but then think better of it. Decorum and all.

She continues, "But at what price come these benefits? Wendy and I debated this deal for months. I thought I'd finally convinced her not to sell, but the network execs got to her. Sure, she exacted promises to uphold the spirit of the show, but she also signed away all the rights." She pulls up a palmful of sand, allowing the grains to slip between her fingers. "Dust in the wind, that's what a network promise is. And deep down, I fear that Wendy knows it."

"But you two are like sisters," I argue. "I mean, she's built her entire career on the concept of sisterhood. She'd never let you down."

A shadow of something unrecognizable flashed across Patty's face. "Wouldn't she?"

CHAPTER FOUR

Running Away

I close my e-mail and slam shut my laptop because this news calls for a run.

I attach my iPod to the device that tracks my pace and pulse and weave my hair into a fat braid. My hair's probably the one frivolous thing about me—to appear my most professional, I should sport a neat, swingy, shoulder-length bob. Instead, I have the thick, dark tresses of a country music star, or possibly Wonder Woman. Actually, I heard the comparison a lot as a kid since I also have light blue eyes rimmed in gray and pale skin, much like Lynda Carter in those old reruns. (Minus the leotard, golden lasso, and ridiculous jugs, mind you.)

Geri's always saying my long hair dates me, and then Mary Mac will chime in about that being impossible, as no one wants to date me.

Yes, ha-ha-ha!

P.S. That's why you're not in my will.

Those two have always been envious of my looks. Whereas I'm a contrast in darks and lights, with long, toned limbs, they're short, red, and rotund and appear predisposed for guarding pots of gold or bitching about "me lucky charms."

My point is, I feel my style suits me, and besides, my hair's always restrained in some respect, be it pony/bun/chignon, so is it truly anyone's business? And Sebastian's always said my hair's my best feature.

Personally, I'd say my willingness to be naked in front of him would be my best feature should he finally return my call, but let's not split (lovely) hairs.

I slip my keys into a slim nylon waist pouch—fine, fanny pack—and lace up my lemon yellow/dark shadow–colored Mizuno Wave Rider 15s, which are the optimum choice for those with high arches. Right before I head out the door, I douse myself in a second layer of sunscreen and grab a baseball cap and sunglasses. After Hawaii, bits of my face and arms were peeling off for two solid weeks, so now I'm exercising extra caution.

I head down the stairs and lock my door behind me. When I step into the vestibule, I notice that my idiot neighbors have left their mail scattered everywhere. Of course they have. That's the downside of living in the Lincoln Park area of Chicago; you can't escape the influx of all the recent Big Ten grads.

However, I shouldn't complain, as the rent I collect from the Hawkeyes, Boilermakers, Hoosiers, Spartans, Wildcats, Badgers, et cetera in the garden and first-floor apartments covers the entire mortgage on my classic Chicago graystone. That's how I was able to afford it in the first place. Plus, my tenants' parents write the checks, so they always clear. Were these twentysomethings in my care, we'd have a long chat about codependency, but in this case, helicopter parenting works out for all of us.

My goal is to one day have the resources to make this a single-family home, yet when I shared that news with Mary Mac, she was all, "Why? You hate families." No wonder she's always exhausted—that kind of negativity has to be draining.

I skip down my front steps and bask in the brief coolness of the morning. Later today, the city sidewalks will be hot enough to fry eggs, but right now the temperature is still bearable.

I've always been fit, but I've been a dedicated runner since my time at Pepperdine. Between the stress of my program and the year-round spectacular weather, it made sense to take advantage of the outdoors. Actually, that's how I met Boyd in the first place. I was running on the Malibu Lagoon State Beach, which is one of the premier surfing spots because of a wicked right break. I was halfway through my five miles when this massive bandanna-wearing dog came out of nowhere and plowed into me. The mutt somehow hit me in the solar plexus and completely knocked the wind out of me, and I couldn't even catch my breath to shout for its feckless owner.

As I spat out sand, this—for lack of a better description—bronze surf god materialized to see if I was okay. The first thing I saw was his abs.

Holy guacamole.

Not only did he sport an insanely chiseled six-pack, but he had that V-cut musculature that you see only in underwear ads or old Marky Mark videos. FYI, the men at University of Chicago? Did not look like this. His dark hair had turned tawny in the sun and the surf, and his skin was perpetually golden, offset by eyes the color of a Tiffany box.

Turns out Boyd was as beautiful inside as he was on the outside. And he was smart, too. Originally from Long Island, he'd attended NYU and spent his summers surfing Ditch Plains in Montauk. He'd come to Pepperdine for his MBA, but after a semester, the lure of the waves was too much and he went from Future Master of the Universe to Part-Time Bartender.

We fell for each other hard and were inseparable . . . until his presence in my life jeopardized all my goals.

Like I said, you can't sustain yourself with ice cream for dinner. And that was a long time ago. Point is, even though Chicago isn't Malibu, my love for an outdoor run is everlasting.

Today my plan is to take a left down the densely tree-lined street, even though I'd much prefer to head right. I live a couple of doors away from the Caribou Coffee on the corner of Clark and West Arlington, and normally, nothing would make me happier than an iced green tea. But I have some frustration to process and the endorphin rush of a quick five-miler will serve me well.

I've run this route so many times, I could do it with my eyes closed. Today, like always, I stretch out on the stairs before starting a leisurely jog heading east down Arlington. Then I take Lakeview south, which borders the park, down to Fullerton and turn right on North Lincoln Park West. Sometimes I have to stop here and catch my breath. Today my *gastrocnemius* (the outer calf muscle) is tight, so I pause for a quick round of toe lifts, bracing myself on a bench at the intersection of North Lincoln Park West and Fullerton.

By the time I reach the Shakespeare statue a few blocks

down, I'm all warmed up and I loop back up to Stockton until I can cut over to Cannon Drive by the Lincoln Park Zoo entrance. Depending on the weather and time of day, sometimes I can hear the sea lions. I have no desire to see them, however. If I want to see a bunch of surly creatures flailing around in water, I'll watch Mary Mac's kids swim in my parents' pool.

After I cut over in front of the zoo, I run the length of the lagoon. No matter what time of year it is, I can count on seeing old men fishing in that spot. Never seen them catch anything, but I admire their commitment.

By this time, my heart's really pumping and I've entered the zone. Although with all the adrenaline already coursing through my system, I'm not surprised. I mean, I'm not angry at losing my summer off—this is the price we pay for prime-time exposure. And trust me, we're about to be well compensated for this sacrifice. But to cut Patty loose after everything she's given to *Push*? This show was as much her baby as Wendy's. I can't even fathom what the network brass at DBS was thinking in replacing her. How are we going to function without our spiritual center?

And will the new executive producer allow me to keep my prime parking spot?

Patty must have sensed this was coming, hence her being so upset on the beach that night.

Driven by my fury, I keep moving.

At North Ave., I cross over to the Lakefront Trail and keep going until I turn around in front of the Drake Hotel, which is my halfway point. On my way back north, I turn up the heat and do a tempo run all the way up the lakefront. Even though it's early, the beach is already busy, with cooler-toting families having staked out the prime spots. Sun dappled though the lake may be, I'd never actually dive into Lake

Michigan, having seen the number of saggy-swim-diapered toddlers on any given Sunday. *Cryptosporidiosis*, anyone? Thanks, but no thanks.

Despite this being a lake two thousand miles from where Boyd lives, I find myself inadvertently scanning the horizon for him anyway. Old habits, eh? I admit it; I miss him. After I decided we couldn't be a couple, we remained friends until I met Sebastian. Seb was so gung ho about being the only man in my life that I slowly stopped responding to Boyd's e-mails. It's better this way, though, or would be if Sebastian weren't sending such mixed messages at the moment.

This stretch is where I challenge myself, and my goal is maximum roadkill. (Passing slower runners. Of which there are many.) I keep up the velocity until I hit the volleyball courts on North Ave. I slow down a bit to see if I can spot any friends. Then I realize it's a weekday and anyone I'd recognize is at work, so I accelerate again. I maintain that pace until I hit Fullerton. From there until I reach Arlington, I do my recovery run.

I find it almost impossible to be upset after hitting the pavement. The runner's high is a real and powerful phenomenon.

So maybe I overreacted to hearing Patty's news. To be fair, Wendy was equally upset and she whisked Patty away for some quality time at Canyon Ranch. Seems like Wendy could have added the proviso that Patty run the show when she sold it to DBS, but her business is none of mine. Yet I'm confident those two will make it over this blip in their relationship . . . after all, they're like sisters. (Technically not a selling point in *my* world, but still.) And I hate to broach the possibility, but what if *Push* could benefit from fresh blood? Perhaps DBS is bringing in an executive producer who'll shepherd us to the next level. I guess I'll find out at the staff meeting this afternoon.

As I reframe events, I can feel my spirits lifting. Everything will work out as it should, and the universe has a plan.

Then I laugh at myself. I swear, Deva's starting to rub off on me. I wouldn't say we've become bosom companions since Hawaii, and I don't buy into her ridiculous beliefs like astral projection, but she's not without charm and I recognize that now. Just last week, we had dinner at the Green Zebra, a vegetarian, farm-to-table concept restaurant. Apparently she's friends with the owner, who wouldn't let us pay for a single bite. I'm a big fan of free.

As I slow my pace to a walk up my street, I blot the sweat from my brow and check the numbers. Twenty-nine minutes— bravo! I'm delighted with today's stats and make a note to run angry more often. I shaved a minute off my usual thirty. It's iced-tea time!

Except my good humor vanishes as soon as I see what appears to be an angry leprechaun perched on the wide cement railing by the front door, holding a foil-wrapped dish.

"A *Cubs* hat? Jesus, Mary, and Joseph, where did we go wrong with you?"

I lean down to kiss her cheek. "Hello, Ma."

"What, it's bad enough you have to live up here with all the quiche eaters, but you've gotta support their team, too? Your grandfather Murphy is rolling in his grave right now." My mother then stands to her full height of five-two—in heels—yet she carries herself like a giant. Her once flaming red hair is now shot with white patches, and her freckles are beginning to fight for real estate with her wrinkles. She refuses to try any of the fine antiaging products I've gifted her, saying she won't "put on airs." I hardly think moisturizing is "putting on airs," but it's simply too exhausting to argue.

Her still-vibrant green eyes are boring a hole in my stupid hat, as I've inadvertently reminded her of the crosstown rivalry that's been raging for a century. "Okay, okay, I'm taking it off," I tell her. My hair's damp with sweat, and I do my best to smooth it down.

"What I don't understand is why you'd put it on in the first place." Do I even need to mention that the rest of the family bleeds Sox black and white?

I try to remain patient. "Because I wanted to keep the sun off my face and it's the first thing I grabbed. Besides, it's not even mine—I think it belongs to Sebastian." Note to self: Have his assistant schedule us some time together over the weekend.

"Him," she snorts. Of course my family worshipped Boyd and they've never forgiven me for ending things. Geri was all, "But I love ice cream for dinner!"

Of course you do, sweetie.

Ma clucks her tongue, and she's still glowering as I toss my damp hat into the vestibule. "You know, your sister's already been to a dozen games at the Cell so far this year."

"I'm sure she's maintaining her girlish figure with a constant influx of ballpark hot dogs and giant beers."

Naturally, my mother defends her precious baby Geri. "You wouldn't know because you haven't seen her." Pfft. By design. "Besides, Geri's been busy working out. I hardly ever run into her anymore."

"Ah, so she's finally moved out of your basement?"

Geri is five years younger than me, but in that time period, everything changed in regard to how parents related to their children. I've no concrete evidence—yet—but I suspect the transition to helicopter parenting has something to do with those damn yellow Baby on Board decals that became so prevalent in the mideighties. I wasn't even made to wear my seat belt when I was little, but suddenly, Geri comes along and she's so valued she merits a sign? I remember my early summers when Ma would be all, "Go play in the vacant lot. The drifters and stray dogs won't bother you if you don't bother them." By the time Geri was five, my folks had fenced in the yard, constructed a massive swing set, and installed a swimming pool so she wouldn't ever want to roam from our yard.

Ma shoots me yet another disapproving look. "Nobody likes a smartass, Reagan."

I find myself clenching my fists. "Better than a fat ass, *cough *Geri* cough.*"

"Is that what they taught you in your fancy mental health college? To mock your sister's underactive thyroid problem?"

"Oh, so it's her underactive thyroid that makes her eat all those nachos? Noted." Then I stop myself. I hate when I get like this, but there's something about my little sister that brings out the worst in me. "You know what, Ma? That was inappropriate and I apologize. Please send Geri my best."

I don't mean it. But I have to say it.

"I'll do that."

We reach a tentative truce.

"Hey, what are you doing on this side of town? What's caused you to venture north of Madison?"

She shrugs. "Eh, there's a something at the Notebaert Museum and I promised Richie I'd swing by." I do admire how my mother's so thoroughly unimpressed by anyone that she has no problem referring to the former mayor as "Richie."

"Is Dad joining you?"

"Nah, he's over at Mary Mac's. One of the kids tried to flush a box turtle and now the plumbing's all jacked. The turtle's fine, though. Little pissed off . . . largely at being pissed on."

My mother cracks herself up at this.

(This incident does nothing to disabuse me of my notion that those children are trouble.)

"Anyways, the closet bend in the toilet? It's messed up, so your dad's working on it and couldn't come." Dad sold his plumbing business a few years ago and grudgingly retired, so he leaps at any chance to roll up his sleeves. Ma glances at her simple Timex. "Listen, gotta go. But here, this is for you." She thrusts the foil-wrapped pan at me.

"Um, thanks. What is it?" If I were a betting person, I'd wager whatever it is contains canned cream of mushroom soup, chock-full of MSG and sodium.

"Turkey tetrazzini."

"You made it with *turkey*?"

"That's why there's 'turkey' in the name, dear. Didn't they educate you on anything at *Battle of the Network Stars* school?" And then she snorts to herself again.

"Thank you, Ma, but did you forget I'm a pescatarian?"

She shrugs. "That's why there's no beef in it."

"Can't argue with that logic." Fortunately, the Nittany Lions who live on the first floor are going to love this dish, so I'll save it for them.

"Take care, Reagan."

"Okay, Ma. See you soon."

I kiss her cheek again and open the door to the vestibule, sure to retrieve my hat before it's usurped by a neighborhood Golden Gopher. I watch as my mother strides confidently down the stairs in her sensible shoes.

In terms of familial interaction, this wasn't so bad. I maintained my cool, and we didn't get into it over Geri. Mission accomplished!

But before I step onto the stairs leading up to my unit, I realize my mom's at the door.

"Hey, Reagan, I won't see you *soon*; I'll see you Sunday. We're having a birthday party for Finley Patrick. Plan to be there."

And with that, she totters off to her Buick, neatly and completely annihilating any positive energy created on my run.

After I shower, I grab the casserole and knock on the first-floor apartment's door. One of the boys occasionally telecommutes, so I take a chance that he's there.

Trevor answers the door clad in Penn State boxers and a rumpled hockey jersey, his early-days-of-Bieber 'do hanging even more in his eyes than usual.

"Trevor, did I wake you up?" I glance down at my watch. "It's almost one p.m."

He stretches and his shirt pulls up over his stomach, which he then scratches vigorously. "Yeah, I like to sleep in on the weekends."

"It's Wednesday."

He shrugs. "'S the weekend somewhere."

"Actually, it isn't."

"You sure?"

I nod. "Pretty sure."

"Shit. Anyway, wanna come in?" I step past his foyer and then into the living room. The layout of his place is identical to mine, with a large living room surrounded by bay windows. Whereas mine is arranged with low gray linen couches and butter-soft cashmere throw blankets, his entire room is taken up with a leather couch the size of a boxcar, positioned in front of the television altar. I have ecru silk dupioni curtains on top of feathery sheers, whereas he and his roommate, Bryce, have nothing. I don't know why this generation cares so little for the concept of privacy, but I suspect it has something to do with sharing every aspect of their lives on social media. Today's not the first day I've inadvertently seen this kid in his underwear.

Beyond the living room is the dining area. I have a vintage-look Parsons table from Crate and Barrel, whereas they've opted for the more traditional billiards table. Our units differ in that I renovated my kitchen and swapped it with the front bedroom for better flow. In his place, there are a couple of bedrooms and baths between the dining room and the kitchen, which made no sense. Now my master is over their kitchen. As they've no idea how to cook, I never hear them in the back of the house once I'm in bed, which works out nicely for all of us.

"Listen," I say, "I won't keep you from your, um . . . busy day. But I have this casserole I thought you might want."

Trevor snatches the container out of my hands. "Sweet! What flavor?"

"Turkey tetrazzini made with canned soup." I shudder involuntarily at the idea of the preservative-laden, gray-mushroomed, goo-topped noodles.

"Thanks, playa! Did you make it for us?"

"My mother brought it over. She knows I'm a pescatarian and yet she insists on bringing me a dish made with *turkey*."

He angles his head, looking down at me. "Thought you were Catholic."

I weep for this generation.

"Lapsed. And 'pescatarian' means I don't eat anything but fish. So turkey? No. No way. I'm sure it's not organic, pasture-raised, antibiotic-free turkey, either. Whatever's cheapest at the Jewel? That's what she used."

His whole face lights up. "Badass! How cool is it that she makes you dinner and then takes the time to drop it off? You have the best mom in the world, son!"

That's his takeaway from this situation? Here she completely disrespects my lifestyle choice and he thinks it's "badass"?

I point out, "Your mother pays your rent."

He rotates his head and I can hear the vertebrae in his neck popping. "Yeah, and I appreciate that. But anyone could write a check. It takes, like, *commitment* to make a dinner. I mean, my mom's my best friend, but she never learned to cook for me. That's love."

Yeah, *love*.

Or passive-aggressive.

CHAPTER FIVE

Big Time

For the sake of the show's continuity, DBS is leasing space from Wendy, so our offices are still in the South Loop WeWIN studio. We'll continue to film audience segments here, too.

I find a seat in the back of the conference room and set my purse down on an adjacent chair, saving a spot for Deva. As I settle in, I notice there's a steady buzz of conversation, and it all seems to be centered around the same topic.

"Where's the fruit tray?"

"Probably with the croissants. Which is to say, not here."

"Seriously? No one stocked the Keurig machine? Seriously?"

"I'm starving! Are the sandwiches coming soon?"

For the first time in *Push* staff history, the credenza behind the conference table is not groaning under the weight of all manner of treats—muffins, scones, bagels, doughnuts, cookies, cream cheeses, an assortment of nut butters, six kinds of juices, platters of fresh fruit, sandwich fixings, and ice baths brimming with boxed salads, yogurt, kefir, and individual servings of cottage cheese. In fact, there's not a morsel anywhere. Personally, I'm fussy about my food's origin, so I had a spinach salad and some hummus before I arrived and *I'm* fine, but still, it's odd not to see the usual spread.

"What are people going to have for lunch?" I say, more to myself than to anyone around me.

"Whatever they buy for themselves," says a masculine voice behind me. I whirl around to see an attractive man, maybe in his mid- to late thirties, leaning against the wall. I don't recognize him, but there are some new faces here. A few of the *Push* staff opted for the contract buyout, and a couple went to the scripted-television division, so we're an equal mix of old and new. Yet outside of the lights/camera/sound guys, we don't have a ton of male employees, so I'd definitely have seen him before if he were a returning staffer.

This particular gentleman is a shade over six feet tall, deeply tanned, with an almost imperceptible smattering of gray at his temples blending in with his short blond waves. The brown eyes are an unexpected twist. I'm normally a fan of light eyes/darker hair, like Sebastian, but I could see how others would find him handsome. He's broader than Sebastian, too. (All that biking and volleyball keeps Seb on the lean side.) My point is there's something decidedly rugged and outdoorsy about him, and I wouldn't be surprised to find, say, a kayak strapped to the roof of his car. I bet he owns one of those sloppy, friendly breeds of dog, too. Maybe a Lab or a retriever. There's something vaguely familiar about him, but I can't quite place my finger on what it is.

I'm distracted by admiring the cut of his blue gingham

shirt with the cuffs rolled up just so (is it possible to be attracted to someone's wrists? Because his are prime specimens; I suspect he could dig a well or smack a tennis ball like no one's business) when what he's said sinks in and I snap to. "But that's ridiculous," I argue. "Wendy's a fanatic about making sure snacks are available. She grew up poor and that forever changed her view on hunger—that's a big part of her story. In fact, combating hunger is her battle cry. Over the years, she's done dozens of shows on food insecurity and the chronic link between malnutrition and obesity. Surely you're familiar?" Huh. That is one square jaw he has there. Not quite as magnificent as the wrists, but fine all the same.

Sebastian's wrists are the tiniest bit dainty for my liking. You'd think they'd be, I don't know, *meatier* maybe, from playing volleyball, but they're not. He wears a couple of bracelets, too. Not a fan. Sometimes I think, "Hey, nice arm party you've got going on there, Johnny Depp." Of course, the last time I teased him about something innocuous—maybe the Drakkar Noir in his bathroom?—he went off the grid for a solid three weeks. Sensitive, that one.

"People are fat *and* malnourished? That dog don't hunt."

Is he flirting with me or is he actually dense? I'm generally attracted to intellect, so clearly this would rule him out. Clearly. Is he one of those guys who isn't aware of his looks or their impact on people?

"I assure you, I'm right. Are you at all acquainted with the concept of food deserts? People in low-income areas don't have ready access to many unprocessed foods, so even though their caloric needs are being met, their nutritional needs aren't."

He merely shrugs in a manner I find intensely annoying, so I press on. "Wendy's been a board member for a number of hunger-fighting charities and she's a tireless advocate for SNAP—Supplemental Nutrition Assistance Programs. The— let's face it—convenient by-product of her passion is that no one here has to buy his or her own lunch ever, and not just on the days we film."

He smiles and I'd be blind not to notice how straight and white his teeth are. *Somebody's* parents invested in orthodontia. Did I already award bonus points for not wearing bracelets? Then he says, "I don't believe in free lunch."

And like that, any charm this man could potentially have held suddenly dissipates.

I give him a tight smile. "I guess we'll leave that up to the new executive producer."

"Guess we will." Then he ambles off, presumably to annoy someone else.

Deva arrives moments later and settles in next to me. "Salutations, Reagan Bishop."

I quickly air-kiss her cheek. "Hey, Deva, I'm glad you're here. We've apparently hired yet another obnoxious staffer and I already hate him."

She studies my face and then looks me up and down. "Are you sure? Your aura is radiating clear red right now, which is more indicative of passion."

As if! "Then you're reading me wrong."

"If you were a murky red, I'd sense anger and . . ." Then she takes in the set of my mouth and my crossed arms and decides not to pursue the reading. "Okay, Reagan Bishop. I'm sure you know what's in your own heart. Let it be full of hate if that's your preference."

The conference room is packed to capacity and the meeting was supposed to start a few minutes ago. We've all been summoned here, but it occurs to me that I have no idea who's actually running the show now that Patty and her team are gone. As we're burning daylight, it's hot, and I'm sure we're violating fire code, I feel like it falls on me to finally ask, "Excuse me, who's in charge here?" We all crane our heads to see who's stepping up to run the show, both literally and figuratively.

And Mr. Outdoorsy Handsome Wrists replies, "That would be me."

Shit.

"The key word this season is *big*. I want big stories about big lives with big results. You follow?" declares Benjamin Kassel, our new executive producer (and free-lunch antagonist). He's been sent here from LA to run the show, or possibly ruin it; I'm presently undecided.

I glower from the back of the room. Actually, no, Benjamin Kassel, I *don't* follow you. I'm too distracted by the sound of everyone's rumbling stomachs and your refusal to use our given names.

Am leaning toward "ruin."

He points at Mindy, who's wearing a black T-shirt embossed with the words "Hail to the Thief" in white lettering. "You! Radiohead! What's this season going to be?"

"I don't know?"

Oh, come on, kid. This isn't exactly an SAT question or remembering your date's name before you take the walk of shame in the morning. She looks around for help and Craig mouths the answer to her. "Is it . . . big?"

Kassel claps so loud I jump in my chair. "Yes! And what's going to make it big? Anyone?"

I mutter to Deva, "His ego, perchance?" ("Wrists" would also be an acceptable answer.)

Benjamin "call me Kassel" spent the first twenty minutes of this meeting telling us all about his illustrious career, the highlights of which include dropping out of UCLA after his junior year and executive producing a show called *Make 'Em Eat a Bug*. Color me not impressed.

He points to me. "Something to share with the group back there, Peace Corps?"

My hackles are instantly raised. "I beg your pardon?"

"Seems like you have input. Love to hear it."

I sit up straight and level his gaze. "I absolutely have input. First, I believe I speak for the group in saying it's offensive to not be called by our given names. Dehumanizing, in fact. For example, I am Dr. Bishop, so when you call me 'Peace Corps' it diminishes everything I've accomplished as a professional."

His amusement fades and he puts on a serious face.

That's more like it.

I'll not have my credentials mocked; I sacrificed too much to earn them.

"Sorry. From now on, I'll call you Dr. Peace Corps." The shit-eating grin returns. Stupid orthodontia. "When you're finished giving the world a hug, *Doctor*, how will you contribute to making this show big?"

Definitely "ruin."

With as much control as I can muster, I say, "As I've done most successfully for two seasons, I plan to continue using cognitive strategies to help our pushees achieve maximum behavior modification through evidence-based treatment. In my experience—"

"Boring! I need asses in seats. Anyone else have a bright idea? Anyone?" He begins to point at various staffers. "You, Sideburns?" Our hipster/muttonchopped sound engineer simply shrugs. Then he gestures toward the dark-haired makeup artist who arrived late and is still wearing her backpack. "How 'bout you, Dora the Explorer?"

Under my breath, I tell Deva, "You want an ass in a seat? Then maybe you should sit down."

Deva replies, "For what it's worth, Reagan Bishop, I'm seeing the murky red now."

Kassel begins to pace in front of the whiteboard at the head of the room. "Here's the deal—everything about this show is wrong." At that, the audience starts to grumble, except for Mindy, who's mentally spent from answering such a difficult question and is now surreptitiously sending texts.

I whisper to Deva, "Why? Are our pushees not eating enough bugs?"

One of the preppy blond production assistants raises her hand. I'm perpetually intrigued by her vast collection of embroidered belts and gravity-defying collars. She's as sharp as a tack and ambitious to boot, so naturally Dr. Karen grabs her first whenever she can. "Wendy said we were doing God's work!"

"Bup, bup—don't get your panties in a wad, Muffy." Ironically, her name *is* Muffy. "Let me amend my statement. *Push* is at a five in terms of drama. That's being generous. We need to turn it up to eleven."

"How do you propose we do that?" I say, louder than I intended.

"First of all, we need better guests."

Craig volunteers, "They're called pushees."

"Uh-huh, they were, and now they're called guests, Horn-Rims. About the guests—boring! Bulimic ballerinas who don't let us film them bingeing and purging? Boring! Families who can't communicate their feelings? *Boring!* A hoarding grandma? Listen, if there's no flattened cat under that rubble, then she's wasting all of our time. Hoard big or go home."

Everyone's mouth is hanging open at this point. I can't be the only person in the room wondering if Wendy's just punked all of us.

Backpedaling a bit he says, "Don't get me wrong—no one wants to see a flat cat. Do you want to see a flat cat, Tank Top?" He points to the second cameraman, who replies, "Nope."

"Me, neither, I don't want to see a flat cat . . . well, at least not until sweeps. Point being if we're not in cat-flattening territory, then we haven't gone far enough! That grand-mother who was able to hide so much of her disorder? Bor-ing! I want trash up to the windows and spilling out the door. Understand? I want neighbors testifying about the smell in front of city council. I want to see bony ballerinas pirouet-ting knee-deep in empty Ben and Jerry's cartons and Doritos bags. I want families tossing chairs, all right? I want crazy on the outside where the audience can see it, am I right, Radio-head?"

To which Mindy replies, "Big?"

"See? Radiohead gets it. The rest of you will, too. If we're going to change everything, we have to change everything. Now, how do you guys normally find guests?"

"We filter requests from our Web site and viewer mail," says Ruby, one of the associate producers. Ruby used to run a YouTube channel and gained a bit of a cult following with her webisodes, so Wendy snapped her up, looking past her Goth-girl exterior, saying talent like hers shouldn't be wasted on the Web. Bar none, she's our best associate producer.

"You don't source them yourselves?" Kassel asks.

"That hasn't been necessary," Ruby replies. "We've had a lot of luck with the pool of applicants who contact us."

"Well, Nose Ring, your pool is shallow and boring, and that changes today. For the first month while we build an audience, we need to go big, big, big, so I've lined up some celebrities. Mostly D-list. Okay, entirely D-list. I'm talking ex–reality show people, aging teen stars, has-beens, basically anyone who's willing to bare their soul for a chance to be on TV again. And a check, of course."

Faye, a senior producer and Wendy Winsberg veteran, interjects, "We never pay our pushees."

"Which is why we've gotten what we've paid for to date. The new strategy is we use those famous enough to garner ratings, but not so famous that they can afford the house makeovers on their own."

I don't even realize my hand is in the air until he calls on me. "Problem, Peace Corps?"

I'm so rattled that I'm practically sputtering. "Since when do we do *home makeovers*? This program is about pushing individuals to change their behavior, not . . . product placing refrigerators."

I will *not* have my work upstaged by a guest receiving a free Ford F-150.

Kassel snaps his fingers at Carol, the office manager, sitting at the head of the table, who's done nothing but take minutes since the minute he started talking. "Yo, Note Pad, write that down. We need to approach Sears about a sponsorship. They're in bed with *Extreme Makeover: Home Edition*, but maybe their deal isn't exclusive. Okay, covered that. Who can tell me how you guys divide into teams once you've picked your guest?"

Ruby tells him, "We employ a collaborative approach. As a group, we choose who we're going to help and we make assignments accordingly. Once we decide on the lead producer, we assign according to everyone's interest and level of commitment."

Kassel nods. "So that's ridiculous. Antiquated. You looking to form a trust circle or are you trying to make powerful television? Well, we're done with the old ways and we're changing everything from the ground up. Radiohead, what do you have to say about that?"

Mindy glances up from her iPhone. "I'm hungry?"

Kassel high-fives Mindy. "Yes! That's right! You're hungry. We're *all* hungry—hungry for change. And the time for change has come. First up, enough with the management by committee. You'll work in small groups and you'll like it. We're going to specialize. There's no need for everyone to have their hands on every aspect. We'll divide and conquer! This is going to be great, I promise."

Then why doesn't it feel great?

I'm beginning to fear Patty was right—maybe you really can't trust a promise from a network guy.

CHAPTER SIX

Party Girl

I love *parties*!

I *love* parties!

I love parties!

Nope, no matter where I place the emphasis, I can't seem to psych myself up about this thing.

Under what circumstances might I be able to avoid the whole ordeal? I wish *Push* was already in production because I could claim to be shooting in a different city. But I opened my fat mouth and mentioned we weren't starting until next week, so that excuse is officially off the table.

Hmm . . . I could not go because I was sick. What a relief that would be! Summer colds are the worst, right? Everyone's at the lake or riding bikes or having drinks outdoors, except for me, who's at home, alternately freezing and sweating beneath the down comforter that covers my couch-bed.

And my coffee table becomes a mini organic pharmacy, with all the bottles of echinacea, goldenseal, honey and ginger tea. Time my illness right and I could catch up on an entire season of the more obscure *Real Housewives*, like DC or Miami. I never did quite hear the full story of the White House party crasher. And Sebastian could bring me sweet-and-sour cabbage borscht from the Bagel in Lakeview, even though matzo-ball would be better, except I don't eat chicken broth.

Actually, that sounds like a fun day.

I should make a mental note to not wash my hands after riding the El.

Although . . . *eeeew*.

Also, I'm not sure Sebastian would bring me soup.

Okay, what if I simply *pretended* to be sick? That might be doable. I could start planting the seeds right now on my Facebook fan page, mentioning that I feel a touch of something coming on. I'd lay the groundwork for skipping the party by describing a new symptom every day, all, "Hey, is anyone else experiencing postnasal drip?"

Then my coming infirmity would get back to the family because Geri follows my page. I'm aware of her presence because occasionally she'll "like" one of my comments or photos. Ugh. I wish I could block her from seeing my profile without causing a familial shitstorm, the likes of which would wipe out the entire north side of Chicago.

But nooooo, I have to endure her faux support. "So cool!" "Nice picture!" "Way to go!" Be a little more insincere, why don't you? Her running commentary absolutely incenses me because she's just doing it to be noticed.

Oh, I'm sorry, Geri—do you not already receive enough 24/7 attention from our parents, who love you so darned much that they believe your living in their basement is the totally normal thing for an adult child to do?

Or what about Mary Mac, who's also so deeply enmeshed that she bought a house two doors away? This is *not healthy*. Most families don't live in each other's backyards by design. They need distance. They need separation. They need the chance to miss one another once in a while. My parents even keep Mary Mac's husband's woodworking magazines in their bathroom in case Mickey has to make number two while he's there.

Go poop in your own house. It's two doors away.

What is *wrong* with you people?

And yet this is my lot in life. I'm obligated to be a part of their big, obnoxious, happy-family celebration. Now I won't have time to do the full thirteen-mile training run I'd planned on Sunday, followed by an afternoon of recovery and iced beverages at the 'Bou. And I'll be hard-pressed to settle into my research and organization for my preproduction meetings with my new team this week. Instead, I'll be forced to make pleasant conversation with my asshole sisters, and if I'm not polite, Ma will drag me by the ear into the laundry room to yell at me. I'm thirty-three years old and I have a doctorate degree, yet the second I walk in the front door, I'm a child all over again.

I am a *party girl*!

I *am* a party girl!

I am a *party girl*!

It's official—I can't positively affirm myself into not dreading the day.

I wake up feeling like there's an anvil on my chest. For a second, I wonder if I didn't accidentally manifest my dreams of bird flu into reality, but then I remember it's Sunday and I have to attend the stupid birthday party.

At least I'll have the confidence of having picked the perfect gift. I spent an hour at the Building Blocks Toy Store on Lincoln trying to find something awesome for little Finley-Cormack-Liam-Patrick-pick-a-name-already. The clerk and I settled on a motorized erector set. He's already expressed interest in being a builder like his old man, so I'm confident he'll love it.

I won't hold my breath waiting for a thank-you note, though.

I pull up to my parents' classic Chicago bungalow, my heart in my throat. Why do I have to do this? I'd rather be anywhere but here. Like, perhaps getting a Pap smear. Possibly from Captain Hook. I'd kill to be draped in nothing but a sheet right now, my gynecologist urging me to scoot a little bit closer to the edge of the table.

Or maybe I could be taking my SATs again.

Wait, I *enjoyed* taking my SATs. Poor example.

The front door's open, so I let myself in, walking through the living room, which has barely changed a lick since I lived under this roof, save for my mother finally, *finally* removing the plastic slipcover from the formal floral sofa. Have you any idea what it feels like to sit on a plastic-covered couch on a sweltering July day? Your skin fuses to it and practically peels off when you finally stand up. Of course, Princess Geri requires central air for her delicate constitution, so my parents upgraded from ineffectual window units only after I left for college.

This room is a moment frozen in time. Almost every doily, every knickknack, every occasional table has been in the exact same spot for as long as I can remember. The shelves on either side of the fireplace and mantelpiece are still filled with all the old photos and trophies, too. What's ironic is I've given them a dozen photos of Sebastian and me, yet they refuse to replace the antiquated shot of Boyd teaching me to surf on Zuma Beach. (I do rock the bikini, though.)

The rest of the house is more modern, and Dad's always upgrading the size of his television, but this particular room is a living Bishop family time capsule. I peer at the shot of Mary Mac clad in her Irish dancing outfit. She looks so young! She's always weary now, slouching around in yoga pants and a ratty ponytail, so it's odd to remember her all fresh faced, not being surrounded by half a dozen kids and covered in oatmeal.

In this photo, her hair's pushed back with a mini-crown, and she has hundreds and hundreds of perfectly formed copper-colored ringlets. My mother struggled with the curling iron for years before finally saying, "Screw it," and investing in a wig. Said it was the best decision she ever made.

I remember how much I admired Mary Mac's Irish dance solo dress, which you couldn't just buy. Instead, the right to wear that garment had to be earned through competition and participating in exhibitions. And then it wasn't a matter of simply picking out whatever the dancer preferred. Instead, all the candidates had to model dozens of options for the dance mistress. Dancers ranked their favorites and then the mistress matched up which girl should be with which dress. Mary Mac briefly joined a sorority in college and said the rush process wasn't nearly as intense as the dress selection.

God, I loved her solo dress. It was the most magnificent piece of clothing I'd ever seen. The top was perfectly fitted due to the lattice of silken ribbons running down the back. The deep cobalt blue velvet fabric was embroidered with what looked like peacock feathers cascading in a multicolored waterfall down from the shoulder, forming a handkerchief hemline. The skirt was full and swingy due to layers and layers of petticoats, while the bell sleeves added a dash of worldly elegance and sophistication. The fact that no two solo dresses are the same only added to its mystique.

While I study the shot, my jaw inadvertently clenches. I remember how I couldn't go to language camp the year Mary Mac received her dress because it was so expensive. Then, within six months, she stopped competing on the weekends in favor of hanging out with Mickey. Yet was I allowed to borrow her glorious garment for trick-or-treating? Of course not! Mary Mac was all, "Sure, you can wear it—as soon as you earn the right."

Do I even need to mention how ten years later, Geri happily Riverdanced all over the neighborhood in the damn thing on Halloween?

I force myself to head into the party because this little trip down memory lane isn't helping my mood. At all.

I pass through the kitchen, and even though my mother's about to feed forty people (most of them Mary Mac's kids), I have to admire how there's nary a cup, plate, or fork out of place. Everyone's out in the backyard, on the deck, in the pool, or—and I never understood exactly why—in the garage. How is this an appropriate gathering place? Dad parked the Buick on the street, so now the whole area's filled with neighbors sitting in lawn chairs around the buffet.

"Well, lookie here, it's President Reagan! Hey, would you like some jelly beans?"

"Heh, hello, Mr. O'Donnell. Wow, that joke never gets old," I respond, trying my best to smile. Mr. O'Donnell bears an uncanny resemblance to former Speaker Tip O'Neill, from the dense patch of snow-white hair to the broken capillaries in his ample beak. He's lived next door to us my entire life. He's kind of like an uncle, in that I don't particularly like him, and yet I can't seem to avoid him at family gatherings.

"Where's your boyfriend?" he asks.

That's a damn fine question. Seb made some noises about joining me, yet he's not returned a single text since then, hence the solo appearance.

I share the most likely scenario. "Working."

"Is he still surfing?"

I nod, because it's easier than explaining that the only surfing this particular boyfriend does is on the Joseph Abboud Web site.

He pinches me on the cheek and it's all I can do to not slap his hand away. "You're so skinny! We need to fatten you up! Have one of the sausages—your sister made them from scratch. Oh, that fennel!"

There's quite a crowd gathered back here, made possible by my dad having the foresight to snap up the vacant property next door about twenty years ago. Now they have a rarity in Chicago—a double lot. I keep telling my folks that Bridgeport is red-hot real estate now and they should sell, but they never will. At least, they won't until the yuppies move in. (There are two Starbucks within walking distance now—I keep telling them gentrification is imminent.)

Eyeing the crowd, I spot almost everyone immediately. My dad's working the grill, while Mary Mac hovers watchfully by the side of the pool. I'm not sure why Mickey can't play lifeguard, freeing Mary Mac up to enjoy herself for once. After all, the pool's only five feet deep and he's taking up half of the surface of the water on his inflatable boat. I admire his ingenuity in realizing that he could float a small cooler next to him. Very convenient.

Kids are running all over the yard, each one making more noise than the other. One of the ginger boys dashes up to me, demanding, "Where's my gift, Auntie Reagan?" I hand him the festively wrapped package, which he immediately tears open. I hope he understands the time and thought I put into this present.

"What is this crap?" he asks.

I bristle. "It's a motorized erector set. So you can build stuff, just like your dad."

He dumps his present on the cedar picnic table, covered in checked red-and-white oilcloth. "Lame! I wanted Call of Duty."

It's not that I dislike children; it's just that I dislike these particular children.

Which is why it's not my fault that I'm compelled to lean in and whisper, "Then I guess it sucks to be you."

His eyes widen for a minute before he careens off and cannonballs into the pool next to his father.

"Hey!" Mickey calls. "You're getting chlorine in my beer! Mary Mac, I need a towel. And gimme one of those sausages, too. Oh, that fennel!"

My mother spots me and ambles over. She reaches up to give me a quick, dry peck on the cheek before she admonishes me. "Party started an hour ago."

"Sorry, Ma, there was a lot of traffic." A lie, but it feels true. I can always count on the vagaries of the Dan Ryan to buy me a late arrival. As I scan the crowd for a glimpse of my nemesis, I reply, "I'm here now, though," with a bright, insincere smile painted on my face.

"You hungry?"

"Not really." I make it a rule to eat before attending a family event; otherwise, I have to make a meal of garnishes. Nothing about their choices meshes with my lifestyle. Case in point? My cheese does not come in a can.

"Grab one of the sausages your sister made. They're fantastic—oh, that fennel!"

"That's the word on the street."

My mother tries to detect whether or not I'm being sarcastic, but in the spirit of the day, she decides against grilling me. "Have you said hi to everyone? Of course you didn't. Go talk to Ethel. Maybe you can shake some sense into her. Ya know, 'therapize' her. You're always bragging about how you're a doctor. Do me a favor and use your skills to make a difference for once."

Argh.

Jack and Ethel Culver have lived across the street from us for twenty-five years. No one likes Jack, but he's tolerated for Ethel's sake. Over the years, the neighborhood's been playing armchair therapists, speculating that Mr. Culver has a borderline personality disorder. Listen, I've studied BPD and treated afflicted patients. Trust me when I say he's not symptomatic. More and more often, society looks to official diagnoses to explain and understand abhorrent behavior, but the truth is, sometimes folks are just jerks.

Jack happens to be one of those folks.

Everyone on the block is at a loss to explain why Ethel refuses to leave him. His verbal abuse is legendary, and I remember having to close our windows on summer nights to suppress the sound of him berating his wife over some minor offense, such as not having swept the front porch or cooking a dry meatloaf.

The verbal abuse is but the tip of the iceberg, too. Whenever Ethel visits her sister in Madison, Jack invites strange women to the house, not caring in the least that the entire neighborhood witnesses his infidelity. Over the years, we've easily seen fifteen different makes and models of mistresses' cars parked in front of his place.

Given how tight my parents' block is, and how much everyone hates Jack Culver, I'm perpetually shocked at Ethel's reticence to listen to reason or accept help. More than one Tupperware party–cum-intervention has been staged to convince Ethel that he's a bum.

At Ma's insistence, I offered to work with her pro bono when I was first licensed, but she didn't care to upset the applecart that was her life.

I have to take a deep breath before answering. "I do use my skills to make a difference, Ma. But in this case, I can't counsel anyone who doesn't want my input."

My mother looks at me long and hard. We're at a stalemate here and she knows it. Resigned, she says, "Well, the least you can do is grab some more Jungle Juice drinks for the kids."

"Mmm, nothing says 'pure refreshment' like high-fructose corn syrup and artificial red dye number five," I reply. "Are you all out of arsenic and need a less expedient way to poison the kids?"

"They add vitamin C," Ma argues.

"Which they could get naturally from actual orange juice instead of this science experiment gone wrong."

Ma's nostrils flare as she exhales. "Just bring up the damn juice, Reagan. It's in the utility room downstairs."

"Will I have to pay the basement troll a quarter for permission to cross her bridge?" I ask.

Ma's eyes narrow into little slits. "If you mean your sister, she's not here, Dr. Smartypants."

"Really? Geri lives for gatherings like this. Where is she? There's no home game at the Cell, is there?"

"Her girlfriends gave her a Mexican cruise for her birthday! She left two days ago and comes back next week. I guess everyone at her salon pitched in and surprised her."

"That's amazing!" I exclaim.

Ma beams. "Right? Our Geri, everyone fights to be in her orbit."

"No, I mean that it's amazing that she's found an entirely new group off of which to sponge." Before Ma can grab my ear, I duck and skitter backward. "Okay, getting the Jungle Juice now!"

I take the back stairs into the basement. When I was in junior high school, my parents finished off a couple of rooms down here, so not only is there a bedroom and full bath, but there's also a whole living area and a kitchenette. A lot of the houses in the neighborhood are two-family dwellings, so my parents are already zoned to rent this out as an apartment, if Geri would only leave already.

I pass the living area and approach Geri's bedroom. I ease the door open and I'm immediately assaulted by the sickly-sweet smell of her perfume. Pfft, more like Lady *Gag*.

Even though she's out of the country, her presence is practically breathing down the back of my neck. This must be how Batman feels when he happens upon the Joker's lair.

Anyone else would assume a teenager lived down here due to all the pink furnishings and the unicorns. I'm sorry, what kind of adult still collects stuffed animals? Her bulletin board is filled with stubs from seeing football games and crappy bands, with ropes of Mardi Gras beads and placards from various hair shows.

Geri's floor is littered with shoes and purses and clothing, much of it turned inside out. I imagine this is what the dressing room at Forever 21 looks like every night. Her bed's unmade and her desk is piled with magazines and catalogs. I shudder to imagine what's in the space between the mattress and the floor.

When my dad finished the basement, this was originally my room, so he turned two entire walls into built-in shelves to hold all my reading material. Books are how I escaped as a kid. Between my dad watching the ball game in his boxer shorts, my ma smoking with her sisters in the kitchen, and Geri being Geri, sometimes I'd head downstairs with a book on Friday afternoon and not come up for air until Sunday.

Naturally, there are no *books* in Geri's bookcases now. Instead, they're full of trinkets, gewgaws, some profoundly creepy big-eyed Japanese dolls, and tons and tons of snapshots. Seems like Geri's forced every single person she's ever met to pose for a picture with her. Typical. Toward the back of the shelf, I spy a couple of family pictures that include Boyd.

You guys; stop trying to make Boyd happen.

It's not going to happen.

Being in here is giving me the heebies as well as the jeebies, so I start to pick my way over the detritus to take my leave. As I'm about to walk out the door, I notice a newly framed picture hanging on the wall next to her closet. I'd recognize the ocean backdrop anywhere, of course, even if my wearing a cap and gown weren't a heavy clue as to date and location.

Geri and I are standing close together, sun shining on our faces, and the breeze ruffling her long red hair. She has her arm around my shoulders, wearing a huge grin on her face, likely because she was moments away from congratulating me on earning my *Battle of the Network Stars* degree.

But still, in this one moment captured on film, we actually look like friends.

Like sisters.

How have I never noticed that we have the same chin and identical bows on our top lip? Her eyes are green while mine shift from slate to blue, but we have a markedly similar dark ring around our irises and a matching arch in our left eyebrows.

I guess I've always concentrated so hard on what makes us different that I've never taken the time to appreciate what's the same.

And for one brief second, I wonder if I've not misjudged Geri, and maybe misinterpreted her intentions.

Before I can process this thought, I feel a pinch in the vicinity of my earlobe and I find myself being dragged into the laundry room, face-to-face with my mother's fury.

"Did you just tell your nephew that it 'sucks to be him'?"

And just like that, I'm nine years old all over again.

"Thank you for joining me."

"It's my pleasure, Reagan Bishop." Deva and I are sitting outside at Caribou Coffee. I called her when I returned home from the south side. I have other friends, of course, but there's something calming and comforting about Deva, and I needed to feel anchored to someone after yet another stressful parental visit.

Sitting across from Deva, I already feel cheered.

Or maybe it's just that it's hard to be in a bad mood when

your coffee date is dressed liked Princess Jasmine/I Dream of Jeannie (depending on your generation).

She sips her tea and appraises me. "I'm seeing a blockage around your heart chakra." She pulls out her enormous carpetbag and begins to rifle through it. "Have you experienced feelings of loneliness and anger? I may have some ylang-ylang essential oil, which will help. You may also find that completing a series of the Ushtrasana posture will loosen your blockage, Reagan Bishop."

"Or we could have a conversation," I offer.

"Isn't talking about your feelings new age nonsense?" she asks with a wry grin.

"Do people realize you're funny?"

"I had everyone in the Lakota sweat lodge laughing last week, Reagan Bishop," she replies. "My one-liner about tai chi and chai tea had them rolling in the aisles." Then, more to herself than to me, "Or maybe that's because it was a hundred forty degrees in there."

"Your karma ran over my dogma," I quip.

She clutches her massive hand to her chest. "Oh, Reagan Bishop, I'm so sorry, I didn't realize. We must mourn the loss immediately."

"Um, Deva, I was kidding."

She laughs so hard her turban shakes. "Zing!"

See? Cheered. I didn't get my run in today, but I am sitting outdoors with an iced beverage, so it's not a total loss.

Deva leans back in her chair and folds her legs underneath herself. "Tell me about your childhood, Reagan Bishop."

"Are you doing another bit?" I ask.

She cocks her head to the side and peers at me. "No, I was asking about your childhood."

That catches me by surprise. "Oh. What do you want to hear?"

"What do you want me to hear?"

I sigh. "I don't know."

Deva nods. "Then I don't know, either."

"Then I guess we're at loggerheads."

Deva grabs her bag again. "Okay, then, Reagan Bishop, essential oils and yoga it is. Would you prefer we do Camel Pose here or shall we take it indoors?"

I clap my hands together. "Conversation it is!" I hesitate before I begin to speak, unsure of how what I'm going to say will be received. "Let me give you the caveat that I don't want to sound like a spoiled brat. For all intents and purposes, I had an ideal childhood. I was fed and clothed and educated. We had enough. Or, close to enough. I suspect our occasionally having to share resources is why I don't get along with my sisters now. They always seemed to wheedle their way into just a little bit more than they deserved, and it made me crazy. But still, people built bookcases for me. I was loved."

"I can see why you're troubled, Reagan Bishop."

"Sarcasm is not part of the therapeutic milieu," I retort.

Deva is completely guileless. "I'm serious. There's no problem like a first world problem, Reagan Bishop. There's a tremendous amount of guilt associated with a feeling of unhappiness despite having ample resources. I see it all the time in my line of work. You have everything, yet you feel bad about not feeling good and then you feel worse. It's a vicious cycle. Some of my clients have every luxury at their fingertips, yet they're soul sick over the smallest slights. I work with a gentleman from Texas who has a G550. Then his nemesis bought a G650. Even though both airplanes can fly from

Seoul, South Korea, to Orlando, Florida, in a single trip, my oilman's depression was palpable."

"How did you help him?" I ask.

Vaguely, she replies, "Sometimes my solutions are unconventional and subject for a different conversation. My point, Reagan Bishop, is that a problem feels like a problem, no matter of which world it's a part. So this is a safe space. Please share." Then she clasps her mighty paws into prayer position.

I swish the ice in my drink with the straw. "I'd say everything boils down to my childhood. As you know I have a couple of sisters; one of them's just like my mom and the other's exactly like my dad. I'm not the same as anyone else in the family. For years I was sure that I was switched at birth. The rest of them have red hair with scads of freckles, and they're all short and, let's be honest, a bit tubby."

"Have you any suspicion of adultery, Reagan Bishop? Tell me about your mailman."

I wave her off. "No, nothing like that! My parents are about the two most upstanding people on the face of the earth. Apparently I resemble my great-grandmother, who was already gone before I was born. But it's not even about physical features. I'm so *different* from them. On the inside. They're all content to live in our old blue-collar neighborhood and do the same things and see the same people. Personally, the idea of never living more than three blocks from my family home makes me feel so claustrophobic I can't even breathe."

Deva nods, saying nothing, so I continue.

"Mary Mac was satisfied to dance and chase boys and Geri reveled in being the life of the party. Neither one of them ever have had lofty goals, no huge aspirations. But I wanted more and I was made to feel like an outcast because of it. Plus, both my parents worked, so we didn't have a ton of time with them. We girls were always jockeying for their attention. From a very early age, I realized that what made me special was academic performance, so I threw myself into studying, and when I wasn't studying, I was reading."

"How did you get along with other children?"

"No problems. Kids seemed to like me. I wasn't bullied, nor was I a bully. I was sort of . . . removed from it all. I was too focused on grades and books to really worry about school-yard politics. How about you?"

Deva swallows hard and replies, "About the same," and yet I'm not sure I believe her.

"Anything you want to discuss?" I ask. She seems like she's hiding something.

Breezily, she replies, "Perhaps another day, Reagan Bishop. But I'm curious as to why you chose the profession you did."

"Promise not to laugh?" I ask.

"Indeed."

"Frasier."

She cocks her head. "As in the fir?"

"No, as in the psychiatrist from *Cheers* and then from *Frasier*. I was just hitting my teens when the spin-off show came on, and it was the one program on which the whole family could agree. Of course, my folks loved it because they thought the retired-cop dad was so great, but I identified with Kelsey Grammer's character. He breathed life into what I felt every day—like he was a lotus who grew out of the mud."

"I thought your parents had a pool in their yard."

I reply, "Nice mud, solid middle-class mud, but still. Mud. Outside of Mary Mac's feckless year at Northern, no one's educated, no one's white-collar. Financially, my parents have made a number of sound decisions, but try explaining that to the snotty little shits at Taylor Park. I knew I was out of my league socially when I got there, so I threw myself into academics to avoid potentially being ostracized."

A flash of something darkens Deva's features for a moment, but she blinks hard a couple of times and it quickly passes. "The best thing about high school is that you never have to go back," she says lightly. "But at least you love what you do now."

Deva's statement almost comes across as a question, so I confidently reply, "Indeed."

Of course I love what I do.

I mean, I feel like I love what I do.

I definitely love the benefits that come from being on *Push*. I love feeling like I'm changing lives in front of an audience. I love the travel and how it's never the same show twice. Plus, I love meeting fans in the grocery store. I really loved having access to Wendy Winsberg.

Back when I was in private practice, I truly enjoyed assisting others in finding resolutions, even though sometimes I could get a bit distracted. I'm not always as patient as I should be in certain situations, either. And yes, sometimes it's frustrating that I can't just take the damn reins already and force my patients into the right direction. But overall, therapy is the best job I've ever had, and it's only been made better by being on camera.

I think.

I did adore the work-study I held in the U of C writing lab, but that was a million years ago.

Of course, I never considered whether I'd rather hold another job, because this is what I've been training for my entire adult life, and I have another ten years' worth of student loans to prove it.

I'm doing what I should be doing.

Of course, Boyd would disagree, but he no longer has a say.

My point here is I got ninety-nine problems but the job ain't one.

At least, that's what I tell myself.

CHAPTER SEVEN

Adventures in Awesome

"Here are half a dozen Twitpics of her modeling a thong. Wow, that mesh front doesn't leave a lot to the imagination, does it? Clamshell-city."

Ruby's scrolling through her iPhone and narrating the most alarming status updates from Ashlee Austin, our show's first official guest, while the rest of us listen. I wasn't terribly familiar with Ashlee's body of work, but according to Faye, she was a huge teen star on some kids' network years ago. Ever since her TV show *Ashlee's Adventures in Awesome* ended, she's made a series of questionable decisions, which have recently escalated in severity.

Ruby winces as she thumbs past entries. Despite all outward appearances—piercings, dyed black hair, dominatrix boots, et cetera—she possesses the moral compass of your garden-variety Mennonite. "Good God, Ashlee. *Please* tell me you didn't do this."

"What now?" I ask. After hearing dozens of disturbing tweets, I shouldn't be surprised by this one.

Ruby reads, "'*LAPD r bulshet*'—I think she means bullshit—'*and I waznt drinkin much. Am just supr skinnie from juice cleanz and low toleratin.*'"

"Her DUI is a matter of public record, as are all her hit-and-run accidents," Faye says, not looking up from her almost constant knitting. She quit smoking last year and now she channels her nervous energy into her needles. She made me a gray cashmere pashmina recently—it's gorgeous! "That's why she's agreed to appear on the show. The judge said she could come to *Push* or go to jail."

Ruby replies, "Yeah, but the arrest itself isn't the most cringe-worthy part. I'm referring to the fifteen subsequent tweets to the Speaker of the House demanding he grant her diplomatic immunity. She keeps calling him 'Congressman *Boner*.' I feel secondhand shame for her. Is this about the drinking? Is she an alcoholic?"

"Possibly, possibly not," I reply. "I won't have a clear picture until we begin therapy. Diagnoses aren't always so cut-and-dried. Her binge drinking may be an offshoot of something else, say, an accommodation for a social anxiety disorder, rather than a true addiction."

"Ashlee seems like she'd be superfun," volunteers Mindy.

Ruby, Faye, and I exchange weary glances. None of us are thrilled to be saddled with Mindy. I suspect she was assigned to our team because each of us took umbrage with Kassel at the initial production meeting. We've tried to limit her participation in today's strategy session, but we've already sent her out for hot beverages three times in the past two hours. I don't know which is worse, the prospect of Mindy catching on to our collective contempt or my bladder exploding from consuming so much green tea.

Mindy adds, "TMZ reports she's been stalking Ol' Rat Nasty. Wonder if that's true. I guess I can ask her later, right?"

"I'm sorry—who?" I ask. I'm missing the better part of a decade of pop culture familiarity from when I was busy with grad school and my internship. At the time, I had no idea shows like *Gilmore Girls*, *Veronica Mars*, and *Battlestar Galactica* even existed.

"Ol' Rat Nasty! Don't let the name fool you, he fiiiiine," Mindy gushes.

Faye explains, "He was a child star, too. His given name is Clarence Floyd and he was on that sitcom where the alien family crash-lands in South Philly. *Marz 'N the Hood*? Sound familiar?"

I shake my head. "That was real? I assumed it was a *Saturday Night Live* parody." At the time, I vaguely recall Boyd used to quote something like, *"Martians? In Philly? I won't hear of it!"* which now makes more sense.

"Huge hit," Faye assures me, inspecting the length of stockinette-stitched baby blue alpaca yarn. Satisfied with her work, she continues. "Really massive. Was syndicated in something like eighty-three countries. Clarence was positioned to make the leap to film and become the next Will Smith. Then he dropped out of the public eye in his late teens."

"Did he snap?" I ask. Sadly, they almost always snap. One day, they're cashing a residual check, the next they're robbing a dry cleaner.

"Far from it! He went to Cornell and then enrolled in

USC's business school. Got his MBA at Marshall and he's since reinvented himself as the rapper Ol' Rat Nasty. He owns a record label now, too."

"And a line of energy drinks," Ruby adds. "I just read in *Forbes* that NastyWater grossed a hundred fifty million last year."

Mindy exclaims, "NastyWater's sick!" I'd inquire if "sick" were a positive or a negative, except I don't care. "Anyway, I'm pretty sure Ashlee wants to get her Nasty on."

Ruby nods. "Ah, hence the following tweet. Brace yourselves—'*I wish Ol' Rat Nasty would slay my panty hamster.*'"

My skin crawls.

I hear a commotion in the hallway, immediately followed by a firm knock. "Hello, hello! Your star is here!" Kassel materializes at the door of our conference room, followed by the other staffers on our team, including a hairdresser, a makeup artist, an interior designer, a fitness guru, a wardrobe stylist, Kassel's assistant, a couple of interns, and Deva. The last person in the room is a very pretty girl with a very bald head.

"Everyone, meet Ashlee." I notice Kassel has no problem calling *her* by her given name. Typical.

I'm not sure what to make of Ashlee's naked pate. She doesn't appear to be ill and there's a healthy amount of stubble, leading me to believe she's not undergoing chemotherapy. That's when I notice Mindy's gawping, complete with an open mouth, and I realize that this 'do is both new and unexpected.

After a round of introductions and greetings, Kassel whips out his iPad and begins to rattle off the schedule. The hair on his wrists is particularly sun-bleached and downy.

Not that I care about that kind of thing. I equally admire

Sebastian's slender wrists. (That is, when they bother to operate his hands and dial me back.)

Everyone takes notes except for Ashlee, who stares forlornly out the window, occasionally running a hand over the barren landscape that is her skull.

"You." Kassel points to Marcy, the interior designer. She's all done up in Pat Benatar eye makeup, shoulder pads, and fluorescents. She looks like the physical embodiment of a Nagel print. Are the eighties back again? I can never keep up with this stuff. "You're heading to Brentwood to work on Ashlee's condo. Your sketches have been approved and supplies are ordered. The contractors are on-site already and they've started the demo. You're set, get out of here."

Marcy scoops up her portfolio and fabric-sample binders and exits in a cloud of Christian Dior Poison.

"The rest of us will stay here in Chicago. So here's how the next week shapes up." Kassel's assistant then hands out hard copies of the schedule and tells us she's also sent each of us electronic copies. "Starting Monday, Ashlee's working out with Jimbo every morning from nine a.m. to twelve p.m. She'll break for lunch until two p.m., and then she's doing a hair consult Monday afternoon—you have a wigmaker lined up, yes?"

Marco the Roman hairdresser offers us the thumbs-up. "*Sì!*"

I'm so glad we're covering the most important elements first.

"Excellent. Makeup on Tuesday, wardrobe Wednesday, therapy Thursday, and Friday you do your voodoo. Heh." He gestures toward Deva, who places her palms together and gives him a slight bow.

"Sound like a plan? Everyone understand their role?"

I glance down at the single sheet. "Where's the rest of our schedule? Or will our time with Ashlee vary from week to week?"

Kassel frowns at me. "What week to week? This is it."

"But that can't be."

"I assure you, Peace Corps, it can and will."

I'm gobsmacked. "I'm sorry, what? Is your expectation that I have *an afternoon* to help this girl? That's it? A few hours on a Thursday? Are you kidding? How do you expect me to miracle any sort of results in an afternoon? The whole point of *I Need a Push* is having the time and resources to instill real change. I can't do that in an afternoon." Venom (and panic) practically drips off my every word.

And, not to split hairs, but what of my screen time? I pretty much was the entire show, and now I'm going to be what? A segment between picking out paint and shopping for sneakers? Unfair!

Kassel nods and begins to scroll through his schedule. "I hear what you're saying and I wouldn't expect you to solve everything in an afternoon."

That's more like it. The idea of trying to—

He continues, "Feel free to work through dinner."

"I have no idea what Ashlee's problems are and I certainly can't treat them in half a day!" My blood pressure has shot through the roof and I can feel my heart almost pounding out of my chest as hopes for my spin-off slip away.

Deva whispers to me, "So murky red, Reagan Bishop."

Kassel shrugs. "All I'm saying is Dr. Phil can do it in an hour. With commercial breaks."

I leap out of my seat. "Then maybe you should hire Dr. Phil."

"Like we could afford him!" Kassel cracks himself up

over this line. "Besides, Dr. Karen said the timeline was no problem."

"Because I'm sure she'll medicate the pushees—"

"Guests."

It's all I can do not to slap the bejesus out of this man. "Then she'll medicate the *guests* into oblivion. They'll be too drugged up for recidivism!"

Kassel leans forward and rests his arms on the table. "I'm failing to see the problem here. We get our aha-moment footage, the pharmaceuticals help guests curb whatever behavior brought them to us in the first place, and the audience thrills in the big reveal at the end of the show. If they need it, we'll pay for therapy afterward. This formula has Emmy written all over it. Trust me, I've won six."

"This is utter and complete . . . six, did you say? You've won six Emmys? *For eating bugs?*" His news completely stops me in my tracks.

Not that recognition of this sort would change my treatment plan, but six Emmys is more than a little impressive. What would it be like if I were part of the team who won six Emmys? What would my family say? Maybe they'd finally have something to talk about other than Mary Mac grinding her own sausage for the birthday party. *Mary Mac—these have so much flavor! And they're so tender! You're so talented! Oh, that fennel!* Really? A homemade encased-meat product garners that kind of praise? Correct me if I'm wrong, but the process of stuffing your own sausage isn't much more complicated than putting on a condom.

Then again, Mary Mac has, like, a dozen kids. Perhaps anything related to using contraception *should* be cause for celebration.

When I graduated from Pepperdine, everyone said, *This*

doesn't give you license to psychoanalyze us, Reagan. No *Great job!* or *What a stunning achievement!* Where were my sausage-stuffed kudos? Why does the bar have to be set so much higher for me? How is that fair? I'm killing myself here and Mary Mac gets a parade for having made lunch.

Kassel's continued to talk while I've been lost in thought, but I manage to catch the end of it. ". . . then why don't we ask Ashlee? Ashlee, are you able to extend your treatment more than a week?"

Ashlee curls her delicate lip. "No way. That'd cut into my time filming *The Bitches of Brentwood.*"

"I can't wait to watch!" Mindy enthuses. Then she explains, "It's a reality show, kind of like the *Housewives,* only trashier." According to *Us Weekly,* which I might read at the gym on occasion, it's supposed to be *Keeping Up with the Kardashians* meets *Mean Girls.*

Who'd want to watch *that*?

(I mean, if they weren't home sick with a summer cold and all the rules were temporarily suspended.)

Ashlee smiles for the first time. Personally, I'm concerned that she doesn't consider "trashy" an insult. I mentally place "self-worth issues" at the top of my list.

"Ashlee," I reason, "I'm fighting for you right now. Help me help you."

"You really want to help me?" she queries.

"In any way that I can," I reply.

She rises from her seat and starts to walk away. "Then come with me."

Before I can even ask where we're going, Kassel uses his wrists (and palms) to shove me out the door behind her.

CHAPTER EIGHT

And Then That Happened

As we exit the studio parking lot, I find myself in the back of a stretch limo with Ashlee and Gary. To this point, I've known Gary as "the second cameraman," as I see him only on the rare occasions when we're shooting on location.

We haven't officially started taping yet, so none of the crew are available in the studio for this mission, save for Gary, who, up until three minutes ago, was napping on the same couch where a pint-sized action star once jumped up and down, declaring his unquestionably heterosexual love for a well-compensated ingenue (like you do). And then, two minutes ago, Kassel loaded him and his camera in the car with us with the instructions to "Film everything!"

"Why were you sleeping in the studio?" I ask.

He rubs a bit of crud out of his eye and says, "I was tired," like this is a perfectly reasonable explanation.

"What's wrong with your house?" I ask.

"It's hot."

"Turn on your air conditioner."

"I'm not sure I have one."

What does that mean? "You're not sure? Have you checked your thermostat to see if you have the AC setting?"

"No. But someone must have checked or I'd have known, right?"

"Do you have roommates?"

"No."

"Then who would have looked at the thermostat and told you anything one way or the other?"

"I don't know." He scratches his chin. "That is indeed a puzzler."

"Maybe until you determine the status of your whole-house HVAC, you could purchase an air conditioner for your bedroom so you don't have to sleep on the couch where we film the show?"

He peers at me as though I've just revealed all the secrets of the universe. "Huh. I guess I never thought of that." As he looks around the back of the limo, he focuses on Ashlee's head. "Have you always been bald?"

She simply scowls in response.

I can't blame you there, sister.

The driver lowers the privacy screen and asks where we're going. Ashlee rattles off an address in the vicinity of the Mag Mile and our ship of fools sets sail.

Minutes later, we're idling in front of the Peninsula Hotel, apparently waiting for Ol' Rat Nasty to make an appearance. Ashlee tells us he has a show at the Allstate Arena tonight, and, like many visiting celebrities and dignitaries, he makes the Peninsula his hotel of choice when in town.

Although considered luxury lodging since its inception, the hotel established itself as the undisputed leader when America's Golden Girl, Jennifer Aniston, checked in while filming *The Break-up*. Which I then heard *all about* because Ma was able to finagle a set visit for Geri. (When the mayor's office asks for a favor? Grant it. That's the real Chicago way.)

I'm told Geri charmed Jennifer, and they ran all over town having margaritas and manicures and massages together, leading me to believe Jennifer is more pretty than smart.

I notice a fleet of Maybachs lined up at the entrance, dozens of paparazzi, scores of groupies behind a velvet rope, and a handful of beefy bodyguards milling about, signifying Ol' Nasty's imminent arrival.

While we wait, I admire the hotel's impressive facade with its giant stone fu dogs standing guard at either side of the doors. Impeccably white-suited doormen in little pillbox hats scurry to and fro, ushering posh guests through the revolving doors. Watching the high-heeled, scarf-wrapped socialites enter laden with bags from Chanel, Gucci, and Cartier, I'd be hard-pressed to discern this Chicago street from one in Paris. That is, until a thickly mustached construction worker strolls by eating a Maxwell Street–style Polish dog piled high with grilled onions and topped with mustard.

So many nitrates.

I'm not really sure what Ashlee's plans entail, so while I wait for some sort of cue, I observe an impeccably appointed family exiting their Rolls. They're immediately set upon by the bell staff. Never in my life have I witnessed so much Louis Vuitton luggage in one place, and I've traveled with Wendy Winsberg, so that's saying something. Watching the privileged clientele conduct their business in front of the velvet rope–contained fans makes the scene all the more incongruous. Yet somehow there's something inherently pleasing about the contrast between the groups. In fact, this dichotomy is one of the reasons I love this city so much—Chicago encompasses so many different worlds living side by side under the same sky.

I've never stepped inside the Peninsula, but it's been on my list of places to frequent. Sebastian and I were supposed to meet up for drinks a while back, but he had to bail on me at the last minute. Ooh, that reminds me—I need to check my texts.

Nothing.

Argh, so annoying.

Anyway, when I mistakenly mentioned our missed connection, Geri prattled on about how the truffle-oil fries in the lounge were to die for and how the whole lobby turns into Chocolate at the Pen on the weekends, boasting buffets full of pastry chef–created delicacies.

Three points to make here: (1) Sebastian and I need to get on the same page about our "break" and soon, (2) I would be very careful about loading up on truffle-oil fries or chocolates if I wore Geri's pant size, and (3) if the Wicked Witch of the South keeps crossing over into my northern territory, I'm going to have to find me some flying monkeys.

As we wait in the car, Gary and I quietly regard Ashlee taking an enormous swig of champagne, straight out of the bottle. Sensing our gaze, she offers a sip to Gary, who refuses only after he feels the weight of my glare.

I have a sinking feeling about this whole enterprise, so I try to offer Ashlee my counsel. "Please walk me through your plan, Ashlee. What I'm hearing you say is you'd like to start a relationship with Mr. Nasty. You believe that the only factor keeping you apart is physical separation, so when you see him, you're planning to"—I pause to make sure I quote her correctly—"'Get down on his jock.' I'm wondering if there aren't more appropriate ways to demonstrate your interest. Perhaps you could post on his Facebook wall."

Then I remember her NC-17 tweets and reconsider the idea.

Regardless, my gentle guidance falls on deaf ears. Instead, she spits, "Why, do you think I'm a whore or something?"

"Ashlee," I calmly reply, "what's motivating you to ask that question? Perhaps you can tell me, how would you define the term 'whore'?"

But the short answer here? Yes, yes, God, yes, I think you're a whore! You tweeted four million Twitter followers in-depth details of your "panty hamster"!

Quick sidebar? It's a myth that mental health professionals don't judge their patients. As human beings, we find it almost impossible not to let our values seep in and color our opinions. The key here is keeping that information/judgment to ourselves. Even though we'd love to say, "You are as effed up as a soup sandwich," we don't.

Yet I wonder what would happen if we did?

Before Ashlee can answer, the first members of Ol' Rat Nasty's entourage begin to materialize. With their shiny grilles and low-hanging pants, they're dressed in stark contrast to the rest of the guests, yet their confidence clearly projects the message *We belong.*

Wave after wave of handsome young men gather outside the vestibule's doors, posturing, smoldering, and posing up and down the sidewalk. Then they do their best Red Sea impersonation and part, allowing Ol' Rat Nasty to step out.

And that's when, in the words of Chinua Achebe, one of my favorite writers, Things Fall Apart.

Seizing the opportunity, Ashlee leapfrogs over me and

flies out the window of the limo, pushing aside a dowager clad in head-to-toe Lagerfeld. Fortunately, the bell staff rights the woman so quickly as they sweep her away, later she won't even be sure that she'd fallen.

Then, instead of, say, introducing herself to Ol' Nasty or perhaps shaking his hand, Ashlee chooses the more unconventional approach of reaching up under her minidress and removing her underwear, which she promptly *tosses in his face*.

My first thought is, Not enough hand sanitizer in the world.

After some contemplation, I find Ashlee's action shocking, largely because I didn't peg her for the kind of person who opts for any type of undergarment in day-to-day situations.

Shame on me for prejudging.

But trust me, we shall cover *this* in therapy. As extensively as time allows.

Then, in an entirely unforeseen turn of events, and like Rafiki displaying baby Simba in the "Circle of Life" song, Ol' Nasty cups the wisp of fabric and holds her undies up over his head for the crowd to behold. While his audience is still gasping, he tucks the panties in his shirt like the world's most perverse pocket square.

This is the point when I reconsider my decision to leave private practice.

The paparazzi are collectively losing their minds, not only for the act in and of itself, but also because this is the first time they're received visual confirmation of the rumor that Ashlee shaved her head in a state of rage over having been seated at an undesirable table at the Ivy.

The moment is captured by a dozen cameras except, ironically, the one belonging to *I Need a Push*, as moments before, Gary discovered the button to raise and lower the privacy screen between the back and front seats and has been otherwise occupied.

I suspect some cognitive delays on his part.

As for Ashlee, I can't speculate on what a mental health professional would normally do in a situation like this because situations like this *don't normally happen.* My first impulse is to protect *Push,* so I rocket out of the car and attempt to grab her. Ashlee feels as light and delicate as a Hefty bag full of chicken bones in my arms, and she offers up little resistance as I try to wrestle her back into the limo. However, my efforts to stanch the humiliation (on both our parts) are waylaid by the groupies as they topple the velvet ropes and we're swept up in the melee.

Instead of Ashlee's act bringing shame down on everyone's heads, the NastyGirlz (a skankier version of the Beliebers) are thusly inspired by her fresh, bold move. Suddenly, the staid East Superior Street entrance to one of the nation's premier properties turns into the Running of the Brides at Filene's Basement. Dozens of attractive women wearing very big hoop earrings and very small shirts start dropping trou right there on the sidewalk. Only instead of baring all in order to snap up a bargain wedding dress, the NastyGirlz begin *tossing their own unmentionables* at Ol' Nasty. I liken this to an explosion at a Victoria's Secret sidewalk sale, with thongs and push-up bras raining lace and leopard-print shrapnel all around us.

I suspect that in the future, when the CDC traces the virology of the plague that wipes out half of the city, this spot will have been ground zero. I fear I'm contracting genital warts from simply watching the scene unfold.

One of the doormen is returning from walking a guest's dogs, and that's when the four prizewinning, Continentalclipped, tightly wound standard poodles enter the fray. Any dog enthusiast will tell you that, despite the poodle's being the smartest of all breeds, there is no panic like Poodle Panic.

Let me repeat, lest there be misunderstanding: *There is no panic like Poodle Panic.*

The dogs utterly, profoundly, and collectively lose their minds in the underwear storm and wrench loose from the hapless bellman. Like giant puffs of cotton candy run amok, they froth and foam and spin in circles, their stray fur floating on the air like so many dandelion seeds. They pinball through the crowd looking for egress, yipping at a decibel more often associated with dolphins.

At that moment, a family of Prada-panted, Disney World–shirted Japanese tourists exits the building, thus alerting the dogs to their escape route. In a cloud of pom-poms, fangs, and fury, the canines immediately dash underfoot toward the revolving door, making a beeline for the safety and sanity of the Peninsula lobby.

As the dogs prepare to force their way into the building, they first have to slip through the legs of Ol' Rat Nasty's entourage, who've since been frozen in position by shock. Many of these men grew up in questionable neighborhoods and are well equipped to not only maneuver but also protect themselves and their boss, having cut their teeth in the highly charged East Coast/West Coast dynamic so prevalent in the last generation of rap music.

But a Westminster Kennel Club throwdown?

Completely unprepared.

Because the men's pants are flying at half-mast, and since a standard poodle can stand twenty-five inches from the tips of his paws to the top of his head, the fifteen-inch inseams prove no match for two hundred pounds of raging poodle.

One after another, the panicking poodles clothesline the entourage in their low-hanging fruit, butting beribboned heads into denim-clad crotches and tumbling the gents like so many bowling pins. Soon the ground is littered with flat-billed hats, unlaced Timberlands, and the shame of the next generation of rap artists.

Fortunately, their falls are broken by a cushion of undergarments, so their only bruises are to their egos.

And there's Ol' Rat Nasty, right in the middle of everything, grinning sardonically and saying, "Okay, gurl, message received. Imma *do* this." He grabs Ashlee and tosses her into the limo, much to the delight of TMZ and much to the surprise of Gary, who's been busy trying to tune in *SportsCenter* on the limo's television. I'm still closing the door as we careen away from the chaos Ashlee created.

"That was *awesome!*" Ashlee squeals as she sidles up to Ol' Rat Nasty.

Gurl, we need to talk about your choices.

But instead of capitalizing on his predicament and turning this moment into the beginning of an X-rated rap video, Ol' Rat Nasty says, "Ashlee, I find your behavior appalling and I'm uncomfortable with your persistent advances."

Beg your pardon, guy who TMZ dubbed the Master of Misogyny?

In the seconds since Ol' Rat Nasty entered the car, his entire demeanor has changed. An imperceptible but crucial shift occurs. Gone is the hip-hop swagger, replaced by an icy calm and competence. In the blink of an eye, he morphs from the dude your parents warned you about to the man who brokered the merger between Bank of America and Merrill Lynch.

He brushes dust and groupie glitter off himself, then adjusts his pants so he can properly cross his legs. He says, "Ashlee, my dear, I urge you to channel the energy and creativity you devote to attempting to seduce me via social media into something more productive. Perhaps you could work with children or take a pottery course? You could change lives, or, at the very least, you'd create an interesting bit of crockery in which to store your keys."

This from the performer who nightly closes his show with the lyrics "Punch the ho in the pussy / Punch the ho in the pussy / Don't be a [f-bomb] wussy, [horrible, terrible, deeply offensive racial slur that I hesitate to even acknowledge exists, except that it's part of the song so I feel I have little choice] / Punch her in the pussy"?

"Your interest is not reciprocated, am I making myself clear?"

Numbly, Ashlee nods. I glance over at Gary to see if he's filming all of this, but he's completely immersed in watching the wind take the cocktail napkins he's tossing out the sunroof.

"Look, Dr. Reagan!" he exclaims. "Floaties!"

Nasty pats Ashlee's knee in a fatherly manner. "I'm not well versed in what brought you to this point in your life, but I recognize your behavior as unhealthy and self-destructive. I implore you to seek help."

"I'm getting help!" she whines before attempting to somehow make *me* responsible for today's debacle. "That's my shrink right there!"

He turns a gimlet eye on me. "You willingly participated in these shenanigans? I'm sorry, which of the APA guidelines are you following right now? Because I'm curious."

I give him the nutshell version of Ashlee's participation in *Push* and the new format of the show, and his attitude changes.

"I thought I recognized you!" he replies. "Hey, aren't you a Pepperdine alum?"

"Yes! Go Waves!" Even though I didn't follow sports, I feel like this is the appropriate thing to say.

"I almost did my MBA there!"

"What's a Pepperdine?" Ashlee asks, clearly distressed at having been excluded from the conversation.

He gives me a sidelong glance. "It's where they used to hold the *Battle of the Network Stars.*"

"Totes cool!"

"Let me ask you something, Dr. Bishop," the increasingly inappropriately named Ol' Rat Nasty asks. "How does anyone expect you to resolve problems rooted in choices in an afternoon? Patients need time to implement behavior modification. The onus is on them to learn how to respond to triggers, rather than react. You're not a witch doctor! You can't give your patients a magic potion and make their behaviors go away! I'm so disenchanted with Wendy for allowing this to happen. The next time she and I are in Southampton together, I'll definitely share my disappointment."

I reply, "You're rapping to the choir here."

As we drive around waiting for the crowd in front of the Peninsula to disperse, Nasty asks for a quick architecture tour. He's particularly smitten with the Mies van der Rohe buildings. "I adore his use of nonhierarchical wall enclosures," he sighs.

We make a loop past the hotel and see there's still a bit of a presence there, so we end up circling the Viagra Triangle, thusly named for the drug of choice of the gentlemen who frequent the area on the weekend. Were it a Saturday night, this whole area north of the Magnificent Mile would be full of hair-plugged men, driving convertibles through their midlife crises, looking to hook up with the plentiful twentysome-thing women angling to quit their day jobs and become trophy wives. But as it's midafternoon, the streets are empty, save for a few Jamaican nannies and their young charges.

When Sebastian and I met, he was living in an apartment down here right behind Hugo's Frog Bar. I convinced him he'd be far better off in Lincoln Park, so when it came time to buy, I helped him find a wonderful condo with a lake view in walking distance from my place. Despite things being on and off between us right now, I'm so glad he's away from here. This place is a spawning ground for bad decisions. I don't even like driving on this block, so I instruct the chauffeur to head south.

That reminds me to check my texts.

Nada.

I wonder if he's in a meeting. He sure wasn't in a meeting last night!

(I mean we had sex, if that wasn't clear enough.)

As we pass the Peninsula again, we note that save for the TMZ crew, it's business as usual, and Ol' Rat Nasty decides it's time to say good-bye.

With a glance at the sullen bald girl, he tells me, "You have a Sisyphean task ahead of you, and I wish you all the best."

I shake his hand, unsure if he means with Ashlee or the show in general. I'm not sure I desire clarification. "It was a pleasure to meet you, and I'm sorry for the circumstances."

"Godspeed, Dr. Bishop. Pleasure to meet you, Gary. And, Ashlee? The Sinead look doesn't work for you." Gary, who has since nodded off, wakes long enough to give him a mock salute.

As we pull up to the curb, Ashlee asks him, "Are we really not going to bone?"

He kisses her on the cheek and replies, "Not in this lifetime, my dear." Then he takes Ashlee's underwear out of his pocket and hands them back to her. "These belong to you. My advice is you put them on and leave them on." Then, almost sheepishly, he adds, "I hope you all can forgive me for what happens next, but I have an empire to protect. There's a reason it's not called NiceWater."

When he exits the car, he seamlessly shifts right back into his public persona, strutting up to the guys from TMZ. "Y'all see that shiz? That was *wack*. I'mma tell you all about it!"

I actually enjoyed connecting with the Clarence behind Ol' Rat Nasty, yet despite my appreciation for his rationale, I can't help but resent how he just threw me, my guest, and my show directly under the bus.

CHAPTER NINE

Blast from the Past

"The network feels I should fire you, Peace Corps."

I wish this news was a surprise; it's not.

Yet the truth is not that I did a terrible job with Ashlee. Quite the opposite, in fact. The network is partially pissed over Ashlee having pulled herself together without our intervention.

Technically, we *did* intervene—it's just that Gary didn't capture a moment of footage. I suspect Ol' Rat Nasty wouldn't have signed a release to use tape of him even if we had any, but it might have been nice if Gary had at least tried. Then, when Ashlee had her epiphany as we drove back to the studio, I didn't have the heart to interrupt her to say we needed to start rolling. She was so forthcoming about her problems with her "momager" and her "frenemies" that I'd have felt unethical in interrupting her flow.

So, like a tree falling in the forest and no one hearing the sound, it's as though her breakthrough didn't happen. At least not on *Push*'s watch.

Now that Ashlee finally has the world's eyes on her again, she's blossoming under all the positive attention. She was witty and engaging on *Good Morning America* earlier this week, and she killed it on *Kimmel* with all the self-deprecation. And the wigmaker worked wonders! All of which would have been fantastic, had *Push* received the credit. (Related note? I could live without the media having nicknamed me Dr. Wack.)

I could have easily weathered the Ashlee storm, had she not been immediately followed by Hurricane Lance Voss.

Lance Voss is world-famous for being the former bad-boy NBA player with three loves in this world: strippers, cocaine, and model railroads. The trains in and of themselves aren't problematic, although I wonder if I couldn't have gotten through to him a little more had he not spent the entirety of our three-hour filmed session struggling to correct a grade he'd built too steep.

After the Ashlee debacle, Kassel and the network were thrilled with the visuals of our session. There Lance was, this shirtless behemoth of man, biceps bulging, covered in tattoos from the neck down, pierced nipples peeking out from under his pinstriped engineer's overalls, matching cap, and a red bandanna, looming like a Japanese movie monster over his tiny town. Yet Lance was sweet and forthcoming on-camera, largely because he wanted us gone so he could do more rails. (The drug kind, not the model-train-enthusiast kind.)

To me, it was clear that he was shining us on, telling us what we wanted to hear, but to the casual observer, he seemed open to change. And I suspect that given the time and the tools the old *Push* would have afforded me, we could have been successful in manifesting healthier behaviors.

Fortunately, Lance is an inpatient at Promises now and receiving the intensive one-on-one treatment he desperately needed. Unfortunately, he was sent there for having tried to commandeer an Amtrak engine after running out on a nineteen-thousand-dollar bar tab at Scores.

Let me just say this: The media has not been kind about the incident, with the lion's share of the blame once again going to *Push*, and I'm just mortified. By itself, the shame is bad enough. But Geri's been calling me all week, no doubt to rub it all in. Each time I see her number, I send the call directly to voice mail before deleting the message without listening. I've no desire to hear her gloat. Naturally, Sebastian pulled yet another one of his disappearing acts. Why is he perpetually busiest when I need him most?

As I was pacing last night, I was so desperate for some reassurance that when the phone rang, I picked up. At that point, I didn't even care if it was Geri on the line. A smug hug is still a hug.

"Hello?"

"What do you say, Ray?"

I'd have known that voice anywhere. Deep and smooth, with the slightest trace of a New York accent.

"Boyd? What . . . how did . . ." I was at a loss for words. I hadn't spoken to him since the early days of Sebastian, almost three years ago, and certainly not since I bought my house and installed the landline.

I could feel him smiling all the way out in California. "How'd I get your number? A little Geri told me. No, no—don't be mad. I Facebooked her to see how you were doing and she said you were avoiding everyone. I figured you could use a friend, so here I am. Hello, friend."

I couldn't help but feel a tiny bit better. "Hi, back."

"I assume Sebastian's not there or he'd make you hang up."

I snapped, "I don't need him here to hang up on you."

"Whoa, Ray, I promise I come in peace. Just figured you could use an ear. No judgment. Just love."

I sank down into the couch. "I also don't need your love, Boyd."

He snorted. "Yeah, you made that clear when you left me standing on the beach back then."

I winced, remembering how I went directly to Surfrider after my adviser read me the riot act. Although I'd done exceptionally well in my classes, I'd sort of . . . misplaced the passion I should have been funneling into my dissertation. Ironic, because writing was kind of my thing.

He said, "Let me start over. Hi, friend. I'm calling to see how you are. You okay?"

I took a deep breath and began my tale of woe. "I'm not. I have a meeting with the show's executive producer tomorrow and I'm afraid he's going to fire me. What's going to happen to me if I lose my job, Boyd? I'm already a national laughingstock. I definitely won't be able to work in television. *Good Morning America*'s never calling me again."

"Stephanopoulos was flirting with you last time you were on."

"Right?" I exclaimed. "I thought so, too! And by the way, did anyone in my family even bother to watch my episode?"

"You're trying to make a cat bark, Ray. Your folks love you and they're proud of you, but they're never going to demonstrate the level of validation you want. You're never getting a parade. That's not who they are. They'll show you in different ways, though. Your dad'll upgrade your garbage disposal and gas up your car. Your mom'll trek to the north side to bring you a casserole, cursing the whole way. That's what they do."

"Well, that's neither here nor there," I said, trying not to feel guilty about the chicken à la king I found in a cooler on my porch earlier and immediately donated to the guys. "The bigger issue is that this scandal could be a career killer. Who'll book me for a speaking engagement now? And I can't imagine private patients lining up to see *Dr. Wack.* I'll be ruined. I'll never be able to show my semi-famous face in Whole Foods again."

"Is being recognized—and subsequently mocked—in the grocery store really a big deal?"

"No." *Yes.*

He laughed. "You're a terrible liar. But it's okay, you can still be my friend."

"Does that title come with dental and a generous base salary?"

"Maybe."

As much as I've tried to deny it, I miss bantering with Boyd. We used to spend hours having silly little arguments about the most ridiculous stuff, like whether I was Mrs. Robinson or a pedophile for having a crush on *Catcher in the Rye*'s Holden Caulfield.

"What are you up to now, anyway?" I asked.

"Little of this, little of that," he replied in his usual noncommittal fashion.

"Any chance you've gone back to business school?"

"These feet were not meant to wear wing tips, Reagan. Give me flip-flops or give me death."

What I really wanted to know was if he was seeing someone, but I wasn't sure what I'd do with the information once I had it.

Some questions are better left unasked.

"Are you happy, Boyd?"

"Every day, every day. Can you say the same?"

"On the eve of being fired? Probably not." Pondering my fate, I could feel my stomach knot. "Seriously, what'll I do with myself if I lose my job? Sit around and watch television and get fat? Become a hairdresser? As is, I've been so distracted that I can't do the marathon this year because I haven't kept up with my training."

He sighed into the phone and I could picture him running his hands through his hair. "Reagan, baby—when'll you learn to cut yourself a break? Take a breather? Would it be so bad to have an open schedule for the first time since you wrote your dissertation?"

"You mean, when you had me so distracted being your little surf bunny that I completely procrastinated writing it?" I think back to the beach with Boyd and how his pals would tease me for wrapping myself in the terry-cloth equivalent of a burka. Sometimes I miss those days so much it's a physical ache.

"Guilty as charged. I'd do it again, too."

I curled into the corner of the couch and inadvertently wrapped myself in a throw, remembering how he'd laugh about the SPF properties of terry cloth.

"What am I going to do, Boyd? My only skill is counseling people."

"Not true," he countered. "Your writing always impressed me, Ray."

Even though I was heartbroken when I finally sat down to

begin my dissertation, I can't help but remember the joy I felt putting words to page. I always wanted to write a book, yet I assumed that would happen after I'd had some major accomplishments. Losing my job, even if it's through no fault of my own?

Hardly an accomplishment on which to base one's literary career.

"Thanks, but if you recall—and I'm sure you do—*this* is the choice I made. I mean, I dedicated the last decade and a half to getting here, and it's so wrong that I'm being penalized for things that aren't in my control. The stuff with Lance Voss couldn't have been helped. I had three hours with him! That's not enough time to bake a brisket, let alone address a decade of addiction."

"You back on the cow?" Although Boyd's a carnivore, he never once teased me for my dining proclivities. In fact, he'd perpetually seek out the best vegetarian and seafood places because he knew they'd make me happy. And he's the one who introduced me to the wide world of organics in the first place.

Of course, Sebastian is Captain Steakhouse. But I figure it's a trade-off, what with his career involving more than board shorts and a shot glass.

"God, no. I just couldn't think of anything that might take me more than three hours to do."

"I might be able to occupy you for that long."

And then I blushed, because he was right.

"Listen," I told him, "I have a big, awful day to prepare for tomorrow, so I've got to go. It's been good to talk to you. Thank you . . . friend."

"Miss you, Ray. I'm here if you need me. Take my number." He rattled it off and I parroted it back to him, pretending to write it down.

As smooth as it may go down, I can't eat ice cream for dinner; ergo, the past is inevitably best left in the past.

As for my present?

I'm about to learn my fate.

Kassel leans across his desk. "Relax. I'm not going to fire you."

A wave of relief washes over me. I can feel the tears beginning to well in the corners of my eyes, but I fight them back. I loosen the death grip I've had on my phone, which is now slick with my own terror sweat.

He amends his statement. "At least not yet."

Kassel manages to sound empathetic when he says this, gazing at me from behind his surprisingly old-fashioned antique partners' desk. This heavy, hand-carved piece of furniture is a good six feet deep, meant to accommodate workers on either side, so I feel like I'm sitting a mile away from him. I was shocked when I saw his office for the first time. I'd have pegged him for picking a hypermodern glass-and-steel workspace, but that's not the case at all. This room projects exactly as much warmth as it did back when Patty had draped every surface in tapestry.

He's lined the walls with old books—really, a reader?—and he's covered the floor with a sumptuous vintage Persian rug in a myriad of subtle jewel tones. Deva says she recognizes the pattern from her time in Tabriz. (I haven't a clue as to what she was doing in East Azerbaijan. She called it Persia, which is the politically correct way of saying Iran.)

"Thank you," I practically whisper. I hate how much my voice quavers.

"Don't thank me yet, Peace Corps. I'm in a world of shit because of you. The Ashlee episode was supposed to be our premiere, followed by Lance Voss. Those are both off the table now. I've gotta go with the third runner-up, which is Dr. Karen and the hand washer. Not big. Not at all big." He makes an obscene gesture to punctuate his point, inadvertently drawing attention to his glorious wrists.

As it turns out, tales of the aging soap star's obsessive-compulsive disorder were largely a figment of her publicist's imagination. So it's not like it was particularly difficult for Dr. Karen to capture big changes on film. The trailer featuring Andrea DiAngelo dipping her paws in a compost pile has been running all week, leading up to the show's premiere.

I cast my gaze downward as he continues. "Do not cock this next one up, got it? You have one more shot. This next episode is do or die for you. Keep in mind, if you're gone, then your whole team is outta here. Understand? You're a package deal. Sorry to be harsh, but that's how it's gotta be. I fought the network to keep you, so *do not* make me look bad."

I'm awash with equal parts shame and determination. I'll be devastated if anything happens to Ruby or Faye because of me. Ruby's about to buy her first condo and Faye's been talking about bringing her grandkids back to the resort where we stayed in Hawaii. They used to lobby to work with me because I'm so much more competent than Dr. Karen and her (medicine) bag o' tricks. I can't let them down. I can't allow their faith in me to be shaken, at least any more than it already has been.

And what of my family? The only thing they have to be proud of right now is Mary Mac and her ability to toast fennel seeds. It's my birthright to be the successful one. It's on me to make enough to buy the folks a winter place on the Florida coast . . . because that way I can determine how many guest rooms they need. (Hint—she who pays stays—the rest of you mooches can rent a hotel room if you want to visit.)

Despite how invested I am in where I went to school, my job is what makes me special. Without it, I'm basically Geri. Only not chunky, and with my own house. But still.

I need *Push.*

I need my job.

I need a win.

I need a way to make the impossible possible.

I need to check my messages.

CHAPTER TEN

Swimfan

From the recesses of my bedroom closet, I hear a buzzing. I dash down the hall to press the button underneath the intercom's speaker. "Hello?"

"Salutations, Reagan Bishop!"

I reply, "Hey, Deva. I'll be out in a sec; just let me grab my keys."

After locating them in the crockery bowl I now use specifically to house them (excellent suggestion, Ol' Rat Nasty), I head down the stairs to greet Deva.

I'm ready for my run in a white Nike Dri-Fit tank and Lululemon's speed shorts in Mint Moment Black with the little zippy pocket that rests on my tailbone in the back. However, I'm wearing a waist pack, too, because I require enough room to carry my phone.

Deva, on the other hand, is ready not so much for a jog as

she is to herd her camels across the Sinai Peninsula. She's covered in layers of linen and ropes of tribal beads, topped with a kaffiyeh head wrap. But what really ties the whole outfit together is the matching Pumas.

"Um . . . are you wearing a toga?" I ask.

"Actually, Reagan Bishop, it's a thobe."

Of course it is.

"Might you be more comfortable in a pair of running shorts? I have plenty you can borrow. We seem to be about the same size." Except for gloves, of course.

Deva waves me off. "Not at all, Reagan Bishop. Linen is very breathable and I'll be protected both from the sun *and* sandstorms."

"Have we had many sandstorms in Chicago lately?" I query.

Deva gives me a knowing look. "It's best to be prepared for any eventuality, Reagan Bishop. The Bedouins have been dressing this way for centuries. I believe you'll find that my outfit stands the test of time."

"Then who am I to argue with the sartorial choices of the entire Ottoman Empire?"

I've had a world of stress to process lately, so Deva's been joining me on my usual five-mile loop by the lake. Except we discover she can't really run today without becoming tangled in her cape, so we decide to take a brisk walk instead.

"I notice a disturbance in your root chakra. How are you feeling today? What is your mood? I'm sensing . . . humiliation?" Deva peers at me, her outfit billowing behind her like a sail.

Sometimes what Deva says is pure bunk, and sometimes she's right on the money. "Yes, I'd say my overwhelming emotion right now is rooted in a level of mortification. Of course,

I've been embarrassed before," I tell Deva. "Comes with the territory."

"Therapy embarrasses you, Reagan Bishop?"

While we walk, I loosen up my arms by pulling my elbows back behind my head and pushing down with the opposite hands. I've been carrying an almost paralyzing amount of tension between my shoulder blades and this simple stretch works wonders.

"On occasion, yes. For example, one time when I first started my practice, I was at the Lincoln Park Target buying— what?—Kleenex? Toilet bowl cleaner? Something innocuous. Anyway, I spotted one of my patients coming down the aisle with someone else and I didn't want to make eye contact."

We're heading down North Lakeview on our way to the spot where I loosen up my hamstrings on Fullerton. The sky is a bit gray, so we're not suffocating in the stifling Chicago summer heat. That's something no one from out of town ever fully understands—the summer temperatures are inversely proportional to the winter cold. I had a roommate at U of C who was from Galveston, Texas. She showed up without a single short-sleeved shirt, expecting late August snow. She was sorely disappointed.

In fact, more than seven hundred citizens—largely the elderly and the poor—tragically perished in the heat wave of 1995. The mayor was roundly criticized for his response to the crisis, so this is one of those Subjects That Are Not Discussed in the Bishop household.

I consider it a small blessing that today's overcast and breezy with the threat of rain, which makes for a pleasant walk. I tell Deva, "You're likely aware there are stringent HIPAA regulations regarding confidentiality. I was worried I might inadvertently greet my patient and then she might be forced into a conversation with her companion on how she and I are acquainted. I wanted to avoid all of that. So, to circumvent the potentially awkward eye contact, I pretended to be very interested in the display in front of me and started randomly grabbing products without even looking at what I was taking. I just wanted to seem like a regular shopper."

Deva assures me, "There's no shame in taking advantage of Target's competitive pricing, Reagan Bishop. I purchase paper towels there. You'd be shocked at the splash zone created by certain types of Reiki healing."

I glance over at her. "Do I want the details?"

Deva's thoughtful for a moment. "Probably not. Please, go on."

I shudder as I recollect. "I'm still mortified when I remember that day. There I was, trying to do the right thing, and it completely backfired. I was so hypersensitive to my patient's needs that I didn't realize I was inadvertently buying Astroglide in bulk. So my patient comes up to me, says hello, introduces her friend, and then she notices all the lube in my cart and she says, 'Big plans this weekend, Dr. B?' I wanted to die."

"Would you typify the recent incidents as worse, Reagan Bishop?"

I snort. "Not even in the same stratosphere. At least I could explain my rationale when I saw my patient the next time. How do I justify myself to the entirety of the TMZ viewership?"

Deva waxes philosophic. "Those who matter will know your truth, Reagan Bishop. It's hard when you're up to your armpits in alligators to remember you came here to drain the swamp."

I give her a sidelong glance. "Did you just quote President Reagan to me?"

"Are we still not doing that?"

"We are not."

When we arrive at the corner of Fullerton and Lincoln Park West, I position myself behind a bench and work through my litany of running stretches. After I loosen up my *soleus* (inner calf muscle) and Achilles tendon, I grasp the back of the bench and execute some leg swings. Swing back, kick front, swing back, kick front, repeat twenty times on each side, really working the joints. To maintain my balance, I fix my gaze on the condo complex across the street. I notice one of the units has recently added a row of flower boxes on the deck and it's filled with red geraniums and some greenery. Personally, I wouldn't obstruct a lake view with cheap flowers and vines, but different strokes, eh?

Satisfied with my range of motion, we move on. "The upside with Ashlee is at least there's no footage of me counseling her. Yes, everyone still blames me, but at least she imploded prior to therapy." I roll my shoulders as we walk. "But with Lance? I have no excuse for Lance."

"Then how will you handle tomorrow, Reagan Bishop?" Deva asks, chugging along next to me. I'll be damned if she's yet to break a sweat. I've already saturated my T-shirt.

I feel my stomach twist itself in a knot because this is my last chance. "Magic? Miracle? Maybe I can simply astral project into Tabitha's body and do it for her?"

We're filming a Very Special Episode of *Push* tomorrow due to Kassel's coup of landing an actual star. Tabitha Baylee's a true A-lister and she's come to *Push* not because she needs a publicity stunt, a makeover, or a free Ford F-150, but because she has crippling acrophobia, which is a fear of heights. What's problematic is that she's starring as Parker Peter in the female remake of the movie *Spider-Man* (don't ask) and she has to film a scene at the top of the Willis Tower.

(FYI, Ma still refuses to call it anything other than the Sears Tower. *Quelle surprise.*)

One of Kassel's pals from his *Make 'Em Eat a Bug* days is the movie's director, and he's desperate to capture the shot where a moody Parker Peter gazes out on the city below, while coming to terms with having become a Spider-(Wo)man. Richard Holthaus, the director, is so desperate, in fact, that he called us after hypnotherapy, acupuncture, and drugs failed to assuage the starlet's fears.

"What can you do?" Deva asks.

We cut across the park and head to the walking path next to the lake. Even with foreboding skies, sunbathers line the beach. The afternoon smells like Coppertone and charcoal, as the aroma from the outdoor grills at Castaways on North Avenue Beach drifts toward us. I haven't touched anything that wasn't born swimming since 1998, but my God, the scent of those burgers is intoxicating.

I explain, "Thing is, I've done tons of exposure work before, which is how a therapist helps patients with fears. For example, I had a client who was desperately afraid of dogs, having once been attacked as a child. But her fiancé had a big Swiss Mountain dog and the creature scared her so much, she was afraid to go to visit his house, let alone live there after they were married. So we started off small. The first pup she met was a teacup terrier, and we worked our way up from there, graduating to shih tzus, then pugs, etcetera. Over a six-month period, we slowly introduced bigger and bolder dogs. By the time of her wedding, she not only was able to be around her husband's pooch, but even had the confidence to take him out for walks."

Deva has been listening intently. "Cesar Millan sometimes has me perform Reiki massage on his most troubled cases. I worked on a magnificent Basenji named Anubis—opened his chi right up." Deva adjusts her thobe, which has shifted as we've walked. "Anubis still lifted his leg on the drapes after that, though."

"What was your resolution?" I ask, trying to imagine exactly which new age treatment would have curbed a naughty dog's behavior. Chanting? Burning herbs? A newly feng shui'd doghouse?

"I filled a Dr Pepper can with pennies and shook it at him whenever he approached the window."

This stops me in my tracks.

"What, Reagan Bishop? You don't need mystical power to discipline your dogs. You just need to show them you're the boss."

This? This is how she's been winning me over. "You are an enigma wrapped in a turban, Deva."

"Namaste." She grins and bows. "I like you, too, Reagan Bishop. I do not desire seeing you fired, so what's your strategy?"

As we cruise past the volleyball courts, I give the players a cursory look. Nope, no one I know. Which reminds me to check my phone. I surreptitiously slip it out of and then back into my waist pack. Nothing. How can there be nothing? I'm sure the phone works out here—I've tested it. And there's a cell tower at Clark and Division, less than a mile down the road. I have three and a half bars, for crying out loud!

"Reagan Bishop?"

"Gosh, sorry—had to check on something."

Deva knits her brow. "Are you waiting for a call? Again?"

"No, it's fine. Sorry. You were saying—tomorrow. What

am I going to do? That's the million-dollar question. I tried to explain my therapy methodology to Kassel and he said, and I quote, 'No one wants to watch a movie star climb a ladder.' That's how I'd begin to desensitize Tabitha. I said it wasn't ethical for me to try to treat her any other way, particularly given what the filmmaker wants, and that I likely wouldn't even capture any usable footage. And he said to try anyway because he couldn't save me if I fail again."

Tomorrow, Kassel and Co. intends for me to attempt the impossible—stick a terrified girl right out on the Ledge of the Willis Tower Skydeck. The Ledge is an enclosed box on the hundred and third floor that extends 4.3 feet away from the side of the tower. People who *don't* harbor a rabid fear of heights feel weak in the knees stepping into the laminated glass enclosure, so there's no way I can coax Tabitha out there.

Patently impossible.

I'm normally not so defeatist, but I understand the parameters under which I'm toiling. I wouldn't expect a wheelchair-bound person to walk based only on my encouragement. There would be months, if not years, of intensive rehabilitation involved first, and even then success wouldn't be a guarantee. I mean, I'm skilled, but I definitely couldn't just tip them out of the chair and say, *Have at it.*

This business with Tabitha is almost a guaranteed failure, and I can't stand failing. I'm not clinically diagnosable with atychiphobia, as I don't *avoid* risk to prevent failure. (Ahem, *person who lives in our parents' basement*, ahem.)

Rather, I'm übermotivated by my desire to exceed and excel; that's why I was such an exemplary student. Well, that and my desire to not be taunted by rich kids. While everyone else was dating and attending prom and playing team sports, I was locked in my room memorizing the periodic table and diagramming sentences. I attained the highest grades because I was willing to sacrifice the most to earn them. But I can't nose-to-the-grindstone my way out of tomorrow, and the notion of bombing is giving me agita.

And won't everyone at the unemployment office be impressed with my credentials. Argh. Maybe I can write a book about how the disinterested clerk keeps calling me "Doctor" when she really means "bitch."

Oh, this can't happen. I cannot be fired. I feel my chest constricting and I think I may vomit.

"Humor me, Reagan Bishop; please stop and take a deep, cleansing breath."

I comply, inhaling so much grill smoke that I can practically taste the burgers and brats. Oh, is that fennel? Then I hate myself for being drawn to the taste of factory-farmed meat. While we're by the snack bar, I dash in to buy us both a bottle of water to wash away any stray flavor.

After I hand her an Aquafina, Deva circles around and stands in front of me. "Repeat, please—*nam myoho renge kyo.*"

I grimace. "I'd rather not." It's one thing to stroll the lakefront with someone dressed like a Hari Krishna, an entirely different one to actually pass out the carnations.

"Do you not desire to open the pathway to awaken your Buddha nature?" Deva clasps her chest with her enormous paws, clutching herself as though I've cast a mortal blow.

"Not today, no."

Deva rights her head wrap, and I can tell she's about to lecture me about her new age hokum. "Nichiren believed that voicing this incantation strengthens our capacity for wisdom, courage, confidence, vitality, and compassion."

"Listen, Deva, gaining wisdom, courage, confidence, vitality, and compassion sounds fantastic, but ultimately will this incantation lure a movie star into a glass box 1,353 feet in the air and prevent me from being fired?"

"Not directly, but—"

"Maybe next time, then."

We keep moving and I check my heart-rate monitor. I'm not quite hitting my target heart rate, yet my blood pressure is elevated due to my stress level. I wonder, will that produce the same caloric burn?

At this point we're back across the park and heading north toward my place. "Hey, give me your water bottle. I can pitch them here." I grab her empty and toss them in the recycle bin behind the condo complex at North Lakeview and Fullerton. As I pass the rest of the bins, I can't help but notice what the residents have so thoughtlessly thrown away. Distressed as I am about myself, I congratulate myself for still looking out for others.

"Deva, come see all this waste—these bananas are barely brown. They're still edible." I pull them out of the can and set them off to the side. I hate our culture of waste in this country, so when I see an opportunity to salvage food products, I take it. "And look at this box of lentils," I say. "It's not even open!" In no time, I've scavenged enough ingredients to provide a day's worth of sustenance for a family of four. I find a clean paper grocery sack in the recycle bin (why isn't everyone using canvas totes yet?) and I bring the bagful of ingredients out front to the bench where a homeless person can spot them.

I tell Deva, "Maybe this one little action won't change the world, but if someone who wouldn't have had dinner tonight now can eat, I feel better about myself."

"That's very noble, Reagan Bishop."

"Thank you."

I often give myself affirmations about my own nobility.

"May I ask you a question?"

"Anything." I zip open my waist pack and dig out my hand sanitizer. After I feel like I'm thoroughly disinfected, I reach for my phone, glance at it, then look back up at the geranium-covered deck.

"Reagan Bishop, how long have you been stalking your ex?"

CHAPTER ELEVEN

Take Her to the Mattresses

"I *beg* your pardon?"

"Stalking. Is that not what you're doing?" Deva seems genuinely confused.

"Of course I'm not stalking him! What would give you that idea?" I'm genuinely appalled at this accusation. Stalking! Me! A mental health professional. A *doctor*. Preposterous.

"Perhaps 'stalking' is the wrong term."

"You think?" I hiss.

"Allow me to share my observations, Reagan Bishop. You're always texting him and calling him, yet I have never witnessed his returning the favor. I've heard you on the phone with his assistant dozens of times. No one takes that many meetings. Not even your namesake fortieth president at the height of the Cold War."

She begins to enumerate my perceived offenses on her sausage digits. "Every time we walk, you make us head south and pass by the volleyball courts, where you mentioned he plays in a league. Why have we never taken the north path, Reagan Bishop? There's an entire beach for dogs at Belmont Harbor, right up the shoreline. Who wouldn't want to walk to a beach entirely for dogs? Big black ones, little brown ones, fat white ones, all frolicking in the surf together. They bark as one. There's a lesson there."

I'm so angry I'm practically hyperventilating. "You're accusing me of being a stalker because I keep track of my mileage by taking the same route?"

She places a gigantic hand on my shoulder in an attempt to calm me. "Of course not, Reagan Bishop. I'm calling you a stalker because of the stalking."

I can barely sputter out a defense as she keeps ticking off my supposed misdemeanors.

"I've seen you pull up his Facebook profile at work a hundred times."

"That's a crime now?"

"No, but when I first noticed this pattern, you were so fixated on his page I assumed he was our next guest."

I can feel my fists clenching into balls. "His page is my home page—what's so weird about that? Do I mock *you* for having FoxNews.com as your home page? Which, what's up with that, by the way?"

Deva purses her lips and cogitates my question. "I like Bill O'Reilly's aura. I'm attracted to his dominant energy."

"I have no response to that."

She keeps pushing her stalking agenda. "Also, you've asked me to accompany you to the bar Cactus again and again, yet you never order a cocktail. By your own admission, your ex works in a building across the street. Stopping by his favorite watering hole once is a coincidence, twice is a pattern. A dozen times, particularly given your distaste for alcohol? Forgive me for saying it, but you're entering *Fatal Attraction* territory."

"Your accusations are truly absurd."

Deva grabs my elbow. "Sebastian doesn't happen to own a pet rabbit, does he? I ask for no particular reason."

I wriggle out of her grasp. "Circumstantial evidence, okay? All of it. Seb's been really slammed at work, so the onus is on me to contact him. I miss seeing him regularly, so from time to time I check in on his social media profiles. If I were to run into him while we're out and about? Then maybe he'll realize how much he misses me, too. We're on a semi-break now, but there have been plenty of times when I do catch him that we get together. I realize in terms of healthy relationships, this pattern isn't optimal, but everything is fine between us and I'm satisfied with the arrangement."

"I feel as though I've angered you, Reagan Bishop, and I apologize. That was not my intention. I don't want to add to your burdens, particularly given the Herculean task you have in front of you tomorrow. Let us never speak of this incident again."

"Thank you. And I'm not a stalker."

Deva grabs me in an awkward attempt at a hug before commenting, "I was harsh to say you're a stalker, Reagan Bishop." We begin to walk in the direction of my house. "I'm sure there's a perfectly logical reason you were just digging through his trash."

"I was in denial," I tell Deva. I'm slumped on the wide cement steps on my stoop, suddenly too weary to even climb the stairs. The cement is cool beneath my legs and I shiver a little, although whether that's because of the temperature or the profound insight into my own behavior, I can't be sure.

I'm a stalker.

How did I not notice I was engaging in the exact same behavior as Dina at the height of her Lorenzo madness? The calls, the texts, the constant monitoring of his Facebook account, the staking out of his house? I didn't reach the restraining-order level, but who knows how I might have proceeded if Deva hadn't called me on my behavior? How did I let this happen? I mean, I'm the one who helps people solve their problems, not the one who causes them. I'm never one to obsess.

Deva sits next to me, attempting to offer comfort. "You saw no signs of your own fixation?"

"Not even a little bit." I fiddle with a loose thread on the bottom of my running shorts and the whole hem unravels.

Great, first I'm getting fired, then I'm a stalker, and now I need new shorts.

I snap off the thread, balling it up and stuffing it in my fanny pack. Just because I'm a loser doesn't mean I'm a litterer. "Thing is, Deva, ultimately I'm responsible for my own behavior. I made the choices I've made, yet I can't help but place a portion of the blame on him. If Sebastian truly wanted to break up, he'd have completely ended it. Why take *some* of my calls? Why respond to *a few* of my messages? Why not just be a freaking man and say, *This isn't working anymore.* Give me closure and I can move on."

Deva sagely nods. "Men are the greatest unsolved mysteries of the universe."

"What's so shaming is this isn't the behavior of a professional, of a grown-up, of a doctor. This is some junior high bullshit, and I'm so mad at myself."

"How did your other breakups go, Reagan Bishop?"

Sheepishly, I admit, "I've only had one other boyfriend and he was a saint in a lot of ways. When we broke up, that was it. End. *Fini*. We kept in contact, but it was clear the romantic portion of our lives together was over. He understood and respected my reasons, even though they were counter to his own wishes. There were no instances of *We're not really together anymore but I'm still showing up at your place at two a.m.*"

"Like a house call, Reagan Bishop. Only for booty."

"That's why it's called a booty call, Deva."

Deva nods, as though soaking in this information. "Then I have learned something today. What do your friends say, Reagan Bishop? Do any of them counsel you about your compulsive behaviors?" Little bits of sun are starting to peek out from the clouds, prompting the Caribou Coffee customers to quickly fill the primo outdoor seating area. (If I weren't so distressed, I'd insist that Deva join me there. Sit at the corner of West Arlington and Clark for long enough, and eventually you'll see the entire city go by.)

I try to remember how my network of friends reacted when Seb and I decided to take our break. I don't have a ton of girlfriends because I've been so career focused ever since graduation, which is fine. Unlike Geri, I don't *need* to be surrounded by my scores of minions who spirit me away to Mexico. But I'm close with a couple of women from my marathon-training group and from the Chicago chapter of the Association for Behavioral and Cognitive Therapists.

Or I *was* close with them.

I admit, "I kind of haven't seen any of my friends for a while. Is it possible I wore them out with my postmortem over Sebastian? Have I become one of those women who struggle to find acceptance and move on?"

"Did you invite any of your friends to come to Hawaii with you?"

I think back to the day that I placed one call after another. "I invited all of them. Each one said they were too busy with work."

Deva nods enthusiastically. "Then, yes, absolutely. A free trip to Maui?" Her words are like a punch to the gut. "Face time with Wendy Winsberg? No one turns that down without a solid reason, Reagan Bishop. You chased them away like St. Patrick did the snakes of Ireland." She suddenly seems delighted with herself. "Did I properly incorporate your heritage in that simile?"

"You did." I slump down lower. "I feel like such a fool."

"Happens to the best of us. When Shaman Bob broke up with me, I was so upset I traveled back in time to—" But Deva can't complete the sentence because she's suddenly coughing so hard.

I jump up. "Shall I grab some water?"

She quickly recovers and clears her throat. "Um, no. What I was saying is that when Shaman Bob dumped me, I traveled back *to a time in my mind* that I was happy. Then it was all fine."

That doesn't make a lot of sense, but come on, this is Deva. Like, how she's dressed for a nomadic trek, and not a walk by the water? Not everything that comes out of her mouth is twenty-four karat.

"Let me ask you something, Reagan Bishop. Was your family more forthcoming than your peer group? Did they attempt to help?"

Pfft, hardly.

Geri the Judas is not only still one of Seb's Facebook buddies, but she had the nerve to sign me up for some Catholic dating service. And Mary Mac suggested I was putting the "psycho" in "psychotherapist." And Ma? Ma said I should "stop being an asshole and call Boyd, for Christ's sake." Thanks for your overwhelming support, ladies.

I reply, "Not really, no."

"Then that is a shame, Reagan Bishop, and I am sorry."

The front door bangs open and Trevor comes bounding down the steps in cargo shorts and an old fraternity barn-dance T-shirt. This is the first time I've seen him clad in something other than his underpants in quite some time. "What's shakin', Dr. B? Going to the 'Bou to get my turtle mocha on!"

"You do realize that drink contains over six hundred calories?" I ask. Sure, he's in fine shape now, but he won't always have his twentysomething metabolism.

He simply grins in response. "YOLO, ya know?" He plops down next to us. "Hey, who's your friend? No, wait—whoa! No way! *No way!*" He bounces back up and runs to the top of the stairs. "Yo, Bryce, get out here! You'll never believe who's on our steps!"

Moments later Bryce staggers out, his pasty belly exposed under a dingy gray hoodie with a goofy plaid neck scarf completing the top half of his ensemble and nothing but his plain white boxer shorts on the bottom.

Excellent. I was so hoping to witness at least one of my tenants in a state of undress today.

"*Devalicious!* What up, girl?" Bryce practically launches himself into Deva's lap. "I owe you, like, a debt, playa." He turns to look at me. "Do you know who this is? This is the Deva-*diggety* and she has, like, powers and shit." Then he and Trevor give each other a complicated series of handshakes and backslaps.

Now, *this* is an interesting turn of events. As depressed as

I feel about my own terrible choices, I can't help but be curious.

"Deva, why are my tenants prostrating themselves in front of you?"

"Hey, my prostrate is cool, Dr. B," Trevor informs us. "No worries. But my old man needs twenty minutes to take a leak."

"I may be able to assist," Deva says. "Would he be willing to soak in a tincture added to the bath, Tenant Trevor?" Her suggestion does nothing to dissipate my level of confusion.

"His prostrate has his jimmies totes rustled, so I'll check," Trevor confirms.

I'd try to explain the difference between *prostrate* and *prostate*, but I lack the anatomically correct dolls to point to. Instead, I say, "I'm sorry—I don't follow how you're acquainted."

Bryce explains, "Dr. B, I got a cousin who knows this dude who has a slampiece who worked in PR or some shit and she said that Deva, like, merked the time/space continuum. I was like, 'I would get down with that.' So me and some of my bros roll to her store, all, 'Whassup?' and Deva goes, 'I'mma help you,' because one of my coworkers is a bullshit swagger jacker and my pops is all, 'Son, I'm disappoint.'"

Sometimes I wonder if English is Bryce's second language, despite his having been born in Pennsylvania. (Don't worry, Philadelphia—I blame MTV.) Fortunately, I worked with enough teens to have a cursory understanding that Bryce was struggling with his job and he somehow sought Deva's assistance.

"Yo, I thought you went to buy a bong first?" Trevor asks.

Bryce cracks his knuckles while he explains and I inadvertently wince because it sounds so painful, but he doesn't seem to notice. "Naw. Well, yeah, but naw. So Deva gives me the fresh hookup and now I'm Scrilla Gorilla. I be rollin' and they be hatin'."

I attempt to piece together his message. "What you're saying is you've since found professional success that is, in fact, lucrative?"

Bryce grins and nods. "Fa sho. Thanks to this biz-nitch up in here." Then he gives Deva a squeeze, about which she looks distinctly pleased.

Affirmative, then?

It's none of my business, but I can't help asking, "Does that mean you'll start paying your rent yourself?"

"Why'd I wanna go and do that?" Bryce asks.

Trevor volunteers, "He's buying a boat that is *off the chain*! I'mma get my wakeboard on! Diversey Harbor represent, son! Yo, baller, come buy me a turtle mocha to celebrate!"

"Lemme grab a Benjamin." Bryce trots back up to the apartment and returns a minute later, wallet in hand, having added flip-flops and large red plastic sunglasses to his ensemble.

"Is this what guys are like now?" I ask, more to myself than to Deva. "Is this what I have to look forward to, climbing back into the dating pool?"

The boys amble down to the coffee shop and finagle outdoor table space by joining a couple of cute girls. The boys raise their cups in salute to us.

"Bryce is still not wearing pants," Deva notes. "It's disconcerting seeing someone so inappropriately dressed for an activity, Reagan Bishop."

I start to giggle because I assume she's made a joke, but then I realize she's serious.

"Hey, what exactly did you do for Bryce? And what was the part about *time travel*?"

Deva raises one tumescent finger. "'Don't ask me about my business. Don't ever ask me about my business.'"

I'm taken aback. "Gosh, Deva, I'm sorry, I didn't realize—"

Deva bursts out laughing. "Aw, Reagan Bishop, I was quoting *The Godfather*!"

"Never saw it."

She's shocked. "What? You've never seen *The Godfather*, Reagan Bishop? It's an American classic. That Francis Ford Coppola is a genius. He's an excellent vintner as well. Terrible dancer, though. Stepped all over my dashiki the last time we attempted a Viennese waltz when we were in St. Barts."

"Enigma in a turban," I state again. "So, back to the topic at hand—how did you help Bryce?"

She explains, "Bryce lacked confidence, so I provided him with an obsidian amulet from ancient Sumer. As you're likely aware, the word 'Sumer' has its genesis in the Akkadian language—"

"Why would I have an awareness of the phonetics used by the ancient Sumerians?"

"Aren't you a doctor?"

"Yes, but—" I lack the tenacity to argue. "Please, continue."

"'Sumer' means 'land of the civilized kings,' so I felt he'd be best served by channeling their spirit, at least on sales calls. But I'm glad to see his royal confidence is impacting all areas of his life. Why, just look at how he holds court! Those women are in thrall, Reagan Bishop! Like a Sumerian prince." We glance down the street and notice that the boys have indeed gotten cozy with the girls. Her eyes shine with pride.

Oh, I see what she did here.

"You gave him a trinket and made him believe it had some sort of influence over him. You harnessed the power of suggestion."

She angles her head as though she's a dog who can't quite discern whether or not its owner said "treat."

"No, I harnessed the power of obsidian."

"You cannot be serious. You actually believe you have magical power?" Come on, universe! I have one friend. One! I knew she was quirky, but I wasn't aware she was actually delusional.

I'm not saying I can't accept this, but still.

While we've been talking, my legs have fallen asleep, so I quickly spring up and jump around, trying to regain feeling.

Undaunted by my hopping around, Deva replies, "Of course not, Reagan Bishop! That would be absurd. I'm neither witch nor wizard."

"I'm glad to see you still dwell in our realm," I reply, vigorously shaking my foot. Pins and needles! Pins and needles!

Deva smooths out her thobe and unties her head wrap before retying it in the exact same fashion. "The power comes from the artifacts. I simply *channel* the power. I'm the medium. Occasionally I'll concoct potions, tonics, and tinctures, although that's not my favorite because sometimes I struggle to source the ingredients. I spent a whole month a few years ago battling the rains of Mount Kilimanjaro, trying to harvest *Impatiens kilimanjari* from the jungle floor. Total nightmare and I ended up with a yeast infection for the ages. For. The. Ages. Oh, the damp, Reagan Bishop. The damp. I told my client the next time she wanted to lose weight? She should just diet and exercise like everyone else. Cut back on simple carbohydrates—they'll get you every time."

I settle back in next to her. "Deva, this seems so far-fetched. And I respect that you believe you have powers, but your claims violate the natural order."

"Fair enough, Reagan Bishop. But let me ask you this—do you truly believe I got rich selling bongs to frat boys?"

That stops me cold. My mind reels and suddenly a million little details begin to fall into place. The beach house? The ski lodge? The massive Oak Street loft? The Viennese waltz with Francis Ford Coppola?

I point at the sunny yellow vehicle parked across the street. "If what you're saying is true—and I'm not saying it is, although it would neatly explain the new Lamborghini you've been driving around like some kind of Saudi sheik—"

"Lambo."

"Beg pardon?"

"Pros call it a Lambo. Appearances seem important to you, Reagan Bishop, and I wanted to make sure you were using the proper terminology as to not be embarrassed."

"Noted." Sometimes talking to Deva is like living in a Salvador Dalí painting. All kinds of stairways, and no clue as to which way is actually up. "Anyway, what I was saying is that if you're not somehow suffering from delusions, then your ability defies the laws of the universe." Then I belatedly add, "No offense, of course."

As I just have the one friend left, it's best if I don't alienate her, despite not being able to wrap my mind around what she's telling me.

Deva clucks her tongue. "*Your* universe, Reagan Bishop. Not mine. Your universe is but a grain of sand on the beach, surrounded by billions of others. And I'm not offended. In fact, I'm pleased you've opened your mind up enough to even consider other possibilities. That brings us to tomorrow."

I'm loath to ask what comes next. "You can't help me with Tabitha tomorrow . . . right?" I can't possibly employ her assistance, and yet the idea of failing spectacularly and being fired is almost too much to bear, so if she were to be able . . .

With much gravitas, Deva replies, "'We've known each other many years, but this is the first time you ever came to me for counsel or for help. I can't remember the last time that you invited me to your house for a cup of coffee.'"

What?

"Didn't we have decaf espresso here last Thursday? Remember? You brought your own agave?"

Deva pokes me in the arm and I almost fall off my step. "Reagan Bishop, I beg of you to borrow my *Godfather* boxed set. De Niro? Pacino? James Caan *and* Robert Duvall? Oh, and a young Diane Keaton! Perfection!" She cups her hand and brings her huge fingertips to her lips before throwing a kiss. "Take a lazy Saturday and watch them back to back. You'll thank me. Possibly two of the finest films ever made. Don't waste your time on the third movie, though. Sofia— good Scrabble partner, bad actress."

I wrap my arms around my legs while I process what she's been telling me. "If I were to ask for your help—and that's a big if—how would we proceed? Just for the sake of conversation."

Deva rubs her chin while she sorts through the possibilities. "Depends on your level of squeamishness. How would you feel about injecting yourself with Tabitha's blood, or, better yet, her spinal fluid?"

"I'd be opposed," I say, before adding, "vehemently."

"Drat. Okay, scratch that. What if we were to . . . I suppose urine is out of the question?"

I cross my arms over my chest. "Uh-huh."

"How attached are you to your hair, say, on a scale from one to ten?"

My hand flies up to my ponytail. "Ten."

"Yes, but in this scenario, does ten mean 'most attached' or 'least attached'? Because I could work with—"

"Most attached. Ten." I clutch my ponytail protectively.

"Huh. I was afraid of that." She ponders and ponders and, finally, snaps her mighty fingers. "Well, I could . . . hmm, wait, no, there's an awful lot of management involved."

"Any exchange of biohazards?"

"No, but it's complicated. I could do a form of astral projection in which you'd briefly inhabit Tabitha's body and you could execute the action of stepping out on the Skydeck for her. The problem is, she'd have to inhabit your body as well. That's an awkward conversation to have when you meet a movie star for the first time, am I right, Reagan Bishop? Would you be willing to ask her?"

The ice I'm on is already thin enough. "Not if I didn't want to be fired on the spot."

"Right, right. There's a couple of work-arounds, but the most effective one is so against your philosophy that I hesitate to even suggest it."

I reflect briefly on my parents' mantelpiece, which is never going to hold my Emmy photo without desperate measures.

"Maybe you could it explain it anyway."

"I've not said yes," I remind Deva, an hour into her extensive explanation. "I've simply agreed to be open to the possibility."

Deva beams at me. "Look at you—this morning, you were a garden-variety stalker about to lose her job. And now? You're willing to accept that yours is not the only universe.

I'm proud of you, Reagan Bishop. You've taken the first step on the path to your enlightenment!"

"Then why do I feel nauseated?" I ask.

She explains, "There's always some turbulence when traveling on the astral plane."

"That would certainly explain— Wait, was that a *joke?*"

"Ha! Zing!" Deva exclaims.

"If I go through with it, and if I'm somehow successful, then I'll owe you a massive debt," I tell her.

Deva rises and brushes off her thobe. "Good. Then, someday—and that day may never come—I might call upon you to do a service for me."

"*Godfather* again?"

Quizzically, Deva replies, "Well, no, Reagan Bishop—I was just stating how favors work."

CHAPTER TWELVE

Lights, Cameras, Action

Deva and I have moved inside to my apartment, and I've been vacillating for the entire afternoon about whether or not to accept her help when the phone rings. I check the caller ID.

"Argh, it's my mother." I glance over at Deva for moral support.

"Then you must honor her and pick up, Reagan Bishop."

"Not really the moral support I'd hoped for, Deva," I grumble. Despite my best instincts, I grit my teeth, pick up, and put her on speaker. "Hello, Ma." I try to not sound resigned.

Breathlessly, she replies, "Reagan, you're never going to believe it!"

"What, Geri was selected for *The Biggest Loser*?" Deva raises an eyebrow, and I bell my arms out around me, puff my cheeks, and wobble back and forth. I thought Deva would laugh at my impression, but instead she seems perplexed and a bit disappointed.

"Your sister is a beautiful girl and doesn't deserve your crap."

I can't help but roll my eyes. "Fine, maybe she's not that tubby, but let's just say no one would be surprised if her gym placed her photo on a milk carton."

After a chilly silence, Ma responds, "Do you want to hear the news or not?"

"Sure, whatever, but can you make it quick? I have a friend over and I don't want to be rude."

Ma immediately shifts gears from surly to incredulous. "What? Did I hear that right? You have a *friend* over? Hold on." I can hear her placing her palm over the receiver before she calls to my dad. "Tommy, hey, Tommy—Reagan has a friend over!" Dad mumbles something indecipherable.

When she returns to the line, Ma's decidedly tense again. "Reagan, what friend is this? It's not Sebastian, right?"

I distinctly hear my dad asking, "She didn't slip him one of those roofers, did she? The guys at the lodge were just talking about the roofers people put in your drinks that make you black out before they take advantage of you."

From across the room, Deva points to me and mouths, *Stalker.*

"Damn it, no, Ma! I didn't slip Sebastian a *Rohypnol*! The date rape drug? Please. I can't believe your mind would go there, particularly since I've moved on."

Granted, I decided to move on only today, but this is not information she requires.

She presses, "Are you sure? You're not spending your days buying coffee at his Starbucks and walking your nonexistent dog past his house?"

This is mortifying.

Apparently my activities surrounding my relationship with Seb did not go unnoticed. I bet Geri's been having a field day at my expense.

"Is there a reason for your call, Ma?"

"Oh, yeah, I almost forgot—the Culvers are getting divorced!"

This tidbit is surprising for a number of reasons, but primarily because my mother isn't one to share gossip. At all. In any way, shape, or form. She was privy to every bit of this city's dirty laundry over the years, yet she's never shared a single detail, no matter how salacious the story. The Hired Truck Program? The Sorich conviction? Daley's son Pat's involvement in Cardinal Growth? Our family learned of these scandals only from the *Sun-Times*, just like everyone else in Chicago. To this day, she won't give us any of the inside scoop on the Blagojevich conviction, which is a shame because that family is someone's doctoral thesis based on the hairstyles alone.

"I can't believe it. Wait, did something happen? Is Ethel okay?" Jack's abuse never branched into physicality, although with his anger, I wouldn't have been surprised if he finally lost his tiny modicum of control.

Ma tells me, "She's more than okay. Thing is, Ethel decided to cover her grays. She saw a television program with Marilu Henner—she's from Logan Square, did you know that? She went to Madonna High School with Dad's cousin Terry. Nice girl. Very talented. She was on *Taxi* with Judd Hirsch years ago, but you were just a baby when that show ended and wouldn't remember."

Dad chimes in, "Danny DeVito was her costar. Who'd have predicted he'd become the biggest celebrity from that whole ensemble? I'd have laid money on Jeff Conaway, God rest his soul. He was one good-lookin' fella."

Ma continues, "Saw on *Good Morning America* that Marilu has one of those autobiographical memories—she can recite the details from every day of her life."

"Wait," I can't help but interject, "you watched Marilu Henner on *GMA* but you forget to tune in when I'm on?"

From the background Dad says, "She was on *Celebrity Apprentice* twice! Why don't you go on *Celebrity Apprentice*, Reagan?"

"Marilu's a U of C alum, too, ya know," Ma adds.

This?

Right here?

Is why I wanted to let the call go to voice mail.

Tersely, I reply, "As are Kurt Vonnegut, Roger Ebert, Saul Bellow, and Tucker Max, but how does any of this relate to the Culvers' divorce?"

"Oh, yeah. Anyways, Ethel was watching the show with Marilu—"

"Probably *Celebrity Apprentice*," my dad adds. "'You're fired! You're fired!' That Donald Trump is hilarious. Hate that he tore down the *Sun-Times* building, but he's still hysterical. He keeps trading in his wives for newer models, too. Kind of like I do, only with Buicks."

"Ma?" I beg. "Point? Please?"

"So Ethel's watching and she says to herself, 'My hair used to be that color.' Then she runs into Geri right after she sees the show and they get to talking."

I already don't like where this is headed.

Ma can barely tamp down her excitement. "Geri convinces her to come in for a free cut and color, telling Ethel that everyone deserves a lift once in a while, right? So Geri styles her up, and you know what she says to her when they were finished? She looks her right in the eye and goes, 'Ethel, you're far too hot with your new hair to put up with Jack's shit. Drop him like a bad habit.' And she did! Threw the bum right out! You should have seen ol' Jackie boy sitting on the curb yesterday in his ratty old La-Z-Boy, with all of his bowling trophies in boxes, waiting for one of his girlfriends to pick him up. That sorry son of a bitch won't be missed, I'll tell you that. Thirty years of bullshit! She put up with his foolishness for thirty years and all it took for Ethel to come to her senses was an hour in the chair with Geri. That girl—"

I jump in. "Well, I'm thrilled for Ethel, but I really have to go, Ma."

Ma sighs. "Fine. All I'm saying is you have to stop discounting Geri. She was able to work her magic in a way that, come to think of it, you couldn't. You don't give her enough credit sometimes."

Brightly, I respond, "Okay! Love to Dad! Bye!"

I notice that Deva is watching me intently as I stab the disconnect button again and again. "Might I assume, Reagan Bishop, that you've made a decision about tomorrow?"

Without hesitation, I respond, "Oh, *hell* yes."

I can't believe we're doing this.

Further, I can't believe it's working.

I catch a glimpse of myself in the ad hoc dressing room's mirror, before I part the curtains to cross the Skydeck. Like every other day, I expect to see my solemn blue-gray eyes gazing back at me, dark hair neatly confined, skin the color of parchment (save for a bit of hyperpigmentation I haven't been able to exfoliate away since Hawaii), and whatever neutral-colored garments were on sale at Talbots skimming my trim figure.

Today?

I am buff.

I am a fitness goddess.

I am Linda Hamilton in the second *Terminator*, minus the weapons and the silly sunglasses.

I could feel how powerful Tabitha's body was the second we made the swap. Climbing into her skin feels like shimmying into a wet suit, or a full-body pair of Spanx. Everything is so firm and tight and ripped! I always see tabloid photos of her running the stairs in Santa Monica with a trainer—apparently those weren't just staged for PR purposes. She was actually putting in the effort and now she, and by extension I, is as strong as an ox right now. I'd read that Tabitha spent an entire year in the gym for this role and I can feel the extent of her dedication.

I slip the leather jacket from my shoulders and spin around to admire my temporary, gorgeous deltoids and trapezius underneath this skimpy tank top. I am *so* adding heavier/higher weight reps to my workout. I've always been light and lithe, but I had no idea how it might feel to be a badass. I flex my/her/our? legs and am simply delighted at how solid the adductor magnus muscles are.

Tabitha's skin is absolutely flawless, too. I've always appreciated my own creamy visage, but I have to admit that her café-au-lait coloring is beyond beautiful. I read that she's some kind of Nordic-Cuban-Japanese blend of ethnicities. Someone at the UN should set up class trips for young residents of these countries to meet because, damn.

I peek down inside the tank top.

Whoa!

Can I just take a minute to congratulate Tabitha's plastic surgeon? Her rack is magnificent. I give them a quick squeeze—these are the ideal size, shape, and consistency, and I am not kidding.

Or . . . are these possibly real? Surely no one is this perfect without professional assistance.

Before I can admire myself/herself/ourselves anymore, I'm pelted by a dream catcher, hurled from where Deva's chanting and standing over me . . . or technically is that considered Tabitha?

This is so bizarre.

For the most part, I was willing to accept Deva's blathering about channeling metaphysical powers because I felt like I had no other choice. When your only option is a miracle, then you tend to put all your eggs in the miracle's basket. I needed to trust Deva for my own sake, but for that faith to actually have been rewarded? When does that ever happen?

What's most astounding is that she's proved to be exactly who she says she is. When is anyone ever truly who they claim to be? Everyone fibs about something; according to evolutionary psychologists, it's coded in our DNA. We're genetically programmed to protect ourselves and propagate our species, and often the most expedient way to do so is to lie. This is exactly why so many people stretch the truth in their online dating profiles. You're six-two? Sure you are, pal—standing on a chair.

I guess I deal with so much deception every day—largely with people deceiving themselves—that it never occurred to me someone could be entirely genuine.

That in and of itself is borderline miraculous.

Last night, before Deva's abilities morphed from theoretic to actual, we discussed a number of different scenarios on the hows of today. She walked me through a couple of different ways we could pull off the swap. Since I need to inhabit

Tabitha for only a quarter of an hour—max—Deva decided we should go the least invasive route.

I mean, as uninvasive as briefly wearing someone else's skin can be.

Because our plans seemed so speculative and abstract, I didn't consider what the swap would feel like. Which is why I can't stop studying my new self in the mirror; the experience is too surreal, too existential. I'm looking at my reflection and I'm not looking at myself.

Can I actually still be considered me right now?

Theologians argue that the body is just a vessel—a mere collection of flesh and bone—and it's our souls that make us who we are. But I believe part of my physicality makes me who I am as well, be that good, bad, or indifferent. I mean, as strong and stunning as Tabitha is, I bet she doesn't have my level of endurance, and there's no way she could complete the Chicago marathon.

Also, my mortal form is what it is because of every single choice I've made. I'm the one who's eschewed alcohol. I'm the one who assiduously avoids GMOs and refined sugar and wouldn't touch a chili dog on a dare. The freckles on my shoulders are a direct result of my drinking on the beach without sunscreen. My eyes scanned those thousands of pages of textbooks in school. My hands are the ones that gather my hair into a ponytail every day. My body is the one that fit so perfectly in Boyd's arms.

In regard to my actual, corporeal being, I'm curious if my skills have been transferred to her and vice versa. Like, say I were a piano aficionado in my regular self—would I be able to play while inhabiting Tabitha? Or is there an inherent amount of muscle memory proprietary to the body? Certainly when I agreed to attempt the swap, I was concerned with ethical issues, but at no point did I give consideration to the philosophical ramifications.

As I ponder, I'm pelted with a votive candle. With one mighty paw still on her/my/our back, Deva uses her other hand to gesticulate toward the clock on the wall and mouths, *Go! Now!* Remembering my task, I scoot out the curtains and speed walk over to where the crew's set up by the Ledge.

Richard Holthaus, *Spider-Man, Part Femme*'s director, swans up and places his arm around my (seriously, admirably strong) shoulders. "Tabby, are you up to this?"

I open my mouth as if to speak but hesitate before answering him, not because I'm not up to this, but because I'm not sure if I'll be answering him in my voice or Tabitha's.

"Five minutes, that's all I ask," Richard pleads. "Please, do what it takes to give me five minutes. Then I'll never make you participate in anything like this again. Promise. Everything else will be handled by your double or superimposed on the green screen. I just need those gorgeous peepers of yours to look out over the city for a solid thirty seconds."

These eyes are stunning, aren't they? They're almond shaped and topaz colored, framed with the thickest, darkest lashes I've ever witnessed. I was sure they were fake, but when I gave them a surreptitious tug, I realized they were one hundred percent real.

(Which makes me wonder about the boobs.)

I lower my chin and blink up at him through the thick fringe, and Richard practically melts. This is amazing! My God, if I had the ability to turn a grown man into a puddle simply by blinking, I'd never have spent that much time in the library! It's a shame I'm only squiring Tabitha around for the next five minutes or so. What I wouldn't give to drop by Sebastian's office and show him what he's missing!

Except that wouldn't really make sense, as he's never met Tabitha, and also, I own the fact that I may have been a bit stalkeresque in the past. Plus, I pledged to Deva that I was going to break the cycle of insanity and I'm no longer going to try to contact him. So approaching him again, even if it's in someone else's (amazing) body?

Kind of counterproductive.

"I'm ready." The voice that comes out isn't my own shrill (according to Mary Mac) tone, but instead is a husky, velvety, melodic, Kathleen-Turner-back-in-the-day sound. (Note to self: If possible, record outgoing voice mail message before returning Tabitha's bod to its rightful owner.)

"Do you need your doctor with you on set?"

"*No!*" I bark, before I quickly clarify. "I mean, Dr. Reagan said I'd do my best if I, I mean, she weren't watching."

Also, Tabitha . . . kind of hasn't been informed of what we're doing right now, so she's in no position to fake being me. She's in the dressing room with Deva, wearing an ancient amulet, eyes clamped shut to ensure she doesn't look down and realize she's not in her own skin. We told her that this was a creative visualization exercise, but at the end of it, she'd have completed her task with no real memory of actually having experienced what terrified her.

I know, I know.

If the APA ever caught wind of my shenanigans, I'd never . . . well, I can't even consider the repercussions right now.

Richard calls, "Places, everyone!" and his team scrambles. They've all been warned that they only have moments to capture the shot, and woe be to them if they're not ready. From the corner of the room, I spot the *Push* team as well, and I have to catch myself before waving to our crew. Pfft, like Kassel needs the ego boost of having been acknowledged by a movie star, especially one as undeniably hot as I am.

Granted, I've never had a desire to . . . dine at the Pink Taco before, but my God, look at me! This face! This skin! These tits! I'm a total game changer.

"And we're rolling . . ."

Okay, Tabitha's body, let's do this.

My only task is to sit here in the corner of this clear box, one hundred and three stories above the rest of Chicago, using nothing but my face to communicate the whirlwind of emotions my character is feeling. Not only has Parker Peter recently discovered her new superpowers stemming from a radioactive spider bite, but she's also just learned she's tasked with saving the city from her new arch-nemesis, Venom, played by a catsuited Charlize Theron.

While the cameras are on me, my goal is to project equal parts fear, resolve, and hope.

Easy-peasy.

I fear being found out, while I resolve to keep my job and license to practice, and I hope to wheedle the name of Tabitha's surgeon out of her.

I emote the hell out of the scene, somewhat inadvertently.

As excited as I am that this is actually working, a part of me is racked with guilt. Although technically psychologists don't take a Hippocratic oath, we govern our practices by it. The first-do-no-harm business is no joke. I've been wrestling with myself over this deception, as I'm not doing harm so much as I'm helping Tabitha keep a hundred-million-dollar movie on track.

Yet I'm motivated by my own self-preservation, which is at cross-purposes with all my training and values.

When I asked myself if Maslow, Jung, or Freud would ever

perpetrate what I'm doing right now, the answer was no, never, under no circumstances, even for the purpose of research.

But what about Dr. Phil?

Pfft, in a heartbeat.

So that causes inner turmoil—do I want to be a psychologist who happens to be on television or do I want to be a television psychologist?

If I choose the latter, then I wonder if the rules shouldn't be relaxed a bit.

"Cut!" calls Holthaus. He comes over to where I'm perched and eases down next to me. "Tabby, baby—that was incredible. I'm so proud of you. Whatever your doctor did worked." To the rest of the crew, he calls, "It's in the can!" The whole Skydeck, which is filled with cast and crew, begins to cheer.

Which means I'm not fired!

I glance over at Kassel, who's conferring with a cameraman who isn't Gary. (Like I'd trust Gary with a nickel, let alone my career.) He pumps his fist in victory—apparently the *Push* crew nailed the shot as well.

As I still have a couple of minutes before the jig is up, and for the entirely selfish reason of wanting to walk around in Tabitha's superhero shoes for another moment, I find myself asking, "Do you want a take from a different angle?"

CHAPTER THIRTEEN

The Ego Has Landed

The episode airs on Thursday night, one week after having been filmed. The team had to do a crash edit to pull it all together, but Ruby and Faye made it happen.

I mean, after *I* made it happen.

(Yes, I'm giving myself affirmations again. I deserve them.)

Normally, the whole staff would stage an episode-watching party, but after everything that went down with Lance and Ashlee, and following the soft opening of Dr. Karen and the not-exactly-OCD hand washer's episode, everyone's understandably afraid to jinx tonight. I'd have invited Deva over, but she's taking a mini-break at one of her other houses since we're not shooting this week. As she completely saved my hide, I begrudge her nothing.

I'm just about to settle in on the couch to watch the episode when there's a knock at my door. This is odd, because no one can enter without having been buzzed.

"Who is it?" I demand, my voice coming out sharper than usual.

"Yo, Dr. B! It's Trevor and Bryce. Got something for ya!"

I open the door, and not only are the boys completely dressed, but they come bearing gifts: a bottle of whipped-cream-flavored vodka and a six-pack of sugar-free Red Bull.

"'S'like a housewarming dealie," Trevor explains. "Only for your new show. Bought you sugar-free. You know, for health."

I look at the guys, grinning from ear to ear, and then at each of their offerings. "That is really"—don't say disgusting, don't say disgusting, don't say disgusting—"very sweet. Would you like to come in?"

"Naw, gots to go, playa," Bryce explains. "Three-dollar Fireball shots at the Dark Horse and half-price apps, yeah! Gotta get my Thursday night on!"

"Well . . . thank you for this thoughtful gesture, and I won't keep you."

Trevor salutes and says, "Yeah, gratz, Dr. B!" They begin to clatter down the stairs when, as an afterthought, Trevor adds, "Next time your buddy Tabitha's in town, maybe you give us the fresh hookup?"

"Sure thing."

If my time with (and being) Tabitha Baylee taught me anything, it's that she would absolutely jump on every semiliterate, inexplicably ESL frat boy who crosses her path.

Not.

I shut and lock the door behind them.

I glance at my whipped-cream vodka (why, God, why?)

and sugar-free Red Bull, you know, for health. I'd likely drink paint thinner before allowing any of this near my lips, but I'm still oddly touched by the gesture. They certainly could have asked me for a favor without the sickly-sweet hooch and sugar-free rocket fuel.

I shove the libations into the hall closet. At some point I'll regift this all back to them and they'll never have been the wiser.

I grab the remote and sit down, but before I can even kick off my shoes, I hear the phone. I jump a little, as it's so rare for my phone to ring, particularly with anyone with whom I'd like to speak. The sound is somewhat foreign between these four walls and echoes the length of the apartment.

Tentatively, I pick up. "Hello?"

A familiar voice comes on the line. "Hi, Reagan . . . it's Bethany."

"Bethany? Bethany *Walker*? Long time no talk."

I'm not mad about hearing from my former marathon-training buddy after a whole summer. Rather, I'm pleasantly surprised. I thought our bridge had long since been burned.

Rather sheepishly, Bethany says, "Reagan, I know it's been a while, but I saw that you're on tonight and I just wanted to say congratulations and I'm sincerely happy for you."

I perch on the corner of the couch. "Thanks, that's very kind of you. With all the weirdness leading up to last week's premiere, I'm thrilled that we're finally starting to find our way."

I don't add that I'm delighted to not have been fired, as that's no one's business, regardless of how true it may be.

"Well, I'm definitely rooting for you. Anyway, I'm sure you're busy, but I wanted to say hello. Um, listen—I'm doing an LSD this weekend"—meaning long, slow, distance run, as opposed to Lake Shore Drive or Timothy Leary's drug of choice—"so give me a jingle if you're up for joining."

Huh. I've decided against doing the marathon this year, but it couldn't hurt to step up my distance runs. "I'll have to check my calendar, but pencil me in with a possible yes," I say.

"Super! I look forward to it. See you soon!"

I find myself smiling.

"Sounds like a plan. Bye!"

Now, that's both surprising and serendipitous. However, I don't even have time to process our conversation when the phone rings again.

I'm less hesitant this time. "Hello?"

"Hey, Reagan, it's Caroline. Saw the preview for your show and I thought, *I haven't spoken with Reagan forever.* How are you?"

Caroline, rather Dr. Caroline Kenner, has a bustling North Shore practice where she specializes in working with teens. We met through a professional association a few years ago and we bonded over common philosophies. She's the only other psychologist I've met who shares my reservations about pharmaceuticals, and she's always on CNN advocating against overmedicating children.

"Everything's great," I reply.

Because at the moment? It really is.

"Kudos on the program," she says. "Have you seen it yet?"

"I'm just sitting down to it now. I mean, I viewed the final cut in the edit bay, but there's something so gratifying about watching it on television between the Taco Bell and State Farm commercials and all."

On the WeWIN network, *Push* was always buffeted by low-budget ads for local carpet retailers and Life Alert buttons and Bumpits. Nothing says "big" like a name-brand soda commercial.

"Absolutely," Caroline agrees. "I shan't keep you, Reagan. I just hoped to say hello and to wish you well. Apologies for having been so swamped. It's back-to-school season and all the parents want extra time to help their kids gird their loins for the coming year. I'm telling you, the bullies are buying my kids an Ivy League education. However, my schedule's opening up, so please give me a ring when you're free. I'd love to hear your thoughts on the book I'm working on—it's about the overuse of psychotropic drugs in the Louisiana State foster care system."

Sounds like *somebody's* not considered Dr. Wack anymore!

I enthusiastically reply, "That sounds fascinating! Let's talk soon." We lob a couple of dates back and forth and decide to meet up next week.

Well, isn't *this* an interesting turn of events?

I should probably be suspicious of suddenly hearing from people, but if I'm to be perfectly honest, I'm not concerned about anyone's motives. I'm tired of feeling ostracized and I'm grateful to be invited back into my friends' lives. And if I had to perpetrate a small but effectual fraud with a movie star before they'd have me back? That's a price I'm willing to have paid.

My phone vibrates and I read the incoming text:

Congratulations beautiful person! Knew it would all work out! Feeding Greater Chicago Ball @Metropolitan Club this Saturday—let Janie know if u want to be on the list! Besos, WW

I can feel a massive grin spread across my face. Wendy Winsberg, whom I haven't heard a single word from since Hawaii, wants *me* at her charity event? Network must be an even bigger deal than I thought.

An infinitesimal part of me is angry about how she hung us out to dry, and yet, I'll admit I adore being privy to her inner circle. I don't hate appearing on the party pages of *Chicago Nouveau* magazine or rubbing elbows with the rest of the city's glitterati. I make a mental note to call her assistant, Janie, in the morning.

I feel another buzz and glance down.

me and you at the bou?

I recognize Rhonda's number—she's a former U of C classmate and current neighbor. Funny, but I could have sworn she looked right through me in front of the coffee shop a couple of weeks ago. I thought she was being a megabitch, but now I wonder if she legitimately didn't see me.

At the same time, my landline and cell phone begin to ring, and I can hear the incoming bing of e-mail on my laptop. This is crazy! Unsure of how to prioritize, I allow everything to go to voice mail.

This never happened when *Push* was on WeWIN.

Bzzt, bzzt.

gr8 job, girl!—S

Oh, my God! *Sebastian's* watching the show? And thinking of me? Unbelievable! I'm not even sure of how to react. I feel like I'm finally moving on, and yet, the idea of *him* being in contact with *me* gives me butterflies in my stomach. What would it be like if *he* were to come crawling back to *me*?

My phones keep ringing. I scroll through the caller ID on my mobile and am pleased to note all the old friends and classmates who are suddenly back in touch. I imagine this is what it must have felt like to be popular in high school.

Which . . . don't even get me wrong—I'm so proud of having graduated from Taylor Park. Yet I wonder how much more I'd have enjoyed the experience if I'd ever stopped studying long enough to eke out a minute of fun. Pep rallies, bonfires, homecoming dances—never made it to one of them. I wasn't unpopular so much as I never even allowed the other students to give me that consideration.

I was always That Girl in the Library.

By the time second semester of my freshman year rolled around, people stopped even trying to invite me to events, confident I'd never attend.

Would I be a different person if I'd figuratively let down my hair?

Maybe some of the Taylor Parkers would have scoffed at my solidly middle-class status, our Bridgeport bungalow, and my blue-collar family, but surely there were others there on scholarships? In retrospect—and given the school's commitment to academia—it stands to reason I could have found like minds in students who cared more for books than boys.

Perhaps this is one of the reasons I fell for Boyd so quickly? He and his friends instantly welcomed me into their social circle. Sure, the guys would tease me about bringing bags of books to the beach, but they were always respectful. And their girlfriends became my friends, sharing stories and seeking my counsel. It's little wonder that I found myself so distracted.

My point is, would I be so eager to forgive those who dumped me so easily if I'd learned to be social earlier in life?

Of course, all I need to do to affirm my choices is look at Geri's life. At St. Francis Xavier (where I guarantee she was accepted due to nepotism, not merit) she was the queen of all she surveyed. Despite not being particularly cute or academically gifted, she managed to rule her school.

And where is *she* now?

Standing in a pile of someone else's hair.

Pretty sure I win.

Bzzt.

```
watchin ur show! pls pls let me cut some
lyers in ur hair, at least aroun ur face. Is
2 severe. wll stll b bouncy, but wll have +
lift/- heft XOX, ur lil sis
```

Leave it to Geri to be the world's biggest killjoy. She can't just be happy for me. It's like she goes out of her way to find a way to criticize me. Her jealousy is all consuming. And like I'd *ever* let her touch my hair. The last thing I need is more lift, and is she honestly one to lecture *me* about too much heft? Really? The Stay Puft Marshmallow Sis?

And yet my folks wonder why we can't get along.

Bzzt.

```
Don't be angry that Geri gave me your
digits, Ray. Listen, if the show proves
too overwhelming, you're not obligated to
proceed. Your goal was to be a therapist, not
a pitchman for Ford F150s. Be true to you.
```

Oh, Boyd—why couldn't you be a tiny bit more driven? Trade in your board for a briefcase and we could be great together.

Until then? Delete.

Bzzt.

Halo, Rogain Barkeep!

Deva has the damnedest time texting with her massive appendages. When I hear from her, I have to try to interpret what she means, and not what she actually types.

R ur phonies ringaling?

Are your phones ringing?

A ward of car Sean—

I'm guessing . . . a word of caution?

UR reel fronds r tons how spork tooth

So, my real friends are the ones who *spork tooths*?

Noted.

Not understood, but noted.

As I'm in too fine a mood to try to interpret Deva's cryptic text, I silence everything and arrange myself on the couch to watch the first episode of my new, fresh start.

CHAPTER FOURTEEN

Ancient Chinese Secret

"Do I know you?"

I'm done playing the fake-humble fame game. My status as *Push*'s breakout star is *totes legit.*

According to Bryce and Trevor, that is.

According to Ma, my newfound status is no excuse to skip Thanksgiving with the family. Argh.

Regardless, instead of being coy or retiring when approached by a fan, I've come to embrace my well-deserved notoriety with open arms. With my most brilliant, freshly whitened smile, I turn to the fellow Whole Foods patron and look her in the eye.

"*I'm* Dr. Reagan Bishop."

"Oh, my God, I knew it!" she squeals, and I beam.

This must be what it feels like to be Ol' Rat Nasty.

(Minus being pelted with drawers.)

Yet while I'm grinning beatifically, I can't help but notice her cart is overflowing with wine, bread products, and gelato, which is *so* not the point of shopping here. All those carbs make me feel nauseous. What's with her bushel o' crap? Don't others care to take advantage of the pesticide-free produce and bulk-bin chia seeds, and if they're into that sort of thing, meat classified by its level of animal-centeredness? Otherwise, why wouldn't they just hit Trader Joe's or Dominick's?

However, I'm not judging her, because she's a fan.

Although I bet her fridge is filled with diet soda.

Filled.

Which is none of my business.

She probably enjoys a refreshing Diet Coke while watching me on television.

All I'm saying is I hope she enjoys type 2 diabetes.

She gushes, "*I Need a Push* is the best, the absolute best! My friends and I love your show! I'm Cassie, by the way—hi! Nice to meet you! Yo, Jessica! Jess! Come here!"

A woman with an armload of tortilla chips, presumably Jessica, rushes over to join us. She's cute in that generic, Big Ten–grad, wide-hipped, midwestern way, with straight, shiny hair and a statement-piece necklace, topped with a utilitarian, all-weather North Face jacket. The second the icy Canadian winds start rolling in off the lake in late September, Chicagoans forswear fashion for function. Right now the coats in this store are running about thirty-five percent North Face, twenty percent Mountain Hardwear and Arc'teryx, and fifteen percent Patagonia, with the rest divided between layered hoodies for the trust-funded hipsters and fur for the I'm-so-urban soccer moms who'll remain Team City until the first time someone breaks into their Lexus SUV, at which point they will run like scalded apes to the friendly confines of Wheaton.

"Ohmigod," Jessica exclaims, "what you did with Tabby

Baylee? We were *weeping*! We've loved her ever since she was on the CW? In that show? About the college girl? Who was secretly a member of Homeland Security? Remember? The best! Is she nice? Is she so awesome in person? Are you friends? Is she on your Facebook? Do you guys text?"

I offer an enigmatic reply. "Tabitha is a superhero, and I mean that in every respect."

I'm forever in Tabitha's debt because she proved how easy it would be for us to swoop in and make the switch. At no point during our swap did she suspect anything, largely due to Deva's ministrations.

Deva prepped Tabitha, telling her the three of us were going to do some creative visualization. Tabitha and I sat next to each other and Deva stood behind us, ostensibly to "help harness the negative energy." But really, she just needed to be positioned in a way where she could slip the matching amulets around our necks at the same time.

When I asked Deva about the origins of the amulets, she replied, "Ancient Chinese secret," and it took me a moment to realize she was serious and not just quoting a classic detergent commercial.

Strung on lengths of black velvet cord, at first glance the amulets looked like any other statement necklace sported by your average Lincoln Park resident. The amulets are identical old bronze coins, maybe three inches in diameter, covered in Chinese lettering on one side, and a head with two faces on the other. When I saw them, I asked, "Is this an inscription? Do these characters actually mean something?"

Deva replied, "The loose interpretation is, 'If there is anything that we wish to change in the child, we should first examine it and see whether it is not something that could better be changed in ourselves.'"

"I've heard that quote before," I said.

"Probably because I just said it, Reagan Bishop."

"No, it's quite familiar. Have I read it somewhere?" I pulled my phone out and noticed the shadow cast across Deva's face.

"I'm Googling, okay? I'm not spying on anyone's Facebook profile. No need for panic." Sheesh. You *accidentally* stalk one ex-boyfriend and suddenly the whole world thinks you're filling a panel van full of candy to cruise the parking lot at the junior high school.

My search results populated immediately. "I knew I recognized that quote! Carl Jung said it!"

Deva looked at me quizzically. "Is he a friend of yours, Reagan Bishop?"

"No! Jung founded the whole analytical psychology school of thought."

"Was he Chinese?"

"Swiss."

Deva shrugged. "Then he must have been a fan of the Shang dynasty, Reagan Bishop, because that's where these are from."

As I didn't care to argue whether Carl Jung was a plagiarist or a psychiatrist, I instead focused on exactly what I needed to do for a seamless switch.

Deva told me that the second Tabitha and I touched the coordinating amulets, we'd project into one another's bodies. When the time came, I can't be sure if Tabitha felt the same kind of change that I did when I landed in her skin. But before we started, Deva had clearly explained that any disjointed feelings were part of the process, so if Tabitha felt anything odd, she kept it to herself.

Thank God.

I'm sure if she'd heard my voice coming out of what she assumed were her own lips, the damage would have been irreparable.

As soon as I finished filming, I dashed back to the dressing room. I sat down next to her and Deva removed our amulets. And just like that, we were back in our own bodies.

No fuss, no muss.

The only real management involved Deva making sure that Tabitha kept both her mouth and her eyes closed so she wouldn't look down and suddenly be disappointed in her cup size. Afterward, we explained to Tabitha she'd been hypnotized, which was why she wouldn't remember having been on the Ledge.

Did I feel dirty when the deed was done? *Yes.*

Was I wrapped around the axle in terms of moral equivocation? *Indeed.*

Did I swear to myself that I'd never perpetrate such a falsehood again? *Um . . .*

I *meant* for the swap to be a onetime thing, I truly did. But everyone was so excited about the results, especially Tabitha. She wanted to nail the scene more than anyone. When we wrapped, I referred her to a clinical psychologist in LA to continue with exposure work, so I felt like I did as much as I could given the parameters. And maybe I wasn't the best psychologist on television, but I was an outstanding television psychologist.

That counts, too.

Just ask Dr. Phil.

Cassie enthuses, "What about when the Olympic equestrian climbed back on her horse for the first time since her accident? OMG, waterworks!" She makes spirit fingers up by her chin when she says this.

That was a powerful episode, if I do say so myself. Was I sure to toss in one quick jump over the exact same triple-barred obstacle where the rider had been thrown in the first place? You betcha. Kassel said that episode had Emmy written all over it.

If only they awarded Emmys for giving perms, am I right, Geri?

"How 'bout when the guy who was afraid of flying took that chopper ride around the city?" Jessica adds. I really had to rein in my excitement—I've always wanted to see Chicago from a helicopter. I've flown over it dozens of times coming in and out of O'Hare, but there's something about the perspective from the chopper that makes the whole town come alive.

Cassie grabs Jessica's arm. "Or when the high school mean girl finally apologized to her victims all those years later?" For some reason, Deva seemed particularly invested in this episode. Not for nothing, but that band geek slaps really hard. You'd have thought she played the drums, not the clarinet. I felt a lot of pent-up rage in that backhand. A lot. I'm sure that guest Lissy's face ached for a week afterward.

"Yes, yes," I agree. "It's all a rich tapestry."

I'm sure my professors would be appalled if they had a clue about the sorcery I helped perpetrate. Or they would, if I were a psychologist on television, rather than a television psychologist.

Yet in many ways, I've come to believe my ends justify my means. A lot of people are afraid to fly, or confront their enemies, or try something new and frightening. By showing regular people experiencing victories on such a national platform, I'm surely helping masses of viewers, even if my results aren't exactly lasting for the guests themselves. But they're all given the option of DBS-sponsored therapy afterward, so they're in competent hands.

As it's best to not let anyone genuflect for too long, I must take my leave. "Ladies, I so appreciate your stopping to say hello, and I'm delighted you're enjoying the show. Because it's Thanksgiving week, we won't be airing a new episode, but tune in next Thursday. Spoiler alert, have your Kleenex handy!"

I haven't yet heard what we're filming next, but that's not terribly relevant. Rest assured, I *will* make them cry.

We say our good-byes and I meander over to the bulk bins, where I'm debating the merits of whole flaxseed versus ground when the pocket of my North Face jacket vibrates. I pull out my phone and glance down at the message from Tiffany, the show's publicist.

CHICAGO NOUVEAU MAG WANTS TO DO FEATURE ON
U—U HAVE ARRIVED!

I sigh with contentment.

Indeed, I have arrived.

"Congrats on the *Chicago Nouveau* business, Peace Corps! Great for you, even better for *Push*. See? This is what I consider 'big.'"

"And no cats had to be flattened in the process. Everyone wins!" I quip.

"When's the interview?" Kassel leans back in his chair, placing his hands behind his head. Now that I'm in his good graces, I've come to despise him a whole lot less, and barely dread our weekly one-on-ones.

"Next month," I reply. "They want to include it in their January first 'Nouveau Year, Nouveau You' piece."

"Nice. Very nice." He stretches and I find myself craning my neck to see if I can catch a glimpse of his six-pack. (I don't hold out hope for Boyd's V-cut, though. No one with an actual day job could have one of those.)

You know, it's rare for a man to wear a sweater well. Generally, sweaters add bulk and almost never fit properly, but as he reclines in his chair, I can definitely see the outline of abs beneath the cashmere. Kudos to his tailor. Or trainer. Or parents. Possibly all four.

I modestly reply, "I'm duly flattered by their attention," at no point mentioning my having accidentally shouted, *Who's the favorite now, Geri?* in front of the display of nut butters.

He leans forward conspiratorially. "Listen, Peace Corps, I was saving this news for the next staff meeting, but I'll let you in on it now because you're such a major portion of their decision: Santanos Mills is becoming a sponsor!"

I feel frozen in my chair, but clearly he's waiting for a reaction, so I say, "Wow, that's . . ."

Disturbing? Shocking? Outrageous?

Not only have Santanos Mills soy products been linked to a sudden onset of testicular cancer in laboratory rats, but their factories are the worst offenders in terms of environmental damage due to pesticides and herbicides. They're also the largest proponent of using GMOs—genetically modified organisms—in their products. And their line of Chomp-tastic prepackaged children's meals? Revolting. The sodium alone in one perfectly circular slice of their Hamnificent Hamlike Meat Product exceeds a child's recommended daily allowance by 153 percent!

(Have you any comprehension of how little actual ham

has to be included in a product before the FDA disallows the producer to use the word *ham*? Trust me, this is not knowledge you want.)

(By the way, when I quoted these stats to Mary Mac, do you know what she said to me? "If I have to make seven individual school lunches every day, I will kill self-comma-others. Sometimes a prepacked Chomp-tastic is the only thing standing between me and Susan Smith.")

Kassel rears back to give me a high five, as though Santanos Mills is a victory we should celebrate. "Team *Push*!" he cheers. Then he notices my expression. "Hey, is everything copacetic with you, Peace Corps? You seem off."

I quickly try to cover up my distress. But my God, the Santanos Mills business is worrisome. I can justify my actions with the amulets due to being a television psychologist and not vice versa, but there's little I can do to make peace with their practices.

However, ultimately Santanos Mills will be paying my salary and I'm loath to seem ungrateful. So I quickly come up with a lie that, as soon as I say it, rings true. "I'm just dreading the holidays," I say.

"This is a hard time of year," he agrees. As he speaks, he toys with the small, crude ceramic bowl he keeps on the corner of his desk. The piece is fairly incongruous with the whole turn-of-the-century robber-baron look going on in the rest of the office. He recently brought in a new equestrian oil painting that appears to be directly out of a villain-in-an-eighties-teen-movie's house. Kassel notices me watching him and offers, "My kid made this a couple of years ago in art class. It's an ashtray, even though I don't smoke."

Huh. In all the times we've spoken, we've never once veered into personal territory. Kassel's always such a blowhard that I normally want to remove myself from his presence as soon as possible, regardless of how nicely he fills out a cashmere sweater. But he's giving me this opening, and, well, it's kind of a professional obligation to draw out others.

I ask, "What's his name?"

"He's Walter, named after my dad. He's growing up way too fast! Seems like yesterday he was in diapers, but now? He's embarrassed to hug me."

"Does Walter live here?"

"No, he's in LA with his mom." As an afterthought, he adds, "And with *Brody*. Ugh, what kind of grown-up calls himself Brody?"

I can't help myself. "The same kind who refers to others by personal characteristics rather than learning first names?"

"Ha-ha." Except his laughter doesn't seem to reach his eyes and I seem to have inadvertently struck a nerve.

"Will you be spending Thanksgiving with him?"

He turns the ashtray over and runs his fingers across Walter's large, blocky name etched into the bottom. "No, he'll be in Aspen with his mom. And Brody. I'll be out in LA for Christmas, but this year, I'm on my own for Turkey Day. We're filming a segment with Dr. Karen and a shopaholic at the mall on Saturday. I have to fill in for everyone who's on vacay, so it doesn't make sense to fly back for a day and a half. As of now, my plans involve pizza and *Party Down* on DVD."

I blurt, "I'm so jealous!"

For a second, Kassel seems more vulnerable and less venerable. "You enjoy the suffering of others, Peace Corps?"

I shake my head so hard my ponytail batters the sides of my face. "No, of course not. It's just that I have a command performance on the south side and I'm dreading the day."

Kassel seems rather wistful. "Is it a big family deal?"

I snort. "More like *ordeal.* Ma will be up at three a.m. with the turkeys and the pies and my sister Mary Mac will show up around noon to help, whereas I have to be there at seven a.m. or the world will end. Get this—my sister lives two doors away, yet can her kids stay home with their dad while she's busy prepping? Of course not. So we have to make dinner for twenty-five while a dozen kids careen through the kitchen every thirty seconds. Plus, I'm always stuck with the grunt work of peeling the potatoes and dotting the yams with marshmallows, which may as well be fiberglass for all their nutritional content."

I feel claustrophobic every time I imagine what the day will be like. Between the kids and the football blaring from every television and all the old men smoking cigars and my aunts getting blotto on cooking sherry? Not a selling point.

By the way, does Princess Geri have to raise a finger with the rest of the womenfolk? *Of course not.* My uncles consider her color commentary to be the height of comedy, so while we're slaving away in the kitchen, she's kicked back on the sofa, offering up pithy comments like, "Jason Witten is a tight end? I'll say his end is tight!"

"Everyone likes mini-marshmallows on their sweet potatoes. Fact," Kassel informs me. His humor seems to have improved, likely because *he's* the kind of person who enjoys the suffering of others.

I shudder imagining the glistening, oozy orange lumps piled high on everyone's plates. "Au contraire. The only bright spot is that I'm moving up to the adult table this year. My great-aunt Sophia passed away so I'm slated to finally, finally get away from the kids' table in the basement. That's the only reason I'm maintaining my sanity right now. Well, that and not having to pretend to eat my great-aunt Sophia's Jell-O mold ever again."

Now he's grinning in earnest. "Bite your tongue, Peace Corps, Jell-O molds are classic!"

"In what universe?"

"In every universe!" he exclaims so loudly that it rattles his framed lithographs. "In each and every rainbow-striped, Cool Whip–topped, pineapple-specked universe."

I can't tell if he's teasing me or if he's serious. Both eventualities are vaguely alarming. "Have you ever been served a Jell-O mold filled with canned corn, peas, and shaved carrots? Because I have. Aunt Sophia called it a *salad*."

Hold the phone—I figured out why Kassel seems so familiar. Kassel reminds me of *Boyd*. Maybe it's the California connection, or possibly it's the way we banter. How did I not see this before? Of course, I should say Kassel's what Boyd would have been if he hadn't decided to toss his whole future for "some tasty waves and a cool buzz." (Side note? I was with Boyd for an entire year before I realized that this Spicoli he always quoted was a fictional character from *Fast Times at Ridgemont High* and not one of his beach-bum buddies.) (What? We didn't have HBO growing up.)

Kassel runs a palm over his hair and I catch a glimpse of his wrist. Yep, still golden. Not that I care about that sort of thing, though. "Sweet *and* savory—that's a whole meal right there."

Teasing, then?

"It's my professional opinion that you, sir, are insane."

Was Kassel fun before? I feel like I'd have noticed if he was fun before. Boyd was big fun, ergo it stands to reason that Kassel would be fun.

What kind of fun could we have together?

Until this very moment, I never actually considered Kassel to be a potential romantic partner. But maybe he's exactly what I need? He has Sebastian's professional intensity, yet he appears to embody some of the joie de vivre that Boyd brought to the table.

I wonder if Kassel isn't the best of both worlds.

There's something a bit incestuous about a television crew, and staffers are often drawn to one another, due to both the fraternity and the long hours. Sets are very insular environments. Unlike in a lot of other workplaces, not only is fraternization not taboo, but it's practically encouraged. Wendy used to fix up staffers all the time. Pretty much the only thing *Push* couples have to do is fill out a tiny bit of paperwork for HR, and then? Mazel tov!

I'm not saying I want to date my boss, though.

I'm simply saying that in a world of possibilities, Kassel is one of them, especially since I'm over Sebastian.

Mostly.

There's still a part of my ego that's badly bruised from the whole debacle. What's ironic is I've actually heard from Sebastian a couple of times, but I've yet to return his calls. Hope he appreciates the irony.

I take a moment to admire how comfortable Kassel seems here in his kingdom. He's one hundred percent at ease in his skin and at his desk, and I find his confidence attractive.

"When I was a kid, my gammy used to make a Jell-O salad with Spam and pimento olives."

Look at us, enjoying each other's company. Who'd have guessed?

I joke, "And how does *that* make you feel?"

"Actually? A little nostalgic." Then his chin briefly puckers and his eyes seem a bit glassy.

Okay, so this just veered horribly off track.

Abort! Abort!

I immediately hold my arms up as if to protect myself and as if he didn't suddenly turn melancholy. "FYI, I'll probably hurl all over your fancy antique desk if we continue to discuss Jell-O. So you know. Just to put it out there."

He gives me a wry shrug. "All I'm saying is Gammy's cooking was the stuff memories are made of."

"And all I'm saying is that family holidays may not be as great as you recall. I guarantee if you happened upon a Very Bishop Thanksgiving, you'd be headed back to your place for a DVD and Domino's so fast your head would spin."

Then, before common sense prevails, I add, "You don't actually want your head to spin . . . do you?"

To which he replies, "Tell me when and where."

CHAPTER FIFTEEN
Sister Act

"Yucky! It's touching my sweet potatoes!" One of Mary Mac's twins—no idea which—is in the throes of a fit, having been served a tiny portion of the beautiful salad I made especially for this meal. From the way she's carrying on, you'd imagine I was trying to poison her, and not just add a little non-factory-farmed, chicken-finger-based protein to her diet. To punctuate her point, she adds, "I hate this!"

I try to reason with Kiley Irelyn, but my patience is already shot due to having been stuck downstairs at the children's table a-freaking-*gain*. Yes, this is the year I was to finally make the leap upstairs to the grown-ups' table, lest Aunt Sophia's death—and the loss of Jell-O molds—be in vain.

But no.

Instead, my great-aunt Helen and Charlie, her new octogenarian suitor, are taking the spots earmarked for Kassel and me. Aunt Helen thought it would be a big kick to surprise us on their way down from Milwaukee to Florida for the winter, because who cares about RSVPs? Yes! Let's just throw the seating arrangement out the window! Reagan won't mind being downgraded to the basement! Proper holiday protocol be damned!

And while we're at it, let's park the massive RV we're driving on the street in front of the Bishops' house where it can take up three spaces, causing everyone else to have to hike two blocks carrying the only platters of healthy food anyone will see in this damn place all year!

I paste a facsimile of a smile on my face. "Just try one bite," I suggest. "After all, there are starving children all over the world who'd kill for the opportunity to eat something like this."

Even though I warned Kassel about the potential for this being a dysfunctional family meal, my hope is to keep a lid on as much abhorrent behavior as possible. Or to at least compensate for earlier when Charlie mentioned how comfortable and freeing it is to pilot his RV sans pants. (Although I imagine it *is* more comfortable, what with his current waistband hitting him right below the armpit.)

"No." Kiley Irelyn clamps her lips together. She and her sister could not be more identical today in their matching velvet dresses with smocked tops and lace collars. They're even sporting corresponding hair bands in their shoulder-length, burnt orange curls. Why would anyone do that? What's the point of putting the girls in the exact same thing and styling them in a way that doesn't suggest two individuals, so much as one and a spare?

And yet when I offer Mary Mac this suggestion—coming

from a place of love and concern, mind you—she replies that until I successfully raise a dog/cat/goldfish, I'm to keep my parenting suggestions to myself.

Perhaps the child will respond to reason. I say, "How can you be sure you don't like what I've made if you won't even taste it?"

"Because it looks like barf," she replies, all matter-of-fact.

Across the table, Geri covers her mouth with a napkin to hide her laughter. I point at her. "Not helpful!"

As I'm not about to be bested by a five-year-old (nine-year-old? who can tell?), I say, "I suspect you *believe* you hate this salad because you don't recognize some of the ingredients in it. Allow me to elaborate. The round parts are quinoa, and quinoa is a superfood—it's full of protein and magnesium and lysine!"

She shoves her plate away. "Ewww! You want me to eat *Visine*?"

I'm trying to not raise my voice, but how is she not responding to reason? "No, not eyedrops. Lysine is an amino acid," I explain.

"Kids love amino acids," Kassel quips. "Every time I see Walt, he's all, 'Dad, Dad, can we go out for amino acids?'" Geri begins to laugh in earnest until she spots me shooting daggers at her.

"Quinoa is kind of like rice, sweetie. You love the fried rice from Hunan Garden," Geri offers. I'm not buying this sudden look-how-amazing-I-am-with-children act. She knows Kassel has a kid and she's trying to make me seem like an asshole.

Kiley Irelyn softens because she's only six (eight?) and doesn't realize she's being played. "Oh, okay. But what's the other junk mixed in?"

I have to force myself from sighing in resignation. I'd hardly classify what's on her dish as junk. In fact, it's the opposite of junk. While perusing CookingLight.com, I ran across this salad recipe and thought it would provide the perfect contrast to all things covered in marshmallows and drowned in butter on this day. The organic beets give the dish an earthy crunch and the kumquats offer the sweet tanginess of a bottled dressing, only without all the MSG, sulfur dioxide, and sodium benzoate, which I've read can lead to hyperactivity disorder in children. (Trust me, these kids are already hyper enough.)

"You like oranges, right?" Geri asks. "Remember that time we ate all those clementines while watching *Finding Nemo*?"

Kiley Irelyn nods and snuggles closer to her aunt.

Show-off.

Geri tells her, "Well, there are two kinds of oranges in here. Kumquats are like little-bitty oranges, only you can eat the skin, too. Isn't that crazy? Look at me, I'm going to put the whoooole thing in my mouth! The mama orange cries, *Please don't eat my baby!* but I will anyway!" She takes a bite and makes exaggerated chewing noises before opening her mouth for a split second to show Kiley Irelyn her tongue coated in orange paste.

Charming.

Yet for some reason Kiley Irelyn responds to Geri's antics and she starts to titter.

I guarantee Geri's only being helpful to impress Kassel. Her eyes practically popped out of her head when she saw him come in with me. I explained that we were work colleagues, and when she asked if it was something more, I responded ambiguously.

My relationships? Are none of her business.

Also, I can handle this kid on my own.

I explain, "The other kind of orange is Italian. See the crimson flesh? It's called a blood orange. And who doesn't love the blood orange? They're sweeter than your average citrus fruit and their juice—"

"Ma, Auntie Reagan's trying to make me eat blood!"

I predicted today would go sideways. Damn kids always ruining my credibility. So, in my most calming, professional voice, I say, "Kiley Irelyn, it is never appropriate to yell at the dinner table."

"I'm not Kylie!" She runs up the stairs to the table where I *should* be right now.

Geri shrugs. "Sorry, Gip, I tried."

"Gip?" Kassel looks up from his mountain of mashed potatoes. "Why are you calling her Gip?"

"Like the Gipper? As in 'win one for the,'" Geri replies, batting her eyes.

Okay, please stop flirting with him right now. You're just embarrassing yourself. Side-by-side comparison between us? There is no comparison. Perhaps Geri's shaken off a pound or two of extra tonnage recently, but she'll never have my lean muscle mass or Black Irish coloring. And so what if she's straightened her wild curls today? The second she encounters humidity, boom! The full Bozo.

Also?

Freckles?

No.

Geri explains, "Reagan's namesake is President Ronald, so I've been calling her that ever since I saw the movie."

Intrigued, Kassel leans forward in his seat. "You a fan of *Knute Rockne?*"

Geri reaches into her shirt and brandishes the gold cross she's worn ever since her first communion. "Um, hello? Catholic upbringing? Eff, yeah!"

I'm sorry, but what the eff is it with the *eff* business? Geri drops f-bombs like hippies drop acid and rappers drop microphones. Why is she being such an effing phony right now? "*Knute Rockne*'s only the best football film ever made until—"

Kassel and Geri shout at the same time, "*Rudy!*"

Kassel lowers his voice and says, "'My son's going to Notre Dame!'"

To which Geri replies, "'You're a Ruettiger. There's nothing in the world wrong with being a Ruettiger!'"

"'You ain't here to be no nanny in no kindergarten!'"

"Onward to vic-to-ry!" Geri sings.

They both grin like lunatics and then clink wineglasses across the table. "To the fighting Irish!" Kassel cries.

What's happening here?

Do . . . do I see a spark between them? Because, *no*. Whatever *this* is needs to cease and desist immediately. She's always been like that with every boyfriend I brought home. Or I guess just Sebastian and Boyd, as I never really brought anyone else here. And why would I, seeing how whatever man walks in the door will get the full-court press from Geri?

Although Kassel's far from being my boyfriend, Geri isn't privy to our status. For all she knows, I could have shagged him rotten prior to his arrival.

Perhaps I haven't officially staked my claim, but she should respect the notion that since I brought him, he's off-limits.

My God, it's like the Cabbage Patch doll all over again.

When Mary Mac was packing to leave for college, she began to divest herself of all the childhood crap she didn't want anymore. She had this Cabbage Patch doll named Lillian Lizabeth in mint condition because apparently she wasn't ever that into babies.

(The irony! It burns, it burns!)

I'd coveted Lillian Lizabeth for years, largely because Mary Mac never let me touch her. I always thought she was destined to be mine, as she had my light skin and blue eyes, complete with fat, dark braids.

While Geri was more into stuffed animals, I was a true doll aficionado. Such was my devotion to my doll collection, I hand washed their garments weekly and I kept each member of my dolly family neatly packed away in an old trunk for safekeeping. For fairness's sake, I'd play with each of them an equal amount of time.

I'd created entire journals with their elaborate backstories, too. For example, the blond boy doll with the bowl cut and sailor suit was Hans Maarten van der Maarten and he enjoyed picking tulips when he wasn't busy helping out in his family's wooden shoe factory. He lived right by a dike and he was always sure to plug any developing cracks with wads of chewing gum. He owned a dog named Otto, who was always chasing geese.

Even though Lilly-Lizzie (that's what her close friends called her) wasn't yet mine, that didn't stop me from creating her biography. I believed her to be noble and true, with a scholarly bent. And even though she'd been kidnapped by gypsies as a baby, there was no mistaking her royal bearing. She knew that someday her proper family would find her again, as blood always called to blood. Lady Lilly-Lizzie would indeed ride again.

Anyway, Ma asked if either one of us wanted Mary Mac's doll, which, sweet Jesus, dreams really do come true! As I was standing there trying to decide exactly which doll would be taken out of rotation in order to best accommodate Lilly-Lizzie, and whether or not we should consult an attorney regarding legally transferring the Cabbage Patch adoption paperwork, Geri grabbed her and ran off. I was stunned, yet Ma's response was about how he who hesitates is lost.

What was so infuriating is there was no way I wasn't destined to own that doll, and everyone was aware of that fact. But because of my methodical approach, Geri was able to weasel her way in and run off with my great prize.

Then, within a day, she'd promptly hacked off Lilly-Lizzie's glorious braids, covered her face in Sharpie-based freckles, and then left her floating facedown in the pool like the saddest little corpse in the universe for the rest of the summer.

To this day what makes me mad is she didn't even want the damn doll.

She just wanted *me* to not have it.

Before I can position myself between Kassel and Geri, Mary Mac comes barreling down the stairs like an angry mama bear.

"Why do you insist on tormenting my kids?" Mary Mac demands. Bits of spittle fly from the corners of her mouth.

"Because they're acting like children," I reply, blotting my cheek with a napkin. I mean, isn't it obvious?

"They *are* children. And why can't you just call them by their proper names?" She's standing there vibrating with fury in her awful way-too-soon-for-Christmas holiday sweater, bedecked with bells and three-dimensional felt antlers extending from the top of the embossed reindeer's head.

It's so unfair to be put on the spot like this. "You should have them wear name tags, as no one could possibly remember which is which and how old each one is." When they were all gathered around this table briefly before going upstairs to play Wii bowling, I'd point at whomever I wanted to ask a question. How was this problematic? I asked the one in glasses about school because I assumed she's smart and the zitty one if he had a girlfriend. (Negative.) (And no surprise there.)

Mary Mac hisses, "Geri doesn't have any trouble, do you, Geri? Tell Reagan about your nieces and nephews."

Geri puts on this big act, looking at me, then Mary Mac, like she's all sheepish and truly can't decide whom to support. She hesitates for a long time before replying, "Mickey Junior is turning eighteen right before Christmas, and he's planning on joining his dad's business when he graduates, provided he passes English. That's touch and go for now. *Beowulf*'s a bitch. Sophia's sixteen and has talked about being a nun, or at least she did until she fell in love with Niall from One Direction. He *is* the cutest member, though. Teagan's thirteen and adores YA vampire books and she's even better at Irish dance than Mary Mac was—she's already earned a solo dress."

I try to ignore the rapt expression on Kassel's face as Geri continues. "Brady's just turned ten and plays drums. He's not only best friends but also mortal enemies with Finley Patrick, who's nine. Depends on the day of the week. Today they're BFF. I chalk this up to their being Irish twins. Finley Patrick wants to be a garbage collector and he's always bringing home junk he finds in the alley."

I try not to seem impressed, even though I'd be challenged to come up with half their names, let alone a single interest.

"Kacey Irelyn and Kiley are both seven. Kiley has a tiny freckle under her right eye and Kacey Irelyn is just about the best swimmer I've ever seen for her age. Because she spends so much time in chlorine, her hair is shiner. Connor's the baby, so of course I have a special bond with him. We babies stick together."

I'm literally choking back the bile as she continues, "He's two and a half and is currently going through a stage where he truly believes he's a turtle."

Oh. I guess that explains why he was crawling. I'd just assumed he was a gimp.

Mary Mac flops into Kiley Irelyn's abandoned seat. "Amazing what you can pick up when you're invested in someone's life other than your own." She snorts. "Or the guy you're stalking."

I can feel myself redden, partially from embarrassment, partially from rage.

Naturally, Geri jumps in to offer her faux sympathy. "You can't blame Gip for being busy. Look how much she's accomplished! Compared to us, she's a rock star. I mean, she has a PsyD. Heck, I went to beauty school."

I'm sorry, *heck*? Am I the only one who's witnessing this?

"You're a hairdresser?" Kassel asks.

"Only the best!" Geri fluffs her own ginger mane and giggles. "Or, at least I hope I'm pretty good. But I love doing hair so much—every day I fly out of bed, so excited to get to work. I adore my clients, and my salon rocks! Maybe I'll never be rich, but you can't put a price on having a vocation that makes you so happy."

Really? Is this why you've switched salons *cough* *fired* *cough* four times in the past five years?

So. Full. Of. Shit.

Mary Mac takes a bite of Kiley Irelyn's turkey and chews angrily. She swallows and says, "Why'd you become a psychologist in the first place, Reagan? You don't even *like* people, let alone want to help them. I bet you just wanted an opportunity to judge them on a professional basis."

"Try to be a little more bitter, why don't you?" I reply.

Kassel's head swivels back and forth like he's watching a tennis match.

"Mac, that's not true," Geri reasons. "Gip's amazing at what she does. Remember the episode with the anorexic ballerina? How she connected with the girl? That was genuine. It's almost like Gip knew what it was like to have an eating disorder."

"Of *course* she connected with the dancer," Mary Mac scoffs. "She's orthorexic herself."

"What's orthorexic?" Kiley Irelyn asks from her corner of the table. I try to determine if she has a freckle or shinier hair, but I'll be damned if I can discern between them. Different outfits! God! Is that so hard?

Mary Mac replies, "Well, according to the segment I saw on *20/20*, that means your auntie Reagan is so neurotic about the purity of her food that she ends up restricting her intake."

This is preposterous. I'm not even a little bit orthorexic. Orthorexia is an actual eating disorder, despite not yet being recognized by the DSM-IV. Besides, I watch fat and sugar because it's common sense. I don't restrict animal or dairy products—I eat plenty of dairy, as long as it's certified organic, and preferably raw. And fish is absolutely an animal product. I'm simply cautious as to the process in which the fish are caught. Granted, I wouldn't eat a McDonald's Filet-O-Fish, but that's not just because of how it's farmed, but also because of the gloppy tartar sauce, the refined flour in the bun, the unnaturally orange cheese, and the deep-frying.

"Oh, please," I reply. "There's something wrong with me because I hold myself to a higher standard when it comes to healthy eating? Damn me and my ethics! Forgive me for not climbing on the Chomp-tastic bandwagon."

"No," Mary Mac argues, "there's something wrong with you because you're so insane about additives, preservatives, and genetic modification that you're a massive pill in social situations. Which is ironic, given your stance on prescription meds. Look at your plate right now—there's not a single item on it that you didn't prepare and bring from home."

"I'm a pescatarian!"

Mary Mac slaps the table and the contents of everyone's glasses ripple. "No, you're a pain-in-the-ass-atarian! It's frigging Thanksgiving, the one day of the year that even the most rigid among us indulge. And what does this one bring for dessert? Brownies. But not regular, normal-people brownies, all fudgy and delicious, full of caramel. Hers are made with almond flour, applesauce, and squash. Squash! In a brownie!"

"They sound really interesting," Geri replies sweetly, trying to catch Kassel's eye.

"Then why don't you taste one?" Mary Mac challenges.

"I would but, you know, allergies," Geri says, acting as though she's contrite. And here I almost forgot about the Nut Lie that Geri's been telling for years.

Mary Mac presses on. "Our ancestors who *starved* during the Great Potato Famine would be all, *No, thanks, I'm stuffed,* if someone offered them a squash brownie."

I've had enough of this. "Is that your professional opinion? Because I'm curious, Mary Mac—where did you get *your* doctorate? I'm not familiar—does Northern have a one-year accreditation?"

"Gip, Mac, c'mon, knock it off. We have a guest." Geri slides closer to Kassel.

"Please, don't stop on my account, Peace Corps," Kassel says. He folds his napkin and places it next to his plate. "I live for fights—they make the best TV! I'm popping some corn and waiting for the hair pulling and wrestling."

"Wait, what'd you call her?" Mary Mac asks.

He smiles and his eyes crinkle. Again, he is not my boyfriend, but I definitely find the act of crinkling one's eyes attractive in a potential partner. "Giving nicknames is kind of my thing. Adds to my charm. When we first met, Reagan was so passionate about all her charity work that I called her Peace Corps."

Mary Mac chokes on her wine. "I'm sorry, her *what*?" she sputters.

"You know, the volunteering she does with the hungry and the homeless," Kassel replies.

"Did you start volunteering, Gip? That's awesome!" Geri exclaims, slapping me on the back. "And here everyone always says you never consider anyone but yourself!" Then she flashes a thousand-watt smile at Kassel and he grins back at her.

Do you see?

Do you see what she does to me?

Her passive-aggression is like those whistles only dogs can hear. Just because most humans can't detect the sound doesn't mean it doesn't exist.

Mary Mac slams down her glass and rises from her seat. She begins to bus the plates off the table, bringing them over to the dishwasher in the corner of the basement's kitchen. "Charity, my ass."

Pointedly, I tell Mary Mac, "I'm highly involved with a number of charities. I'm very philanthropic."

Mary Mac rolls her eyes as she separates the good silver from the everyday pieces the kids were using. "*Armchair* philanthropic, maybe. Have you actually done anything other than attend the fancy events we're always seeing in *Chicago Nouveau*?"

"I . . . I . . . have been very busy with the show lately," I stammer. "But I refuse to be put on the spot for my good works. Maybe I haven't done anything outside of attend black-tie charity events in a while, but I live to help others."

Mary Mac begins tossing items into the dishwasher. "I'm at St. Catherine's every Tuesday and Thursday night serving dinner in the soup kitchen. *That's* what helping others looks like, not hobnobbing with Mayor Tiny Dancer. If you care so much about the hungry, Reagan, why don't you stop being such a massive hypocrite and cart your happy ass down here and actually do something productive, like make sandwiches? Or are you afraid to touch white bread?"

Kassel gestures toward Mary Mac and me and asks Geri, "Were they always like this?"

At some point, my mother materialized in the basement, and now she joins us at the table. She pours herself a healthy belt of red wine. "You betcha. These girls are why their father and I drink. They fought all the damn time. 'That's *my* dress! That's *my* doll! That's *my* ham sandwich!' It was constant. They never once came to a consensus. Shoulda seen 'em on family vacations. The only reason Mary Mac and Reagan didn't strangle each other is because they couldn't reach over Geri's car seat."

"At least Geri got a car seat," I note. "You used to let me flail around the cargo area in the back of the station wagon like I was a golden retriever."

Mary Mac whips a dish towel at me, but because it's so light, it barely travels past the counter. "Reagan, you're such a frigging martyr. Don't act like they somehow neglected you. You had a helmet for your bike! And knee pads! They *drove* you to school! I had to take the CTA by myself when I was *nine*. Do you know what manner of perverts ride the city bus, ready to prey on little girls in Catholic school uniforms? My God, Ma was still *smoking* while she was pregnant with me!"

Ma denies nothing, instead calmly sipping her wine. "It was the seventies; we didn't know."

"And you have the nerve to say *I* couldn't raise a dog, cat, or goldfish," I add.

"Didn't say you couldn't, just said you're too self-centered to bother to try," Mary Mac counters.

I think I despise Mary Mac less than Geri because at least she's upfront with her scorn and derision. Geri wraps it up in hugs and affirmations that sound supportive but are truly anything but.

Ma stares down both of us. "If you two don't stop it, I'll ask Charlie to come down and tell you about the miracle that is Viagra. We already heard all about it while we ate. *All* about it. He's apparently a thorough storyteller *and* a tender lover, that one. Big fan of the uniboob, too."

That stops both of us in our tracks, and for a moment, we grimace in solidarity.

"Hey, what's up next for *Push*?" Geri asks. Of course this whole time Geri has managed to deflect any of the conflict off herself, because that's how she operates. And now look at her, changing the subject because she's so desperate for attention.

Kassel replies, "Good stuff! This weekend Dr. Karen's counseling a compulsive shopper. We're filming at Woodfield Mall. After that, Regan's working with an agoraphobic. The guest is a lifelong Bears fan, but he's always been too afraid of crowds to attend a game. So, with Regan's help, we'll be taking him to Soldier Field for the first time. Best part? We're doing a live episode! It'll be huge!"

My stomach instantly knots and I'm pretty sure it's not because of the kumquats. "Beg your pardon?"

Kassel brushes the crumbs off of his crisply starched pinpoint oxford shirt. I bet he smells like cotton and spice. "Didn't Faye already brief you? DBS is broadcasting the game, so we're running the taped portion before the kickoff and then we'll cut to footage of him during timeouts and halftime!"

Slowly, I inquire, "How long is a typical game?"

"About three hours," Geri offers. "Sometimes longer if they head into OT."

To date, the longest Deva and I have been able to keep a guest confined during our swap is about twenty minutes. There's no way I can make anyone "meditate" for that long. Plus, with the added burden of live television, watched by millions of households? There's so much potential for this to go horribly, devastatingly wrong.

What am I going to do?

If I fail on this level, I may as well enroll in beauty school because I'll never work in mental health again.

Shit, shit, shit!

"Can you all excuse me for a moment?" Without waiting for a response, I dash upstairs and grab my phone. I rush outside past the cache of smoking, gossiping aunts and huddle next to the garage. I furiously pound out a panicked text to Deva, and thankfully, she responds instantly.

Is not mayday, Robber Baron—is Thanksgibbing! Goggle, goggle!

I quickly reply, We have a problem—need to swap for at least three hours next week. What are we going to do?

Don't worming, we can hand job

I opt to interpret this as her comforting me and not an oddly salacious suggestion.

But how? I type.

Thanwell

Than we'll what?

I wait, but no further information arrives. I stand there for another ten minutes, but I receive no additional responses. I shiver in my thin silk dress until I can't take it anymore and I return inside.

Back in the basement, the table's deserted, but I hear voices and laughter coming from Geri's room.

Oh, hell, no.

This is *my* potential boyfriend, Geri, not yours. How dare you lure him into your lair!

I swing the door open with a bit more force than intended and I see Kassel on Geri's computer talking to a little kid. Who is that? Is he one of my nephews?

Geri's on the bed with a magazine. She gestures for me to join her. Reluctantly, I walk over to her, but I refuse to sit. "Hey, Gip, we were talking and he really seemed to be missing Walt, so I suggested they Skype," Geri whispers. "He's almost done."

"Wow, that's really"—manipulative? devious? underhanded?—"kind of you," I reply.

"Love you, buddy! See you soon!" Kassel's voice is falsely bright as he bids his son good-bye.

"He asked me to stay while he was online. I think he was trying not to cry. I bet he could use some comforting," Geri confides in me.

I bet you think he does.

Kassel ambles over, his gait less confident than normal. "That was rough, but I needed it. Thanks, Ger."

Ger? *Ger?* What is this "Ger" business? Then they sort of gaze at each other for a second, which, I'm sorry, but how is that even possible? Why on earth would he have an interest in that fatty meatball when he could have something exotic, delicious, *and* good for him, like . . . a quinoa, beet, and blood orange salad?

Seriously, aren't men seeking competent, professional career women, especially those who are national celebrities with brilliant educations and own their own homes? How can anyone find a basement-dwelling hairdresser a more attractive choice?

Geri swoops in for the kill. "That was so hard for you, wasn't it? Come here." She stands up across from me and opens her arms, and Kassel walks directly into them. I watch in impotent fury as she tenderly cradles him in her arms. Clearly he needs a friend right now, and if I were to call out Geri, *I'd* look like the jerk.

Geri seems so sincere in offering him solace that I almost don't notice how she's extending her middle finger at me behind his back. Our eyes lock and she mouths, *Eff you,* at me.

Except this time she uses the whole word.

I'm about to yell, *Ma! Geri's flipping me off!* when Aunt Helen comes to the door.

"Hey, kids, I know we're all missing Aunt Sophia this year. The good news is I've re-created her Jell-O salad!"

CHAPTER SIXTEEN

We're Number One!

"Touchdown by number fifteen, Brandon Marshall!"

I confirm that all the Bears fans are cheering before I raise my giant foam finger in victory. I suffered a small misstep earlier when Patrick Peterson of the Arizona Cardinals intercepted a pass and I clapped. I quickly recovered, pretending that I was simply trying to warm my hands. (Fortunately, the *Push* cameras weren't on me when this happened.)

Let me ask you this—which genius city father decided that Chicago should build an undomed stadium right next to the frigid lakefront? Do you have any idea how cold it is when the wind whips off Lake Michigan? Thanks to the *Push* wardrobe department, I'm clad in what's essentially a Bears-logo sleeping bag over my thermal parka with long underwear and warmers in my boots, yet for all my layers, I'm as chilled as if I were naked.

How is this fun? Why is anyone enjoying hanging out here? At this point, I don't blame Bernie for being agoraphobic if spending time on this icy tundra is the alternative. I used to tell Boyd I'd never live in California permanently, but on days like today, I question my lifelong devotion to this city.

And if I may, a couple of points to make about this football game itself—first, I had no idea the Arizona Cardinals were an actual team. I thought they were fictional, made up exclusively for the movie *Jerry Maguire*. (Side note: Cuba Gooding Jr., what happened? *You* could have been the next Will Smith. What are you doing now? Cell phone commercials?)

Second point? I almost asked the guy next to me whether he was sure the Cardinals weren't supposed to be a baseball team, but I caught myself. After all, I'm supposed to be considered an expert.

Also, why doesn't everyone on the field just try to run faster? Seems like we could have this whole thing concluded a lot quicker if the men would show some hustle, like . . . well, like Cuba Gooding Jr.'s character in *Jerry Maguire*.

Except I suspect he's selling cell phones now.

Why is there no showboating in this game? The players are moving toward the goals in three- and four-yard increments. Boring! I can't say I'm a fan of how the youth of America are being brainwashed about their own mediocrity by everyone winning a trophy at youth soccer games, but my God, at least they scurry! You have an entire field, men—why not use it?

Note to self: Task Ruby and Faye, and to a lesser extent Mindy, with finding an NFL player who needs *Push*'s help. I would happily pilot one of those behemoth bods down the field at double time, with a bonus end-zone dance. Come on, gentlemen—football is *entertainment*. Entertain me already.

As there's zip happening on the field, I take a sip of my beer, which is at least thirty degrees warmer than the air. Then I sneeze when the foam becomes trapped in Bernie's mustache. And BTW, Soldier Field vendors? Would it kill you to sell some green tea? People are freezing out here, and everyone could up their intake of antioxidants! At the very least, why aren't you hawking Eel River certified organic IPA? Not only do they use all natural ingredients, but the brewery is powered by lumber-mill leftovers, so it's clean *and* green. Instead, I'm stuck with Budweiser, which is essentially, what? Bilgewater? However, since these aren't my own taste buds, I find the Bud's actually going down smoothly. Weird.

So, yes, Deva and I were able to perpetrate another swap. Same deal as before with the amulets, but this time we had to take an additional precaution, one that's diametrically opposed to my beliefs. I hate myself for perpetrating this kind of deception, and yet, I'm already down this rabbit hole, with no choice but to go deeper if I'm to come out the other side. (I presume that's how rabbit holes work.)

To prepare for the swap, I had to do the unthinkable: suck up to Dr. Karen.

"How's it going, Dr. Karen?" I asked, sidling into her dressing room. I fought the urge to whip out a measuring tape, even though I'm almost sure her space is larger than mine. But clearly she deserves it, for all the groundbreaking work she's done with the phobic who aren't actually phobic.

I'd have definitely said something about the disparity in the size of our respective rooms, but I needed to win her over to my side. Plus, after Thanksgiving, I was tired of fighting.

"What brings you to my corner of the world, Reagan?" she asked.

Naturally she refused to call me "Doctor." With her, it's all MD or nothing at all.

"Oh, I was passing by and thought I'd tell you what a wonderful job you've done so far this season." The lies felt like ash in my mouth.

She preened and nodded, encouraging me to continue. "What have you been learning from me?"

She patted her couch (she has a couch in her dressing room?) with her bony, spotty claw. The hands are always the ultimate giveaway. I don't care how much poison anyone shoots into their faces to look young, their hands are always their personal portraits of Dorian Gray.

She watched me imploringly, waiting for my answer. Let's see . . . what have I learned from Dr. Karen? Well, now I know how to coach a soap star into acting like she has an actual disorder for the PR bump, how to drug a teen with anger-management problems into oblivion without ever once inquiring as to the root of what was making her mad in the first place, how to exploit former patients for financial gain, and also how to apply lipstick far, far outside my lip line. "So much!" I brightly confirmed.

"I've been meaning to discuss Tabitha Baylee with you," she said. "I felt your approach with her lacked finesse, and frankly when she was on that ledge, she seemed coached. The whole ordeal seemed a bit . . . showy."

I had to ask myself if this was even worth it. But, with my end goal in mind, I proceeded anyway.

"You don't say," I responded mildly.

"Yes, and the equestrian? Did you instruct her to leap over that bar after she mounted her horse? A little pedestrian, don't you think?"

Oh, really? I'd like to see you do better, bi— Ahem. "How might you have approached the interaction differently?"

"Reagan, my dear, I wish I had the time to share the secrets of all my years of experience."

It was all I could do not to issue a smug-storm warning, cautioning local residents to stock up on driveway salt and eggs, milk, and bread.

"So . . . how's your book going?"

"Brilliantly, of course."

Of course. "I look forward to reading it."

"Our entire *nation* looks forward to reading it."

Oh, no! The Homeland Smug-curity level has been raised to red! Take cover!

I had no choice but to proceed. "You've been such a tireless advocate for Thanwell that I've completely rearranged my way of thinking. Obviously, I'm under a lot of stress with the show and I'm struggling with insomnia, so I'm wondering if this drug might help me."

Words cannot even describe the smug-alanche that followed. I was afraid I'd be buried underneath it for days until the ski patrol dug me out.

Suffice it to say, I received not only a Thanwell prescription, but also a boatload of free samples and a couple of Thanwell pens and a handy tote bag. (Sure, Thanwell loves how much she prescribes their drug now, but just wait 'til her stupid book comes out. We'll see who's doling out notepads then.) Much like a street-drug dealer, Dr. Karen wanted to guarantee I had enough supplies to become good and hooked. I had to assure myself that this was a perfectly reasonable way for a television psychologist to behave, even if it violated everything a psychologist who happened to be on television would do.

As soon as Deva, Bernie, and I started to meditate pre-game, I swallowed half a Thanwell, and within ten minutes, I was sedated to the point of sleep. That's when Deva placed the amulets around our necks. My body was out seconds after the swap, so the actual Bernie in his Reagan vessel was down for the count in the supply closet we'd appropriated as a dressing room. I ran a comb through my new mustache, threw on my cold-weather gear, and went out to greet the camera crews.

And now I'm in the stands, freezing my brand-new testicles off.

Which brings me to my next point: I may have a small problem.

Rather, Bernie may have a small problem. At no point did it occur to me that having a tiny bladder might be one of Bernie's myriad issues. Yet here we are. There's at least an hour to go in the game and there's no way I can hold it that long.

Why did Bernie/I drink so many beers? I despise beer.

I try to distract myself with the action on the field, except there is no action on the field. Come on, guys, I've run farther for a taxi. Faster, too.

Despite being full to bursting, I find myself taking another generous swig of beer. Stop it, Bernie's body! Don't do this to yourself! Or myself! Or whichever one of us is actually wearing these pants right now.

Someone in a dark shirt (a Bear, yes?) catches the ball and he actually begins to book down the field. Well, all right! This is what I'm talking about! You! In the white pants! Go! Run very fast! That's it! The whole crowd is on their feet, cheering, and I'm swept up with them.

Touchdown!

Everyone who isn't high-fiving one another is hugging. I never wanted to touch a stranger before, yet here I am, liberally doling out backslaps and fist bumps. Funny, but I sense a bond with the community of fans here, despite the weather and the terrible beverages.

Okay, this football thing is beginning to make some sense. I can see how people might enjoy gathering and observing the spectacle that is an enormous man finally, finally putting some grass between himself and the other players. There's real joy to be had. More so if there were a dome over the field, but still. Maybe if Pepperdine had a football team, I'd have experienced this sooner. (FYI, I didn't even realize U of C had a team until I was a junior.) Granted, my family members are huge football fans, but they also eat at Wieners Circle and vacation in Florida, so it's not like I've ever considered them paragons of judgment.

But this? I could get used to this.

As I sit here, surrounded by a crowd of strangers all rallying together to root for the same goal, I wish it were Bernie who was experiencing this rush. He deserves this epiphany, not me. Yet I'm also acutely aware of how hard this would actually have been for him if he were really here. Suddenly, I want to mourn the fact that this really isn't his accomplishment. After the cameras are put away and the crowd returns home, Bernie won't have conquered anything, and come next season, he'll still be sitting alone in his apartment while all his buddies are at the game. That's not fair.

I pledge to help him any way that I can after the fact.

But for now, I shall chug this beer.

(It's possible, Bernie's body, that we may need to have a chat about your predilection for alcohol consumption.)

When the crew notices I've drained my glass, Faye sends Mindy down with yet another Budweiser. Ladies, enabling? Really? And yet Bernie's hand grasps the glass like a life preserver, much to the chagrin of Bernie's bladder. Because clearly I'm not running this show.

We're reaching critical mass here, at least in terms of Bernie's urethra.

I try to envision warm, arid places, in the hopes that I could possibly reabsorb this excess beer. Isn't that what long-haul truckers do? No, wait, I just read an article on Salon.com about how big-rig drivers have a higher incidence of kidney problems. Damn. I already usurped Bernie of this magical experience called professional football—I don't want to impinge his fluid and electrolyte regulation as well.

I have no choice but to void.

With much trepidation, I shimmy out of my sleeping bag and set down my beer; then I climb the stands until I can exit under the seats. I spot a ladies' room first and begin to queue up until I notice a bunch of women who look like Geri giving me the evil eye. Whoops, my bad, ladies!

The men's room is down a few paces and the line's not nearly as long. For the first time in my life, I'm cheered by this inequity. As I snake my way into the bathroom, I notice there are two options—urinals and stalls. Clearly I want privacy because I've not exactly operated Bernie's equipment before.

I wait for a stall to open. A couple of the toilets are out of order, and the rest of the options appear to be occupied for the long haul. Through the seam of the doors, I can see little glimpses of the men on their thrones, and it would appear that they're all busy on some sort of personal electronic device. Men! Now is not the time to play Tetris!

A hefty guy in an Urlacher jersey with a neck like a honey-baked ham gives me a slight shove. "Shit or go blind, pal," he says, nudging me not so gently toward the urinals. I have no choice but to comply, as I don't want poor Bernie to take a punch. With his agoraphobia and this unfortunate mustache, I feel he's suffered enough.

I position myself in front of the urinal and then I . . . I . . . Huh. I'm unsure what comes next. How does this work? Do I unzip or do I just pull everything up and over my waistband? Does that include the berries as well as the twig? Is it like an udder—is milking required?

From the corner of my eye, I try to observe the moderately intoxicated man on my right. Aha, unzipping is the way to go, followed by a simple grip. Noted.

My goodness, he just goes and goes and goes, doesn't he?

The guy spots me observing his *business*. "Take a picture, jag-off, it lasts longer," he barks, flushing and exiting, without benefit of hand washing.

I'd judge him, except I fear I may have inadvertently eye-raped him.

I unzip Bernie's pants and with a very tentative hand, I reach in and *what is this bizarre force field I'm encountering?* Oh, wait.

Long underwear. Heh. Forgot about the layers. But look at this! The long johns have a flap, as do the briefs. So convenient! So modest! So much less chance of hypothermia! It's as though these bottoms were designed by men for me. I wish men wore bras—perhaps then they could finally engineer a push-up model that doesn't make me feel like I'm wired for explosives.

Now that I've opened all the barn doors, shall I grasp or was that guy simply hanging on because he was drunk? I wonder, do I just put my hands on my hips and freestyle? I feel like if I don't keep a modicum of control, this has the potential to go horribly awry, like a monkey holding a fire hose. As much as I'd like to respect Bernie's privacy, I must look in order to aim properly. And I'm just about ready, so here we . . .

Clearly Bernie is not Jewish.

There's a *child safety cap* on this thing.

How does that . . . do I push down and turn?

Technically I've only seen three completely naked men in my life, so I can't say I'm an expert on the male member. (Where is Geri when I need her?) But of the three I've seen—Boyd, Sebastian, and the brazen homeless guy on the Red Line right before he was arrested by the CTA police—none of them were walking around with their collectibles still in their original wrappers.

This is surreal, kind of like spotting a DeLorean or a Betamax; although there was certainly nothing wrong with those models, they're definitely out of vogue now.

But if my education in biology is to be trusted, the customized trim should have no impact on performance. So I grit my teeth and I assume the position.

Ready, aim, fire!

Or not.

Hmm. I suspect Bernie's bladder may be agoraphobic, too.

Perhaps I just need some encouragement. I know, I'll flush the urinal and then I'll be motivated by the sound of running water. Yes! Genius!

Okay, one, two, three, pull!

Not pull. Go. Go!

Ahh.

The relief I feel is instant, and I congratulate myself for having had the fore . . . sight (ha! I am hilarious!) to keep a steady grip. Although why am I surprised that I have the means and wherewithal to urinate like a proper man? I'm adept at almost everything I try. Good for me!

My stream turns to a trickle and eventually peters out.

(Seriously? With the uproarious puns? I should do stand-up.)

(Get it? Because I can *stand up* to pee now!)

(I suspect I may be drunk.)

(I don't hate it, but I am feeling compelled to hug strangers all of a sudden.)

My job is now to, what? Wipe? Blot? Suddenly I'm aggravated with how private Seb kept his bathroom habits. Help a girl out here; what do I do? Wave it around until it dries? Or if I do that, will poor Bernie end up on the news?

I surreptitiously glance to my left to see how my neighbor's managing and I suddenly realize I recognize those wrists.

I'm not sure if I want to die or stare.

I go with die, with stare coming in a close second.

He says to me, "Hey, Tom Selleck, you know what they say if you shake it more than twice."

Die. Definitely die.

I'm about to pray for the earth to open and swallow me whole when I realize I'm not Reagan gawping at my boss/crush so much as I am a socially awkward systems analyst named Bernie navigating a first-time experience. I meekly reply, "Go, Bears?"

As he washes his hands (bonus points for using soap) and dries them on a scratchy paper towel, he assures me, "You're doin' great, pal, keep it up!" and it takes me a second to realize he's talking about the agoraphobia and not my newfound ability to use the bathroom while standing up.

Which is probably better.

The Tuesday after the game, my team is gathered around the table in the conference room, waiting for the stragglers so we can discuss our strategy for the newest guest.

According to the bio Rudy composed, Georgette's in her midthirties and she's currently living at home with her parents. Although her folks are still fairly mobile, her oppressive siblings are vehement about her not moving out. Georgette feels like she's putting her life on hold unnecessarily, but no one else supports the idea of her leaving. Her married sisters insist because she's the baby, it's her duty to look after her parents, and she feels trapped. She moved home briefly three years ago after living in Asia, planning on leaving as soon as she found a job and bought a condo. However, despite her lucrative work as an interpreter and desire to be on her own, she's essentially been bullied into staying ever since.

"I can't imagine anything worse than living with my parents," I say. Hoo-boy, I'm extra-excited to swap with Georgette so I can tell off her awful siblings! I'm already planning my/her parting speech. Believe me when I say I've already worked out the litany of reasons why adult children should never live at home.

Mindy wrinkles her unlined brow. "Why? OMG, I love living at home! All my buds are still in Winnetka with their fams, too. Plus, my mom does my laundry and lets me drive her Beemer and my dad's got major swag! He has a band with his friends and they practice in the garage on the weekends. And he buys the best weed! The Sonoma Coma from Happy Lil' Trees in Vallejo won a bunch of awards. Home is awesome! I'm never leaving!"

As it would be unprofessional to stand up and shout, *What is wrong with you* and *your parents?* instead I reply, "Alrighty, I need a green tea, Mindy. Anyone else? Green tea? Coffee? Something? My treat!"

Ruby and Faye place their orders, as do Deva and Jimbo, the show's fitness guru. I'm confident that not only will Mindy take forty-five minutes to walk to the corner coffee shop; she'll screw up all five orders, the hot beverages will be cold upon arrival (and the cold hot), and she'll keep my change.

Sonoma Coma? Perhaps.

But it's a small price to pay to be rid of her incessant yammering for a while.

We're supposed to be meeting with the entire team working on Georgette's episode, but neither Marco the hair guy nor Dora the Explorer/makeup artist is here yet. (Some of Kassel's monikers stuck even after he learned everyone's names.) She texted saying her train was late. This would be a credible story if her train from Wicker Park weren't late five days a week. Sometimes the Blue Line is dicey, but never to this extent.

To me? Punctuality is key and I'd fire her in a heartbeat if it were my decision. Plus, I'm not sure Dora's all that skilled. Every single damn guest gets the same smoky eye and it doesn't matter if the guest is fifteen or fifty. Frankly, I'm surprised she didn't smudge kohl all over Bernie, too.

"Who are we still missing?" Faye asks, not looking up from her knitting. Today she's working on a plush fisherman's sweater, covered in a complicated system of cabling. I keep letting her hold it up to me for perspective, in hopes that I'll be the lucky recipient.

"Has anyone heard from Marco?" I ask.

Everyone shrugs.

Ruby asks, "Hey, is Kassel supposed to sit in with us?" She's perched forward in her chair, careful not to press against the back of the seat, having gotten fresh ink over the weekend to celebrate having bought her first condo. (Me? I bought a ficus tree when I closed on my place.) Her right shoulder now sports an almost exact replica of television's most iconic judge with the caption "Only Judy Can Judge Me." She said her regret kicked in the minute the artist applied the final parenthesis and she's already shopping for laser removal. Luckily, our DBS ratings-based bonus will cover the cost. When will everyone learn that skin is not a toy?

"I thought I saw him in the hall," Jimbo says, "with some hot girl. She looks like Jessica Rabbit. Rowr!"

Jealousy strikes me like a flash of lightning, even though I have no claims on Kassel, nor is he yet aware of my intentions. But now that I've seen him a tiny bit naked in the men's room at Soldier Field, I feel a real intimacy between us. Granted, he was a bit puzzled by Bernie's inappropriate gaze, but he was so affable about the whole thing that it wasn't at all awkward.

Or much, anyway.

My point is, I'm positive he and I could be so much more than just colleagues. I mean, clearly he's fine with difficult people because he genuinely enjoyed being with my family, going so far as to eat three servings of Aunt Helen's atrocious pistachio-laden Jell-O salad. Plus, he has that whole Boyd-with-a-briefcase thing, which is fairly irresistible.

Kassel would fit nicely in my life. He's quick and he's funny and I believe he'd be an excellent counter to my more serious nature. We have that whole Ross-and-Rachel bantering thing, too. I imagine we'd be highly entertaining together. People would want to invite us out to dinner—I'm sure of it. Plus, he's won Emmys. If we were married, then I would *legitimately* be able to display his awards on my mantel. While technically a win by default, it's still a win.

You know what? I need to express my interest in Kassel. I must make my newfound affection more evident. I should mark my territory. Going forward, I plan to demonstrate that he's captured my interest.

As of today, I plan to be a flirt in all situations Kassel related. I shall ply him with my feminine wiles.

As soon as I figure out what they are.

While I review various aspects of my own pulchritude—bonus points for my hair and trim waistline—Dora the Explorer bursts in and throws off her backpack. "So sorry, you guys! My train was late."

I try to not roll my eyes.

I fail.

Deva notices and nods. She's a stickler for punctuality, too, largely because of how lateness impacts her ability to time travel. I didn't ask for further explanation, assuming one would make my head ache.

As she unloads her backpack, she asks, "You guys hear about Marco?"

"Is he okay?" Ruby asks, voice full of concern.

"Very okay!" Dora exclaims. "He quit! He's been freelancing for the *Spider-Man, Part Femme* flick and Tabby loved him so much that she hired him to work full-time for her."

"Way to go, Marco!" Jimbo pumps his fist. Jimbo pumps his fist a lot; it's kind of his home-run swing. Well, that and having a wardrobe comprised entirely of Adidas track pants.

I'm not sure how I feel about Marco's leaving the show. On the one hand, he did beautiful work on our guests, and on the other, he was always hounding me to cut layers. "Oh, Missy Doctor, why you want to look like Crystal Gayle?" Marco's from Italy—how is he even familiar with American country music? And by the way, can everyone just leave my 'do alone? Besides, I'm more Megan Fox than Crystal Gayle, so let's cease and desist with the constant comparisons.

I find myself protectively clutching my ponytail, so I flip open my laptop in order to do something else with my hands. "I guess we don't need to wait for Kassel. Shall we begin?"

As the rest of the team digs out tablets and notebooks, the conference room door swings open. Kassel marches in and announces, "Good morning! I assume you've all heard about Marco? Big news. Very big."

Aha! Now is my time to shine! Time to harness my inner minx!

"I assume he didn't flatten a cat?" I ask.

As soon as I say this, I realize I'm not quite bringing my A game to the flirting area.

Truth be told, I'm not even sure how to *flirt*. What does flirting entail? Teasing? Enticing? Wearing off-the-shoulder shirts? The tossing of one's hair? Telling men, *I'm soooo drunk*? This merits further research.

I decide to try batting my eyelashes, having witnessed its efficacy when inhabiting Tabitha.

Kassel frowns at me. "Something in your eye, Peace Corps?"

I immediately want to die but instead mutter something about a piece of fluff from Faye's knitting, which causes her to bristle.

Can anyone explain why dumb girls make flirting look so easy?

In terms of propagating the species, it would seem to me that men would be most attracted to the kind of woman who was more adept at math and science than mascara application. Who wants to breed with gals who consider watching TMZ tantamount to reading the paper? It's simple eugenics, people!

Sebastian always said he was attracted to my brilliant mind. Except we're clearly no longer together and Geri mentioned his current lady friend is a Hooters waitress, which . . . really, Seb? I'm sure all the Hooters patrons are ogling this woman over platters of wings, saying, *Check out the cerebral cortex on that one!*

So disheartening.

Kassel stands at the head of the conference table. *"Push*'s loss is Tabitha's gain. Well, we still have a job to do, and life goes on. So I'd like you all to meet the newest member of Team *Push*."* He looks over to the open door and calls, "Come on in! Everyone? Meet Geri Bishop!"

CHAPTER SEVENTEEN
Bad Dreams Are Made of This

This is a bad dream.

Clearly.

The Thanwell has obviously stayed in my body and I'm having detailed hallucinations, all of which involve me having to deal with Geri in production meetings this week.

For example, in this chapter of my ongoing nightmare, here we are in Georgette's makeover session, ready to start dyeing or ombre-ing or feathering or whatever it is that's Geri's claim to fame.

I'm so glad all of this is a figment of my imagination because otherwise I'd be furious over how quickly the rest of the team has taken to her. Jimbo and Gary the second cameraman have been arguing all week about whether Geri reminds them more of Jessica Rabbit or Christina Hendricks.

Can I vote?

Because I pick neither.

The ladies are sucking up as well. Mindy happily and promptly delivers Geri's proper coffee order (a lardy mocha with extra whip) and Ruby's been all over her, gabbing about the bar scene in Bridgeport, as her place is on the south side. And Faye? Faye thought the fisherman's sweater she was knitting would be divine with Geri's coloring, so she gave it to her when she finished. Just like that! No thought, no deliberation, no consideration for other members of the team who are really lean and could use the added warmth of a fisherman's sweater.

Et tu, Faye? Et tu?

It's like the ham sandwich all over again.

And please don't even start me on the chemistry between Geri and Kassel. Every time I see them chatting, I can feel the bile rise in the back of my throat.

Nightmare.

Absolutely no other explanation.

I'd seek Deva's counsel, but she had to rush off for an emergency with a private client—something about a youth serum?—and she's currently en route to the Philippines to extract the pollen created by bats drinking ultrarare jade-vine nectar. We're about to wrap production until after the holidays, so she's not needed here, except by me. Fortunately, she left the amulets. It'll be tricky to do the swap without her today, but not impossible.

I tried to run my thoughts about Geri's being hired past a couple of my friends, but apparently I'm not interesting to Bethany, Caroline, or Rhonda when I'm not spilling Hollywood secrets.

Fair-weather bitches.

In a moment of weakness, I even turned to Bryce and

Trevor, but they kept pestering me about when "G-spot" would be back in my "hizzouse." From the way those two carry on about her, you'd think she was their long-lost best friend and not just some girl they met for ten minutes on my front stoop that one time she stopped over to gloat after the Sox beat the Cubs in the Crosstown Classic.

Serves me right for even trying with those two.

For now, I'm journaling all my feelings. At some point I plan to pen a memoir about the show, so taking notes helps me remember the specifics. Granted, I meant to fill my Moleskine with tales of my successes, but most of what I've written is more along the lines of *Die, Geri, die.*

I'm sure everyone's opinion on Geri will change today when I give my soliloquy about living at home as an adult via the Georgette swap. If what I say embarrasses Geri? Then perhaps she shouldn't be involved in such shameful basement business in the first place.

Gary's in here to film the whole haircut/color process, even though it's not necessary. We don't need him capturing footage until the big reveal and confrontation later, but he's been buzzing around Geri like a fly to manure.

Technically, I'm not required to be in here, either, but I suspect every minute I'm not with Geri, she's gossiping about me, so I'm staying close. I'm ninety-nine percent sure I heard her and Mindy saying something about Dr. Stick-Up-the-Ass, and my guess is they weren't comparing notes on a proctologist.

Georgette enters the room with Ruby. In my time with Georgette this week, I found her to be articulate and intelligent, albeit reticent. In some respects, she resembles me, with her long, straight, dark hair and ivory skin. I can't imagine that Geri's going to improve on her look. I did my best to boost her confidence about speaking with her family, but she's so stuck that it would take dozens of sessions to break through to her. Fortunately, I have my magic bullets in my pockets, so all will be well upon the post-makeover conversation with her sisters.

"Hey, girl," Geri calls. "C'mere! We're going to have so much fun today! Sit! Sit! Please! Your chariot awaits!" Geri gestures to the adjustable hairdressing chair here in the makeup room and gives it a spin.

Fake! Fake, fake, fake!

Geri begins to muss Georgette's thick locks. "So, sweetie, what are you thinking? I have a few ideas in mind, but I want to hear what'd make you happy."

Georgette bites her lip and gazes at herself in the mirror. "I need a change, but . . ."

"But change is superscary, amirite?"

Georgette cracks a smile. "Right."

Geri fastens a cape at the nape of Georgette's neck and then rubs her shoulders. "Don't worry, kiddo, we're not doing anything that makes you uncomfortable. Today'll be hard enough without having to fret about your 'do, right?" Georgette nods. "So when you envision your life after the show's over, how do you see yourself? Where are you? What're you doing?"

Georgette's voice catches. "I'm . . . not sure."

"Even a little bit?"

"No."

Ha! See? Massage her shoulders all you want, Geri; it's not so easy to wrestle insight out of this one.

"Tell me about the last time you remember being, like, *joyful*."

Georgette appraises herself in the mirror for a moment

before she finally says, "It's been a while. I guess . . . I was out with my colleagues in Changchun—it's a city in Jilin Province—and they were having a going-away party for me at Three Monkeys because I was returning to the States. It was brutally hot and my friends and I were sitting outside. So there I was in the middle of China, at a table with Aussies and Afrikaners and Brits, watching locals dance to Latin music, eating kebabs, and drinking Irish stout."

Geri keeps pawing Georgette's hair. "How'd that make you feel?"

I shift in my seat. Oh, come on! That's is a bullshit Psych 101 question and everyone knows it!

Georgette replies, "I remember how surreal it all was, thinking every culture in the entire universe had peacefully converged in this one spot. And then, almost like a blessing from God, I could feel a coil of air on the back of my neck. In August? In Changchun? There's no wind; there's no relief. The air's as thick as soup, but for this one moment, there was a breeze. I thought, 'Magic truly exists.'"

Geri nods, acting like she's all in tune with Georgette. Trust me, I've spoken with Georgette at length and she didn't offer up any of this neck-wind information. Mostly it was all *blah, blah, blah, my sisters are mean.*

Been there, done that, bought the T-shirt, lady.

"You've been growing out your hair ever since then?" Geri asks.

"I guess so, yes."

"Kind of a metaphor for your world at the moment, isn't it? All of this stuff is holding you down." Geri holds up a handful of silky locks and lets them spill down. "Life was better when you felt a breeze on your neck."

Ooh, thanks for that powerful allegorical insight, Professor Geri. When you're done narrating *The Rime of the Ancient Ponytail*, I look forward to attending your lecture on the History of the Hair Dryer.

An odd expression crosses Georgette's patrician features. "My goodness, I never considered that. But you're spot-on."

Geri shrugs. "I can re-create that style in two snips, if that's what you want. Doesn't solve any of your other problems, but it's a start, right? You know, my ma used to read me this old Irish prayer for travelers that had a line in it about always having the wind to your back and the sun on your face. So I was thinking, maybe if you're sitting on the studio's couches with your sisters and you can feel a breeze on your neck, you'll be all, *I'm ready to reclaim what's mine, bitches.*"

Argh, lies, lies, lies!

Geri hated books! And the only thing Ma ever read was Royko's old columns!

What is Geri getting at? What's she trying to prove? There's an end game here, of that I'm sure.

Georgette makes a grab for Geri's scissors. "Do it. Now. Before I change my mind."

Geri gingerly takes the shears from her. "You sure, hon?"

"No. But please do it anyway."

"Ready?"

Georgette nods. Geri gathers Georgette's hair in a low pony and snips off a solid foot, which leaves me feeling like somehow *I've* been kicked in the stomach. How does that work?

Geri hands Georgette the bundle and she turns the tail over and over in her hands. "The good news is that this is long enough to donate to Locks of Love. You've just changed a life! You're a hero!"

Why is she laying all of this on so thick?

"How's it feel back there?" asks Geri, ruffling what's left of her hair.

Georgette lets out a huge breath. "Like a weight off my shoulders, literally and figuratively."

I glance around the room to monitor if anyone else is rolling their eyes.

Just me then?

"Awesome! I'm really proud of you. Now I'll do your cut next, unless . . ." Geri trails off.

"Unless?"

"Unless you're in the mood for a little color."

"Color's kind of not my thing."

"That's absolutely cool, G." Geri adjusts Georgette's cape and begins to rearrange items on the counter in front of the mirror. It's a haircut, not an operating table—get to it!

Geri strokes her own hair. "But maybe you hear me out on this? It's kind of a cray-cray idea, and you're totally free to say no. You won't hurt my feelings." Geri leans in, all conspiratorially. "Let me just tell you this from personal experience: anyone who says blondes have more fun has clearly never been a redhead." Then she does this little shake that is absolutely mortifying to behold.

Gary inadvertently lets out a wolf whistle, Georgette beams, and I have a small coughing fit. By way of apology, I murmur, "Must be the dry December air. I bet some green tea would help."

Geri asks Georgette, "You game?"

Gary zooms around to pan in on Geri's mug. Why are we bothering with this nonsense? Why film someone having her hair colored? That is literally (and figuratively) one step beyond watching paint dry.

"I've always admired Debra Messing's color," Georgette timidly admits.

"Then that's what we'll do! One Grace Adler, coming up!" Geri confirms with a little clap.

After mixing up some potions, Geri returns and begins to slap various bits of gel on Georgette's head with a pastry brush. Scintillating. Yet from the crowd gathered around, you'd imagine she was splitting the atom.

I wave Mindy over to me. "I'd like a green tea."

"Now?" she replies.

"No, next week."

"Cool." She begins to shuffle back to her seat.

"Of course I mean now!" I snap.

She gives me the whale eye and then makes a big show of taking everyone else's order before she leaves. Perhaps she can tell Daddy all about how bossy Dr. Reagan is when the two of them are sparking up a doobie at the dinner table on the North Shore.

"What's the plan with the fam?" Geri prods.

Don't you worry about the plan, Geri. The plan is handled.

Georgette begins to pick at her cuticles. "I wish I knew. I'm so angry that I'm in this position. I mean, Mom and Dad are okay. They're not as sharp as they were and they need some assistance, but I'm really struggling with my siblings forcing me to take on the whole burden. Two of them live within five miles, and the rest are within a half hour's drive. I want to do my part, certainly, yet there are six of us! Shouldn't I only be responsible for a sixth of the care? It's not fair and it's been nonstop for three years! Do you know what it's like living at home as an adult? It's not an aphrodisiac, that's for darned sure."

"Preaching to the choir, sweetie," Geri says. Of course she's going to try to ingratiate herself. Like she's not toasting marshmallows and singing campfire songs with Ma and Dad every night.

Geri continues, "My roommate got married last year and I couldn't afford our apartment on my own. So I was stuck going back home. Even though it was my choice, it's still weird sometimes. Sure, I'm saving tons of money for when I open my own salon—"

I'm sorry, your *what*? And since when do you have an ounce of business acumen? You know that sea monkeys aren't a solid investment, right, Geri?

"But it really puts a crimp in the ol' dating life, right? Like, if I were seeing someone? I'd have no place to bring a guy back *to* if we were to become serious. What, I'd be all, *Hey, Ma and Dad, you mind if I have hot animal sex down here in my basement?* Awkward."

"I miss sex," Georgette says. "Haven't so much as had a drink with a man since I moved back home."

"That's been three years?"

"Three long, *dry* years."

Oh, please. Don't give me your three-years business. Some of us were twenty-five-year-old grad students before ever doing it the first time. And we turned out just fine.

Geri begins running a squeeze tube full of barbecue-sauce-colored goo in little rows across Georgette's scalp. "For what it's worth, you're pretty much going to be sex on a stick when I'm done with you."

"I'm not even sure I remember how to be social around a man at this point, let alone seduce him."

"I have faith in you. It's like riding a bike—the minute you try again, it's like second nature."

Yes, Geri, but what if you never learned to ride a bike in the first place? What then?

Georgette takes a delicate sip from the water bottle she's been clutching. "What's funny is it's not even the whole physical act that I miss so much, although that's part of it. I miss . . . waking up with someone else. I miss lazy Sundays reading the paper together. I miss all the little intimacies that come from sharing space with a significant other. I miss seeing my guy all curled up on my girly sofa, surrounded by my pastel pillows and scented candles. Heck, I miss my furniture. It's all been in storage ever since I went to China in the first place."

Gary focuses his camera on Georgette.

"Sounds like you're dealing with a lot of losses," Geri affirms.

"Never considered it that way, but you're right. I miss having a bathroom free from my mother's knee-highs drying on the shower curtain rod. I miss throwing dinner parties. I miss quiet and privacy. I adore my folks, don't get me wrong, but I miss . . . having the opportunity to miss them. They won't be around forever, and I hate that I resent their constant presence in my life."

Geri begins removing the little foils, letting each one drop on the floor as she works from the top of Georgette's forehead to the back of her skull. Yeah, sure, just put those foils anywhere, Pigpen.

"I guess I don't understand what's keeping you at home. Is it the financial thing, like me? Maybe you can get a loan or something."

Georgette blinks away a tear. "Actually, money isn't my problem. My problem is I can't handle everyone being angry with me for leaving. I'm trapped and I can't seem to find the words to express how trapped I feel."

Geri spins Georgette around to look her in the eye. "So

what you're telling me is you're willing to subjugate your own happiness because if you don't it'll make your sisters mad?"

Where/when did Geri pick up the word "subjugate"?

Georgette says nothing. A couple of more tears escape and Geri hands her a Kleenex. "Sweetie, you're better than that. You deserve more than that. When you look back on your life you're not going to be all, *I wish I'd made my sisters happier.* They *have* their lives, and they're bitches—lazy bitches—for not allowing you to have one yourself. Don't let them take advantage of your generous nature. I guarantee your folks would rather hire a home assistant or a visiting nurse than live with the notion that you gave up your youth to babysit them just to satisfy a pack of bitches. Guaran-damn-tee."

Geri has Georgette rise from the chair and they head over to the wash sink.

"No." Georgette stops in her tracks.

Geri's puzzled. "No, you don't want me to rinse your hair? Hon, I need to remove the dye so your scalp doesn't stain red."

Georgette pulls off the cape and wraps a towel around her shoulders. "You can rinse my hair in a minute. This can't wait." Without further ado, she marches out of the makeup room and down the hall to the greenroom, where her sisters are gathered.

Gary's hot on her heels with the rest of the crew, but I don't need to follow to catch what she's saying. Pretty much everyone in the WeWIN studio can hear her right now.

Georgette kicks open the door. "We need to talk, bitches."

"To Geri!" Everyone cheers and raises their glasses.

If we toast her one more time, I may have an aneurysm.

Due to today's events, not only am I not to be featured on

the midseason finale, but the entire episode stars Geri, a bottle of dye, and a pusillanimous woman who was suddenly emboldened by a bit of profanity. And here I spent all that time learning the intricacies of the human mind, when I should have simply practiced giving scalp massages.

Geri's reveling in all the attention, wolfing back beers as though drinking and not shampooing was suddenly her chosen profession.

We're at Haymarket Pub & Brewery on Randolph, having our informal holiday celebration. The event is specifically "informal" because we're expected to pay for our drinks ourselves, as the no-free-lunch policy extends all the way up the DBS chain of command.

Although the party was already scheduled for tonight, the event is extra-festive, due to Saint Geri and the Miracle at Losers. Not only did Georgette tell off her sisters; she immediately contacted her old supervisor in Changchun to inquire about open teaching positions. By the time she was rinsed, clipped, and blown dry, she'd arranged a whole new life for herself.

Yet do any of my coworkers give me a moment's credit for my efforts with Georgette prior to her sitting in Geri's chair? Of course not. Much like with a tricky pickle jar, I was the one who loosened the seal before Geri finally pried it open. But you'd never suspect I was even a player considering how everyone else is carrying on.

Also? Georgette's color is garish. There. I said it.

Geri, surrounded by every member of the *Push* staff, as well as a number of our freelancers, climbs up on her chair and holds her glass aloft. "To the Bisshy Sissies!"

Even completely sauced, she's keeping the fiction going that she just loves me sooooo much and any problems I have with her are all in my own head. I wouldn't believe the way she operates if she hadn't already been like this her entire life.

I remember one summer when I was fifteen, I was sitting in my room reading *Anne of Green Gables*. I'd just gotten to the part where Anne saved Diana's baby sister when Geri marched by. She looked at me and at my book and then smirked and yelled, "Ma! Reagan says I'm stupid because I don't like to read!"

No one believed me when I argued that I'd never said that, because the truth is I didn't disagree with her assessment. Later, she admitted to me she'd simply been bored and thought it would be hilarious to "get the Goody Two-shoes" in trouble.

Yes. Ha-ha-ha, I hate you.

Geri's fairly wobbly on her stool and Kassel reaches up to steady her, bracing her with his magnificent wrists. "Steady there, rock star," he says. She laughs, he laughs, everyone laughs, and I want to karate chop the bar in half.

All the guys fight to help her down, and while they do, Kassel meanders over to me. "Hey, Peace Corps, any idea how Geri got here tonight?"

"Broomstick?" I offer.

"She didn't drive, did she?" I'm touched by his level of concern for Geri's well-being. Truly.

I say, "I think she drove to the studio this morning, but she was in the group of us who walked over here." Or stomped, in my case.

Kassel keeps stealing glances over my shoulder. "Well, I want to make sure she gets home. I'm going to offer her a ride."

"*No!*" I shout, and then catch myself. "I mean, heh, no need. She'll be . . . staying with me tonight. I'll make sure she's fine. After all"—I give him my brightest smile and toss my hair—"that's what sisters do."

Geri's now leading the entire bar in a rousing rendition of Journey's "Don't Stop Believin'." "You may want to take her sooner rather than later. Otherwise, she's going to have a very unpleasant tomorrow."

"I'd hate for that to happen," I reply, biting my tongue so hard I practically taste blood.

Kassel rubs his hands together, as though in anticipation. "Yeah, we're having brunch and I wouldn't want her to miss it."

For the second time today, I feel as though I've been sucker punched.

"Don't stop be-leeee-vin'!"

"Listen, can you give her this?" He hands me his business card. In addition to his professional information, he's also written down his cell, his landline, his e-mail address, his home address, his Twitter, Tumblr, and Instagram handles, as well as his Facebook page.

"Are you not on Pinterest?" I ask.

Kassel begins to panic. "Will she need that? Happy to provide—"

"I'm kidding."

"Oh. I really want to hear from her, is all. Do me a proper and remind her that we're on at Original Pancake House tomorrow at noon? The one in Lincoln Park, not the Gold Coast?"

"Of course," I reply in my most compliant tone.

See? *I'm* nice. *I'm* helpful. And I'm cute as can be, so why doesn't he want to take *me* out for pancakes? (Except that I would never eat them, because gross.) What am I doing wrong? Why isn't he into me? Is it because I'm rusty on this whole flirting business?

And how is it that Geri can waltz in, do virtually nothing, be her bullshit self, and then be lauded as the Second Coming? Look at her; right now, men are lined up to talk to her. *Literally* lined up. How fair is that?

Kassel gives me a brotherly chuck on the shoulder. "You're a dream, Peace Corps. A real dream."

Really? Then why does everything feel like such a nightmare?

CHAPTER EIGHTEEN

It's Just Brunch

Immoral. Unethical. Most likely illegal.

I berate myself as I speed walk down Clark Street. I'd sprint, but that's not possible for a variety of reasons.

Queasy. Don't forget queasy.

This is literally the worst thing I've ever done, as a doctor, as a person, and, to a lesser extent, as a sister.

Yet I couldn't stop myself.

There Geri was, head tipped back on my couch, all bloated and snoring. She wouldn't move to a proper bed, no matter how hard I tried to persuade her. She kept saying, "Nooo, is too squishy-fantastic!" in reference to the buttery cashmere throw she was drooling all over.

So anyone who's priced contemporary sofas lately couldn't blame me for what happened next.

Right?

Technically, this is Trevor and Bryce's fault anyway.

"Hey, Dr. B!" Trevor poked his head out into the vestibule after I'd wrestled Geri up the front steps last night. "Kind of late for you. Burnin' the midnight oil, son! Or were you out with a playa, playa?" Then he spotted Geri under my arm and promptly lost his marbles. "Yo, yo, yo—where my G-spot at?"

Which prompted Geri to point at herself and crow, "G-spot's right here, bitches!"

Then Bryce scrambled out and the three of them pretty much danced up the stairs while spouting gibberish, a bottle of their current libation in tow.

Cupcake-flavored vodka.

They were drinking *cupcake-flavored vodka.*

I'd recently perused a journal article about how kids have been imbibing via a method called "butt chugging" which involves a tampon soaked in liquor and a lack of back door inhibitions. At the time, I couldn't understand why anyone would ingest alcohol from that end until learning that *cupcake-flavored vodka* was indeed a thing now. Frankly, the feminine-protection angle seems like the lesser of two evils.

I felt it behooved me to provide the three of them with drinking glasses, given the alternative. They did their shots and brayed like a pack of jackasses until Geri nodded off.

"Okay, boys, I need your help putting Geri to bed," I said.

"Why can't she sleep on the couch?" Trevor asked.

"Because a couch is not a bed," I replied.

Trevor seemed confused. "That's like saying an apple is not a bong. Maybe that's not its intended purpose, but, y'know, ingenuity and shit."

To which I replied, "Trevor, tell me you never vote."

He said, "Nah, no one watches *American Idol* anymore. All about *The Voice*, playa!"

I've said it before and I'll say it again—I weep for the youth of this nation.

"Please help me roll Geri's ponderous bulk into the guest room."

"Totes would, but the thing is? My mom says I'm hypoglycemic, and I can't lift anything until I have a snack." He held up his trembling hands. "See? Weak as a kitten. Couldn't even swat away a fly."

I'm not sure what it was about the word "swat," but it caused something in Bryce to come unhinged. "Swat? You say swat, son?" He burst into song. "*You can do the Brooklyn Swat!*" and then he began air humping my ficus tree while Trevor slapped at the air in front of him as though to simulate a spanking, ironic because I'm sure this kid never received corporal punishment a single day in his life. Even Geri (who I thought was deeply asleep) managed to shimmy her shoulders against the back of the couch.

This continued for a solid thirty seconds until it stopped, as inexplicably as it started, right as I was about to dial 911 to report three concurrent seizures.

Is this some kind of meme?

Is this what I missed by not attending parties in college and not using the Internet for anything but research?

Then the guys both made a mad dash for my kitchen. "Time to bust a grub, son!" Bryce exclaimed, throwing open the pantry door. "Yo, jelly beans!" He opened a glass jar of pinto beans and stuffed a handful into his mouth, before promptly spitting them all over the floor. "Yo, *not* jelly beans."

"Where's all your casseroles?" Trevor asked, his not-currently-chugging butt sticking out of my Sub-Zero.

"Were the two of you raised by Philistines?" I demanded, grabbing a whisk broom and dustpan.

"Yeah, Main Line, baby! Gladwyne represent!" Trevor shouted.

Weep.

"This is a travesty and shit," Bryce proclaimed, examining the spare shelves. "Gonna do a Kickstarter because you broke, son. Otherwise, you'd have snacks."

"I am definitely not broke, first of all. Plus, see? I have Greek yogurt, almond milk, blueberries, pasture-raised eggs, chickpeas, peppers, and fresh kale." I despise feeling like I have to defend my healthy choices, especially to two uninvited guests.

"That's why you've got no junk in your trunk, Dr. B. Time to chow mein! Men like something we can hold on to," Trevor explained. "In bed, I mean."

"So I gathered."

"Mo' booty, mo' cutie," Bryce added, nodding sagely.

I struggle to maintain my composure. "Tell your parents I'm raising your rent at the first of the year."

"'S'cool," Bryce replied. "Obvs you need the dolla dolla bills, y'all, to grocery shop. I'mma introduce you to my friend Joe. He's a Trader."

That's when I reached critical mass. I grabbed my purse and pulled out a twenty. "Okay, kids, party's over! But the Wieners Circle's still open. Char dogs on me!" Then I herded them out the door so quickly and forcefully that I forgot I'd wanted them to carry Geri down the hall.

Related note? I need to convert this place to a single-family dwelling, like, now.

Anyway, after I determined that moving Geri under my own steam wasn't possible, I tried to behave in a sisterly manner, thus proving that I absolutely have more class than she might have demonstrated were our circumstances reversed. I brought her a bottle of water and a couple of ibuprofen and I made her swallow both.

As she lay there on my couch, cradling a cashmere throw, I felt an odd stab of affection for her and I wondered if maybe, just maybe, I hadn't been too quick to judge her. After all, until this week, I had no idea she had even a modicum of ambition, nor was I aware that living back at home wasn't all peaches and cream. Perhaps since every single person in my orbit seems to feel affection for her, it's possible that I've overlooked her better qualities.

Maybe it wasn't so easy for Geri to grow up in my shadow. I set a high bar, at least in terms of academics. Although we went to different high schools, she had all my old teachers from kindergarten through eighth grade. If memory serves, I was quite the little apple polisher. I bet the nuns were all, "Reagan's sister? We expect a lot out of you!" and she couldn't deliver.

My parents have always been quick to highlight Geri's achievements, lowly though they may be, but it's possible that they do this not because she's the favorite, but because they're trying to compensate and protect her self-esteem.

Maybe Geri's more of a delicate flower than I assumed.

I'm not a parent. I've never had to balance the needs of three very different daughters. I'm sure my folks did the best they could. I bet when I'm not around, they champion me like they do Geri and Mary Mac.

What if underneath it all, Geri really loves me and she's never quite understood how to capture my interest? What if her quest for negative attention is simply an offshoot of her desire for my attention? What if she grabbed Lilly-Lizzie because she wanted me to finally play with her and that was her best shot?

Then she opened one sleepy green eye and reached for me. She brushed my hair out of my face and said, "It must suck to be you."

Yeah.

That's when I snapped.

And that's why I'm currently walking down Clark Street in a Geri suit.

I'd planned on running to her/my brunch date because, frankly, she could use the cardio. However, apparently Geri's not that kind of coordinated. Also, I'm battling a monster hangover for her. While she dreams all snug in my bed, I'm trying desperately not to vomit nachos and cupcake-flavored vodka.

This feeling?

Right here?

Is why I never drink.

Perhaps by teetotaling, I'll never lose my inhibitions enough to belt out the best of Steve Perry from an alehouse bar top, but I'll also never run the risk of tossing my cookies in a public trash can.

I'm not entirely sure what my next move might be, after I meet up with Kassel. I probably should have come up with some sort of plan before placing the amulets around our necks and taking a Thanwell.

Yet here I am.

Fortunately, I was able to cram Geri's posterior into one of my stretchiest pairs of yoga pants and Sebastian's old Blackhawks jersey. I threw her hair in a ponytail and didn't bother with makeup because I'm not giving her a single advantage on this date. I didn't even shower. Hope Kassel likes his women *earthy*.

Kassel spots me as soon as I enter the restaurant. He kisses my/her/our cheek. "I was worried I didn't specify which Original Pancake and you'd go to the Bellevue location."

I'm so rattled by his pure joy in seeing Geri that I can't help but respond, "I'm not great with following directions because I'm a bit dim, so frankly I'm as surprised as you are."

But instead of being turned off by my statement, he simply laughs and his eyes crinkle up. Damn it, why is stupid Geri's naked face making his eyes crinkle? "I love your self-deprecation. Rough morning?"

"Why does anyone drink?" I ask.

He places his hand on the small of my back as the hostess leads us to our table. "Believe me, been there. You had a lot to celebrate. You were amazing with Georgette. Life changing. By the way, sent the dailies to DBS and they lost their minds. They *worship* you. Never witnessed such a reaction. Big. So big! Keep it up, and you could find yourself with a spin-off. Someday."

The whole room begins to swim and I have to clutch his arm to stay upright until he can help me into my seat. How is this possible? How does Geri have the whole world handed to her based on one ugly haircut?

Kassel notices my distress and immediately orders us a couple of coffees. "I'd suggest a little hair of the dog, but you may not be able to handle a Bloody Mary."

"Oh, God, no," I agree. A busboy quickly appears with our beverages. "This is just what I need." I take a bracing sip of the steaming liquid. If I drink fully caffeinated coffee, which is rare, I tend to be a purist. I'm never one for sweetener, and if I add anything, it's almond milk, but today straight black is borderline nauseating. I need to cut the bitterness, lighten it up. I reach for the little white pitcher and pour in a splash. I can tell from the thickness that this is heavy cream, which would normally turn my stomach. Yet today, it almost seems like a salve, as does the spoonful of sugar. I stir and then sample.

How can something so wrong feel so right?

I've temporarily gotten my bearings, so I return to the business at hand. "Explain this whole spin-off concept," I say. "What might that entail?"

Kassel laughs. "Ambitious, eh? Let the show air first and then we'll see." He opens his menu. "What looks good to you?"

Um, nothing?

This whole menu is revolting.

I see no indication that they use farm-to-table, local, or organic products, and from the description, everything's either basted in butter, comprised of white flour, or full of pork products. The Three Little Pigs in Blankets are the worst possible offenders. *Our special links wrapped in light buttermilk pancakes and lightly dusted with powdered sugar. Served with whipped butter and hot tropical syrup.*

Disgusting.

So . . . why is my mouth watering?

Kassel says, "There's nothing like a greasy breakfast to cure what ails you. Although in college I was all about McDonald's after a wild night. Fountain Coke? My frat brothers and I were convinced it had healing powers." He peruses the offerings. "Anyway, I'm having corned beef hash, plus a side of chocolate chip pancakes."

The waitress approaches and I have Kassel order first because I'm undecided. And by "undecided" I mean "deeply appalled."

"Do you have any muesli?" I ask.

"I'm not sure what that is," she replies, chewing on the

edge of her pen. Her name is Brandi. There's a little flower drawn over the "i."

Bless her heart.

"Nothing with flaxseed, then?"

Brandi shifts and begins to nervously eye the other tables. "'Fraid not."

"What kind of fruit do you serve?"

"Um . . . we have banana and peach pancakes."

I squint at the laminated menu. "Ugh. No. Is there any chance your eggs are pasture raised? I'll take free-range in a pinch, although some farms do engage in beak cutting, which is certainly regrettable. Also, talk to me about your orange juice—is it freshly squeezed or from concentrate? And it's not artificially colored, right? Because that's patently unacceptable."

Kassel begins to laugh and lightly bats me on the knee. "Your Reagan impersonation is *uncanny*. I assume you're having your usual, yes? You said that's why you wanted to come here." He tells Brandi, "Give her the Three Little Pigs in Blankets. Thanks!" Brandi ambles off and he turns his attention to me. "So . . . are *we* having *fun* yet?"

No, not right this minute, not until the room stops spinning and not until I figure out how to elegantly avoid placing Blanketed Pigs anywhere near the vicinity of this mouth. But it occurs to me Geri's always superannoyingly (possibly artificially) upbeat, so I reply, "I imagine so, yes. This is a social situation and that's my kind of thing."

Kassel nods and I'm struck again by the cut of his jawline. I have to ball my fists in order to keep from running my fingers across his face. I appreciate how even though this is a lazy weekend brunch date, he still took the time to shave. He missed a tiny spot up by his ear, which is oddly charming. And how is this man still tan in December? Is that the end result of having lived in California for so long?

Plus, he must have walked here, too, as his cheeks are flushed. I appreciate a man who's not afraid to hoof it. Even though Sebastian biked and played volleyball, he still used to drive to my place and he was three blocks away. Made me crazy. Lazy is the opposite of sexy. I breathe in and I can smell the fabric softener coming from his chambray shirt. I lean in closer and note he's wearing cologne with undertones of cardamom and black pepper.

This?

This is what I'd like for breakfast.

His dark eyes twinkle as he says, "Speaking of kinds of things, 'I thought I'd go for the "helpful gay pirate" kind of thing.'"

"I beg your pardon?"

"Helpful gay pirate?"

This is sincerely puzzling. I understand each word as an individual concept, but strung together? Not so much.

I ask, "Are you at all familiar with the term *glossolalia*? Because it means fluid vocalizations of—" Wait, Geri would never have any cognizance of the concept of speaking in tongues. But there's weirdness afoot here; that much is evident.

As the waitress approaches with a fresh pot of coffee, Kassel grabs my hand and says, "'Can you look me in the eye and can you promise me that it all means something and that my whole bullshit life is just a bad start to a really incredible Cinderella story?'"

I can feel my heart beating almost out of my chest, and for a minute, I forget that I'm not exactly who I appear to be. In this one moment, it's just me and Kassel and his strong wrists and intoxicating fragrance. He and I should be together and we could have it all—we'd have witty banter and tanned, toned children and a mantel full of Emmys. This could really be my Cinderella story, because if you consider it, she dealt with some awful sisters, too, and—

"Best. Show. Ever!" Brandi exclaims, slopping coffee into my cup.

And just like that, the spell is broken.

She prattles on, "Every day I scan the trades to see if there's anything happening with the *Party Down* movie. Rob Thomas promises there's a script in the works, but no word on an actual movie yet. Hope springs eternal, though!"

Wait, so he's just been quoting some stupid *television show* at me?

"Up on the trades? Must be an actress," Kassel notes. He doesn't seem to be flirty so much as friendly, but the distinction doesn't offer much solace.

"Trying to be," Brandi replies. "'I think maybe I'm going to quit.'"

"'Nobody ever accomplished anything by quitting. What if Ronald Reagan quit?'"

"'Quit acting? He did.'"

"'Yeah, that's actually where I got the idea.'"

Then they laugh and fist-bump and the people at the table next to us join in because apparently *they're* fans, too, and I'm left sitting here like an asshole who's not only incapable of expressing my interest in a man, but also has never seen some esoteric television show because I was busy trying to establish a career.

Story of my life.

Kassel finally returns his focus to me. "Sorry about that.

Could have sworn we'd discussed our mutual love of *Party Down*, but I must have imagined it."

I really did not consider all the ramifications of this whole body swap/date crash before I slid into Geri's body like a pair of old jeans. Granted, I grew up with Geri, so I'm aware of our shared history, but I haven't exactly been paying attention to the rest of her life. I've no clue what she likes or how she spends her free time. (Although I would place money on much couch surfing.) I can't impersonate her because I don't know her.

Kassel smiles at me and sighs like he's so enamored he can't even find words. Realizing it's Geri giving him this reaction and not me makes my heart feel like it's ripping in two.

Okay, that might be a trifle dramatic.

But it's true that his interest in Geri hurts both my feelings and my ego. What's the draw? And it's not just Kassel; everyone falls all over themselves for her. It's . . . almost unnatural and makes no sense. What's it like to live in Geri's world? (I suspect there's a low stress/high snack element.)

How does she hold everyone in such thrall? What sort of black magic does she practice? How is she always so damn happy?

For all intents and purposes, *I* should be the one on top of the world.

I'm the one who put in the effort. I'm the one who made the huge sacrifices to get ahead. Why is no one sighing deeply over my unwashed butt at breakfast?

Well, if Deva's to be believed—and I believe she's proved herself credible—nothing happens by accident. There's no such thing as happenstance. So here I am on hiatus, with a couple of weeks to kill before Christmas and the means to step inside Geri's world to conduct a proper investigation.

This can't be a coincidence. Deva couldn't have given me these tools without a quiet understanding that I'd use them. This is like on those cop shows where someone really needs info and the detective can't officially share it, so he leaves the file on his desk to grab coffee while the sassy private investigator is alone in his office with her mini spy camera.

What's so all-fired great about Geri?

Even if it's immoral, unethical, and most likely illegal, I intend to find out.

CHAPTER NINETEEN
Geri1234

"Jesus, Mary, and Joseph, it's a Christmas miracle!" Ma hugs me to her, which is disconcerting because Ma is not a hugger.

At all.

Also, it's odd being able to look my mother in the eye. I've towered over her since the seventh grade, but in Geri's world, we're on the same level.

Calculating I had at least six hours left until Geri/my body woke up, I figured I should check in with our parents. I don't have confirmation that she's in almost constant contact with them, but I have my suspicions.

I figure the next week or so will be a lot easier if I have some basic Geri intel, so I've come back to our parents' house to gather supplies. I just told them that I'm going to bunk at Reagan's because of our filming schedule, and Ma is happier than I've ever seen her.

"I told your dad that if we gave you enough time, you two'd come together! Here we are, almost twenty-eight years later, and you're on your way to becoming friends! This is all I ever wanted for you both."

Huh. It never occurred to me that our not peacefully co-existing was that big of a deal. Sisters fight. Happens all the time.

. "I look at how close I am with your aunties Mary and Kathleen and it tears me up that you girls don't have that. But maybe now you will."

I'm very uncomfortable with this display of emotion. Stop it! Bring back Iron Maggie, please. Show me the woman who helped close Meigs Field without a second thought.

Ma sits on the bed while I grab items that look useful. I've already stashed Geri's laptop, her printed work schedule for the salon, and the Post-it from her bulletin board, which I assume relates to her passwords as it's labeled "passwords." She frequently uses "geri1234" for her login, but there are a couple of sites where its "1234geri." That's a pretty foolproof system you've got there, sis. IBM's definitely calling you to learn more about all your security protocols.

Ma says, "Now, you gotta promise me that you'll be nice to Reagan."

This should be interesting. "Why's that, Ma?"

"That's what you do when you're a guest."

"Oh." I was expecting more of an insight than just a page from Emily Post.

Ma glances up at the ceiling as though she's collecting her thoughts. "Reagan is a good girl, but she's lost, you know?"

I'd been throwing shirts in a duffel bag, but I stop in my tracks. No, I *do not* know; please enlighten me. I nod, as though to agree.

"She doesn't allow herself to enjoy anything and she only seems happy when she's out of joint about something. Even her hobbies are miserable. Who runs twenty-six miles for fun? People who want to punish themselves, that's who."

I would argue here, except I'm (literally) not myself at the moment. But this is definitely unfair. I'm a runner because I want to challenge myself, to push myself to achieve everything of which I'm capable. How is that not a selling point? And does Ma really see me as someone who's unhappy?

I offer, "Mary Mac says she has an eating disorder."

Ma waves away the thought. "That's a bunch of crap. She's just picky, always has been. And a little pretentious. She gets that from your father's side of the family. Dad's father was an alderman. He never let us hear the end of it. 'As an alderman, I'd have to disagree.' 'The other aldermen and I believe that New York–style pizza is overrated.' 'Alderman Bishop would like more potatoes.' However, Reagan's right— the rest of us *could* eat better."

Ha-ha-ha! In your *face*, Geri! (Except about the pretentious part.)

"Of all you girls, I worry about her the most."

I beg your pardon? Me? The *doctor*? And not the octo-mom or the freeloader? *I'm* your point of concern? Since when do you gossip? Damn it, why are you so willing to share these stories with Geri and not me? I knew she was the favorite!

Ma continues, "Remember how different she was when she was with Boyd? She was fun, she was relaxed, it's like the stick finally disappeared from her ass. She finally stopped looking at herself as a victim. Then she dumped him and for what? Where'd it get her?"

Um, on DBS every Thursday night?

Of course, Geri's there now, too. Damn it!

"I gotta go soon, Ma," I say, anxious to change the subject. Even if Ma is speaking a tiny portion of the truth, I'm not in the right mind-set to hear it. "Hey, where do I keep my clean underwear?" With someone as disorganized as Geri, this is a legitimate question.

"I did a load for you this morning." She exits and quickly returns with a basketful of NastyGirlz-worthy underthings. Then the phone rings and she leaves me to gab with Auntie Kathleen.

I feel like I'm in some bizarre alternate universe right now—how is it that I'm the one who's lost, yet *she's* the one whose mommy still washes her underpants? I don't get it, I truly don't.

I grab Geri's duffel bags and I say a quick good-bye to my parents.

This should be an interesting week.

According to Geri's schedule, she has today off because the salon is closed.

Well, that's just dumb.

Don't people need haircuts on Monday? Sure, I understand that stylists are busier on the weekends, but perhaps everyone's schedule could be staggered so that all shifts could be covered without losing an entire day's revenue. I'll definitely mention this to Miranda, Geri's boss and bestie (at least until Geri screws her over with her nonexistent work ethic and thus loses this job, too).

Not having to go to her job gives me an entire day to familiarize myself with her world. I've double-dosed the Thanwell, so that buys me sixteen hours inside Geri. While she rests in my body, I'll live her life. Then, when the Thanwell wears off, Geri will be back inside her own body and she'll sleep on her own and I can take care of the business of being Reagan.

Every time I feel a twinge of guilt, I remind myself of her perpetually swooping in to take what's mine, whether it's my *Push* spotlight or Lilly-Lizzie, and my guilt magically melts away.

For the most part.

When Geri finally woke up last night, I immediately removed my amulet and we switched back into our bodies. Of course she noticed the necklace, so I explained it as an early Christmas present and she seemed satisfied by the explanation. Then I went into detail about how she had this new kind of neurological flu that was ravaging Asia and under no circumstances should she leave the couch, let alone my apartment.

Pfft, like I had to tell her twice.

With my remote control in one hand and her phone in the other, she acted like she owned the place. Ironically, this was beneficial for me, because I was able to really listen to her speech patterns as well as take notes on her plans.

But now she's snug in my body/bed, so I can begin my research. I open Facebook and I begin to scroll through her wall. After five minutes, I'm pretty sure I have boredom cancer. Why on earth would anyone care what you had for lunch or how your feet look in the sand on your vacation? Oh, hey, here's a shot of a cat in a hat! Hilarious. Not.

What a time suck this is. I use Facebook to advance myself professionally, and not to exchange worthless commentary on why my political platform is better than yours or whether or not Starbucks should be boycotted because they won't stock almond milk. (Although, really, why don't they carry it?)

As I inspect Geri's photos, I see that she is the master of

the selfie. How does she have time to get to her day job if she's perpetually taking all these photos of herself?

I make sure to "like" everyone's entries and I spout her usual banalities of "badass!" and "OMG, u r the best!" and now I feel dirty.

As I tab through, I notice that Geri has a lot of friends. How does she have so many friends? She has more friends than I have likes on my fan page, and as of yet, she's not even been on TV.

Her buddy list bears further investigation. I know she's friends with Sebastian, but who else might I recognize? I begin to scan the list and I recognize tons of people from the neighborhood, as well as a bunch of my cousins. And . . . is that my dad? My father has a Facebook page? His only entry says, "I don't know how to work this thing. Hello?"

Affirmative, that is my dad.

Why didn't he friend me?

I'm about to click off this section when I see a shot of Boyd. I guess I knew he'd finally joined Facebook, but I never searched for his profile. What would be the point?

I open his page and I'm taken aback to see he's only gotten better with age. I feel bittersweet about seeing him. As nice as it is to run across his photo, it's also painful, and I didn't realize exactly how much until this moment. In this picture, his hair is shorter than it was and he has a few tiny laugh lines, but otherwise, he looks exactly like he did the day he drove me to the airport when I left Malibu for good.

I quickly return to Geri's home page. As much as I hope Boyd's happy, I'm not sure I want to delve deeper into his profile to see shots of whatever (or whoever) currently occupies his time or where it is he currently bartends. I made my choice and I live in the now.

I close Facebook and open her e-mail. She doesn't have much in there, save for sale notices at a couple of clothing retailers. I think her generation is too lazy to actually pen an entire note, so e-mail isn't cool anymore. Typical. But she has scores of new texts. If Geri's awake, she's clutching her phone, so if I don't answer them, her friends will assume she's been abducted.

Which is not entirely untrue.

Okay, here goes.

From Catelyn: `where u at gurl?`

In a state of suspended animation.

`Chillin`, I reply.

From Allison: `S'up, s'up, s'up?`

`Nada, nada, nada.`

From Miranda: `How was ur brunch w the hotty?`

Awkward. Infuriating. Enlightening.

`Swag.`

From Mindy: `The bitch makin u mental?`

Delete. Rest up over Christmas break, kid. For that remark, I plan on running you all over the city for green tea when we return to set in January.

From Mary Mac: `cme ovr 4 supper, 7:30. bring wine.`

Oh, *Geri* will be there, all right.

Count on that.

"Auntie Geri, yay!" Kiley dances around me as I throw my coat on Mary Mac's couch. Reagan would have been thoughtful and hung up her jacket, but we're in Geritown now, where all we do is whatever is the quickest/easiest.

Instead of instructing Kiley to please not touch me until she washes the frosting off her fingers, I give her a squeeze. I'm sure the cheetah stripe of Geri's hideous shirt will hide any stains.

I figured if I were coming over here, I'd better bone up on which kid was which or else Mary Mac would instantly be alerted that something was amiss. I made flashcards with all their faces and included their activities, so now I'm completely up to speed.

"Yo, Mickey Junior, *Beowulf* still kicking your ass?"

He glances up from the Xbox and gives me a massive grin. "Nope. Passed the test with a high D!"

I stop myself from saying *congratulations on the bare minimum*, instead replying, "Badass," which earns me not only a mock salute but also an invitation to play *Halo 4* later.

"'S'up, Finley Patrick? Any good garbage pickin' lately?"

"I found a tennis racket without any strings!"

"Awesome, buddy!"

He runs over and hugs me before heading down to watch the big TV in the basement.

So what Geri's already taught me is that if you let children get away with everything and prop up their self-esteem based on a minimum of achievement, they like you. Duly noted.

"Open the wine, please, like right now," Mary Mac says by way of greeting. She slides a corkscrew over to me, even though I don't need it because the bottle is a screw top. I'm not sure how I feel about that. There's an inherent amount of sophistication that comes with drinking wine, largely because of the effort it takes to release it from the bottle. But just un-screwing like it's a soda? Seems like cheating to me.

At the wine store, I wasn't sure what Geri normally drinks, so I perused all the labels and picked the bottle that inspired me the most.

"Hey," Mary Mac says, "Bitch wine, our favorite!"

Nailed it!

I pull up a seat at the kitchen island, scraping aside a mountain of kids' homework, mail, and cotton-ball-and-Popsicle-stick-based artwork. Mickey built this whole kitchen addition, so its bones and the craftsmanship are superb, but it's so full of the detritus that I can barely see an inch of the granite. I also note the custom millwork is covered in frosting handprints. Reagan would have inquired as to where each item would live and then she'd help stow everything before wiping down the cabinets, but Geri has no problem slopping wine in her glass and setting it precariously on one of the stacks.

Okay, not for nothing? This is fairly liberating. Every other time I've stepped into Mary Mac's place, I've grown tense because of the chaos and disorganization and my need to set it all straight. But in living via Geri's dictates, I can simply overlook everything, even Kacey Irelyn walking in and placing her dirty juice glass next to the dishwasher instead of inside it because why take that one minuscule extra step? Whee! It's a party! We can throw our empties anywhere!

"Made your favorite tonight," Mary Mac tells me, pulling a casserole pan full of something orange and gelatinous out of the oven.

Funny, that doesn't look like ginger-soy-glazed salmon with a side of steamed kale and a ramp salad tossed with chia seeds and aged balsamic.

"Mary Mac 'n' Cheese!" she announces proudly.

Oh, Jesus Christ.

"Plus, there's meatloaf basted in extra barbecue sauce!"

Not for nothing, Geri, but this is why you're chunky. I bet your arteries look like the Dan Ryan Expressway at 8:05 a.m.

Given such a repast, Reagan would run screaming into the night, but as this is what floats Geri's boat (and dimples her butt), then I can't quibble.

"Shall I set the table?" I offer, before I catch myself going all Reagan again.

Mary Mac laughs and pours herself a glass of wine in a jelly jar. "Everything else is dirty," she says. Which brings me back to my point of the kids loading their own dishes. Why does she insist on making it harder on herself? "Hey, Mickey Junior, piss off! It's *Bachelor* time!"

Apparently Mary Mac and Geri gather for a sisters' dinner every Monday night to watch *The Bachelor.* I would complain that I'm never invited, but I can't imagine I'd ever willingly attend, so, really, it's a wash.

We sit side by side on the couch with our plates balanced on our knees. Mary Mac cues up the DVR. "Are you ready for an amaaaaaaaazing journey?" she asks.

"As long as you're here for the right reasons and you don't pull a Bentley," I reply.

What? I work in reality TV; it's my job to be familiar with the competition and it seemed like a Geri thing to say.

Mary Mac tucks in to her meal while I assess the situation. I have no choice but to eat some of this, lest I blow my cover. Okay, here goes . . . I take a tiny forkful of the Mary Mac 'n' Cheese and swallow without chewing while only breathing through my mouth. I don't notice any cloying processed cheese aftertaste, so I have another nibble. This is . . . not awful. In fact, it's palatable. The sauce is hot and bubbly and the pasta is the perfect state of al dente.

I can do this.

The meatloaf is another story, though. The last time I tasted beef, Clinton was in the White House. Plus, this barbecue sauce is loaded with artificial ingredients. But I'll give Mary Mac credit—at least she didn't cook it into a petrified meat-log like Ma used to do. Heck, her cooking's the main reason that I didn't miss meat when I stopped eating it. I break off a small bit with my fork and take a small taste.

The only word that comes to mind is . . . transcendent.

Divine.

Heavenly.

I'd like to say this is Geri's body's response to a familiar stimulus, but that's not giving Mary Mac her proper due. This meatloaf is freaking spectacular and worthy of being served at any of Chicago's finest dining establishments.

I take a bigger bite this time, and before I finish chewing it, I stuff in another. Oh, that fennel! Although I'm sure Geri couldn't give a fig about table manners anyway, I'm not even thinking about her right now. I'm just trying to calculate exactly how much cubic space there is inside my mouth, as I would like to cram it as full of this magical meat as humanly possible.

"Mary Mac," I say between frantic bites, "this is the best meatloaf I've ever eaten." Utterly true.

She nods, eyes not leaving the screen, where Bachelor Brendon is tonguing the bejesus out of a bikini-clad Bachelorette under a Tahitian waterfall. "Thanks, G. I added powdered onion soup mix this time."

"Always," I insist, laying my hand on her arm. "*Always* add it from now on."

When a commercial comes on, Mary Mac allows it to play and she begins to chat. "I can't believe you're staying at Reagan's. What'd she do to lure you into her lair?"

I don't have a lair! Geri has a lair! I have an open, airy, tastefully appointed graystone full of lovely couches and dupioni silk curtains!

I shrug my shoulders noncommittally. "It's a *Push* thing, totally for convenience. But I've barely seen her since I've been there, so it's all good in the hood."

Mary Mac takes a leisurely bite and nods. "She called you fat yet? At Thanksgiving, she referred to your weight no less than twenty-three separate times. I counted. That's a new record. The winner of the Passive-Aggressive Olympics is . . . Dr. Reagan Bishop!"

In character, I snort, "I was all, 'Whatevs, bitch.' She's jealous she doesn't have my curves."

"That's what I've been saying for years."

In my defense, sometimes people are in denial, so it's helpful when an impartial adviser points out your shortcomings. If you aren't aware of a problem, you can't fix it . . . right?

Although if I were counseling someone and they told me their sister was always calling them fat, I'd probably consider the sister out of line.

I wonder if that's why Geri flipped me off?

"It's not like this is anything new with her. Remember the time you failed your math test and she spent the next two weeks reciting times tables at dinner? Or how about how she used to lord her mile-high peanut butter pie over you? She bites at your heels whenever she's given the opportunity."

I nod, saying nothing. This really is news to me.

She raises her jar at me. "You notice how her buddy at Thanksgiving couldn't take his eyes off of you?"

That's just mortifying, and now I'm glad I inadvertently mentioned Geri's weight multiple times.

Through gritted teeth, I reply, "I know, right?"

"Do me a favor while you're there, G. Just watch yourself, okay? Reagan always has an end game and you can't trust her for a second. You never know what she'll pull and then find a way to justify. Be careful and don't let her take advantage of you."

"I will protect and guard my heart," I promise, quoting Vienna's squeaky-voiced *Bachelor Pad* paramour.

"That's why you're my favorite sister, G." And then she momentarily rests her head on my shoulder before fast-forwarding over the rest of the commercials. She smells like Bitch wine and baby aspirin and barbecue, which actually pair nicely together.

Overwhelming pangs of guilt take hold of me, not only for possibly being part of the problem in my relationship with Geri, but also because this is about the first nice moment I've ever had with Mary Mac.

Not sure of what else to do, I inhale another bite of meatloaf.

For once, I'm delighted to have the opportunity to eat my feelings.

CHAPTER TWENTY
(Literally) in Her Shoes

"What are you doing here, Geri?" Stylist and manager Miranda glances down at her bling-covered watch.

"Don't I work today?" I assume I have Geri's current schedule. What if I pulled the wrong one? "Thought I was supposed to be here at noon."

Both Miranda and her client eye me. "But it's eleven forty-five. Your appointment isn't even here yet."

"Don't I need time to set up?" Although I can't imagine I have to do much other than locate some scissors, right?

Miranda, who's dressed more for a rave than a day combing clients' hair, steps away from her station and speaks to me in a whisper. "I've never seen you early before. Never once. I'm really glad you took our talk to heart. I hate having to write you up, but the owner's been up my ass about your perpetual tardiness. Thank you for not putting me in this position."

"Of course," I reply. "What are friends for?"

I can barely hear myself think in here with all the thumping techno music. If I really worked here, I'm sure I'd file a complaint with HR saying this was a hostile work environment. There's an actual DJ in here spinning tunes. A DJ! In a hair salon! Way to take yourselves superseriously, ladies.

I quickly figure out that Geri's station is the only unmanned chair, so I head over there and begin to open and close drawers. A young woman with a ton of sparkly eye shadow hands me a sheet of paper. "Your list, my lady."

I glance at her name tag. Allison.

Taking into account Geri's tendency for doing things the easy way, even when it comes to saying someone's name, I reply, "Thanks, Ali."

"No probs, G-spot."

I scan the appointment list and notice that I'm supposed to color someone's hair at four p.m. The cut I can handle because of body memory, but the color will take a working knowledge of times and formulas. It's best to not draw attention to what I can't do, so I say, "My eczema's being a beyotch today. Can I do swapsies with someone else? I need to not, like, touch chemicals."

"Sure, G! I'll give her to Catelyn and you can handle any walk-in cuts."

Crisis avoided!

"Sweet."

As I scan the salon, I notice that all the girls without clients are fooling with their own hair. I'd simply drawn Geri's into a ponytail this morning, which was all I could handle after the trauma of having to wash her generous ass.

Huh.

I really do mention Geri's weight a lot, don't I?

That's not cool.

But now, the frizzy red pony seems out of place in the club-like salon, so I use a round brush to unkink the curls and smooth the whole thing into Rita Hayworth–style waves. I admire my work in the mirror. Not bad!

I mean, not bad considering what I had to work with.

Allison agrees. "Superglammy, G!"

"Thanks!"

My first client arrives and I'm delighted that she's new to the salon, so we don't have a previous relationship. I pieced together what I could from Geri's social media footprint, but clearly there will be portions I've missed.

I do my best to channel Geri. "So what are we doing today?" I ask, running my hands through the client's long, dark, straight hair, which is pretty similar to my own. "I have my own ideas, but let's hear what you're thinking."

Lydia, the client, replies, "I'm sooo bored with this all-one-length bullshit. I want something new and fun."

"Like . . . layers?" I probably should have studied up on actual hairdressing terms, but at least my hands know what to do. I'll whack off some of the stuff around her face, like Geri's always claiming I should do.

I keep running my hands through her hair and holding up little bits, and apparently this seems enough like what a real stylist would do that Lydia doesn't question me.

A staffer named Margarita leads Lydia over to the shampoo bowls, which is oddly disappointing. I thought doing the shampoo would be fun, kind of like washing a dog.

When Lydia returns, I comb out her hair. She sits there quietly, but expectantly. Oh, *I'm* supposed to initiate conversation. On it.

"What do you want to talk about today?"

Lydia glances up at me under her veil of wet hair. "I'm sorry?"

Shit, therapist mode. Try it again. WWGD—What Would Geri Discuss?

"You see *The Bachelor* last night?"

Lydia sadly shakes her head. "Had to TiVo it—my boyfriend was being a pain. He was at my apartment and he insisted we watch the game. I was all, 'But I was looking forward to *The Bachelor*,' and he didn't care. I had this whole night planned for myself with wine and snacks, and Kirk came over uninvited and totally bogarted my plans."

I'm about to inquire about her feelings on the issue when I realize that I'm not encumbered by APA rules. Not only can I ask whatever I want, but I can also offer my unvarnished opinion.

"What an asshole!"

That felt *fantastic*. I've never been allowed to actually tell a patient in no uncertain terms what I really thought. Maybe if I didn't have to mince words so much, they'd be able to change their behavior more quickly?

"Right? Then he had the nerve to try to send me out for beer because he didn't like the wine I bought!"

I'm a little in awe as Geri's hands deftly move through Lydia's locks, almost as though they have a mind of their own. A ton of long strands fall to the floor, which starts to make me feel panicky. But I have to keep my composure, lest Lydia panic as well.

I smooth and comb and snip. "Is this in character? I mean, does Kirk always pull stunts like this?" I ask over the sound of clicking scissors.

"At first I thought he was really into me, being a gentleman and making all the decisions."

"Such a red flag," I say.

Whoops, was that out loud?

Wait, I'm *allowed* to say this stuff out loud! Yes! I remember when I was treating this woman who had a borderline abusive fiancé and all I wanted to do was say, "Honey? Run."

She replies, "I hear ya, but I didn't see it. I just thought, 'Wow, he's so into me.'"

"But then it eventually occurred to you that he wasn't being a nice guy so much as he was being controlling?"

Lydia eyes me in the mirror. "Bingo."

"What's your game plan? Are you at the point where you can talk about this, or is it better to end it?"

She bites her lip. "I'm not sure, honestly."

"Has he ever been aggressive toward you?"

"Nothing like that, no, never!" Lydia quickly exclaims. Then, rather sheepishly she adds, "Well, except that he pushed me over the weekend."

I stop cutting. "He *pushed* you? Like out of the way of an oncoming car?"

"No . . . he'd had a lot to drink and he wanted to drive and I tried to take his keys and we had a little scuffle."

Alarm bells are dinging so loudly in my head that I'm surprised the rest of the salon can't hear them. "So what happened?"

"I ended up letting him drive and I got into the passenger seat," she softly admits.

I spin her around to look at me. "What you're saying is that you not only allowed him to manhandle you, but then you risked your own life in riding with him?"

She hangs her head. "I never looked at it that way, but yeah. I kinda did."

"Do you deserve better?" I ask.

"I do. My friend Scott is always saying so. He doesn't understand why I'd be with someone like Kirk in the first place."

"Then you need to drop him like a bad habit. Go home and change your locks if he has a key—does he have a key?" She nods and I continue, "Then you tell him it's over and if he bothers you again, you'll be filing a police report."

"But what will happen if I'm there by myself and Kirk shows up?"

"Can someone stay with you?"

"I'm sure Scott would. He's like a brother to me. He's always been there for me and he's a constant source of support. He's such a good guy—I don't know why he can't find a nice girl already."

"Then it's settled."

As I begin her blow-dry, conversation becomes impossible, but we communicate by smiling at each other in the mirror and I find myself gently swaying to the beats the DJ lays down.

When we finish, I realize three things: Geri's job actually requires skill and has value, Scott's about to exit the Friend Zone, and I really would look better with a few layers around my face.

I never see Geri without her platform stilettos, so that's what I wore to the salon today. They were fine for the first hour, but after that, I felt like my feet were caught in two separate bear traps. They went from aching to throbbing to screaming to their current state of numb. I give her credit for wearing these with the frequency that she does.

Couple the aching feet with the stamina it takes to work on that many clients, plus the emotional toll of connecting with each person, and I suddenly feel like I have to revise my previous opinion of Geri being lazy. No lazy person would ever hold a job like this.

This profession is draining and grueling and utterly, entirely soul satisfying. Who knew? People come in unhappy and they leave happy. Does a haircut solve deeply ingrained behavior problems? Of course not. Yet the world seems a tiny bit more fresh and hopeful when looking out from under a new fringe of bangs. I feel terrible for having discounted what Geri does for so long. She performs a valuable service and I realize that now.

Plus, I hardly have anyone's hair in my underwear.

(I did learn rather quickly to put a lid on my drink, though.)

All I want to do is go home, slip into a hot bath, and then put my own damn feet back on, but Miranda and company have other ideas. Namely, Brando's Speakeasy for karaoke.

I try to get out of the festivities. "I can't, I'm too tired."

"You say that every week," Ali argues. "Get your shapely behind moving, because we're leaving."

A group of us pile in a cab, even though the bar's less than six blocks away. Normally, I'd walk, but at the moment, I'd pay someone to carry me fireman-style, so the taxi is a welcome compromise.

We arrive at Brando's and I'm pleased to note that it's in a gorgeous old Chicago landmark building and not some hole-in-the-wall Bridgeport pub covered in neon beer signs. The walls are beautiful dark wood paneling with lots of vintage advertising art. There are velvet curtains and flattering lighting, too. If I went to bars, I suspect this is one I might frequent.

We settle in at what's apparently our usual table and the

waitress rushes us over a round of peach martinis. Miranda, who's next to me, asks, "Are you surviving up there?"

"At Reagan's?" I ask. The way everyone's been questioning me/Geri about her accommodations, you'd think she was sent to a gulag and not a gorgeous graystone. I take a sip of my peach martini and I can feel the liquor stripping off a layer of flesh inside my mouth. Yikes. "'S'okay. Why?"

Miranda slicks on some sticky gloss and smacks her lips together. "It's just a surprise, is all. You're so nice to her and she's always such a bitch back. I don't even know why you try." Newsflash? I'm pretty sure that's a lie. "I was curious if she's any less intense when she's on her own turf."

"I'm gaining a whole new understanding," I admit.

Catelyn chimes in, "Remember when your client brought you that amazing shirt back from France and you posted it on Facebook and Reagan was all, 'Stripes? No.' Damn, I wish there were an 'Unlike' button for those kind of comments. Who does that?"

"Y'know, I actually watched one of her old episodes on WeWIN—she was with some girl named Dina? From New Jersey? The whole time they were talking, I was like, 'She's so not listening to that girl. She's smiling and nodding, but she's not processing anything this poor kid's saying.' It's like she was mentally composing her grocery list or something."

I'd argue, but she's not wrong.

Miranda brushes a stray fuchsia-colored feather out of her face. (Did you know there are feather-based hair extensions now? I sort of don't hate them.) "Then, when they're walking down the beach, I saw your sister's backside. I don't care how skinny that bitch is, she has cellulite."

Noo! That wasn't mine! That was from sitting on the slatted bench! Cellulite isn't striped, for crying out loud!

Before I can answer her, Ali yanks me out of my seat. "They have your song cued up! Everyone's waiting!"

"For what?" I ask.

She hands me a microphone. "For this." Then she shoves me onstage and I stare out at the crowd, who are watching me expectantly.

Um . . . help?

What do I do here?

And why is this so scary? I've given plenty of speeches and lectures in my day, but that's always been talk based and scripted. I don't sing. I've never sung. I have a terrible voice! I don't even hum in the shower!

The song begins and my hands begin to sweat. I'm so anxious that I'm actually manifesting Geri's physical responses. Words begin to scroll by on the screen and the audience begins to grow restless when I blow the entire first verse.

I feel like not singing is the only fate worse than singing, so . . . here goes nothing.

The voice that comes out of me is rich and melodic and full of soul and the crowd immediately responds.

I'll be damned.

When Geri's not shit-housed and not screaming Journey songs from the top of a bar, she actually possesses a decent set of pipes.

The crowd goes wild and I'm completely bolstered by their response and possibly also the peach martini. I add a few dance moves and strut across the stage. I flip my hair and the crowd totally loses it.

"Here I go again!"

As I proceed, I channel Tawny Kitaen (before all the unpleasantness) and my performance quickly becomes that of legend.

When the song ends, the audience gives me a standing ovation and her friends are shouting their heads off and collectively it's about the best feeling I've ever had.

And that's when it occurs to me that there may be more to Geri than I ever realized.

CHAPTER TWENTY-ONE

Point Break

A small admission, if I may?

I may have screwed Geri over in regard to her relationship with Kassel.

While he and I were at that brunch, the more we spoke, the more I was struck by how little common ground he and I shared. My intention was to Cyrano de Bergerac him—let him know the real me while I was in my Geri suit, assuming he'd be more about the personality than the package, eventually revealing that it was me he really loved.

Not so much.

As our date dragged on, he insisted on quoting all these stupid movies I never heard of (who is Pauly Shore?) and then we had a stultifying conversation about some ex–Notre Dame football player with an imaginary dead girlfriend who turned out to be a live dude.

What does that even mean?

The lack of commonality wasn't the worst part. Handsome is the great equalizer. Give me broad shoulders and a square jaw and I can overlook terrible taste in entertainment.

Because I'm apparently a masochist, I brought up the subject of *my sister* Reagan. I dropped a trial balloon on how I thought they might have chemistry.

And do you know what that SOB said?

He told me, "Your sister's way too tightly wound. Too intense. I can't deal with perfectionists. Not my jam."

"What about how you two banter?" I asked. Surely that was significant? I mean, Boyd and I could have based a lifetime on our bantering alone.

He made a face as though he'd smelled something sour. "That whole angry-banter thing? Only works for Spencer Tracy. In real life, it's just bickering and it gets old fast. Exhausting, actually. Give me laid-back any day. See, I've been down the high-maintenance-woman route before and it didn't end well."

Then he had the nerve to shudder.

The notion of dating me merited a full-body shudder?

I was so angry, thinking how number one, I'm not high maintenance and number two, I'm not tightly wound and number three, and then I couldn't think of a number three because I was still seething about numbers one and two.

So after pushing my blanketed piggies around the plate for a while, I told him I was feeling ill and I must take my leave.

Okay, that's a lie.

I told him I was afraid I might shart myself and I needed to get home, and thought, *There, is that laid-back enough for you, Kassel?*

I suspect he was so turned off by the whole date that any nascent feelings he might have had for Geri are gone. Again, in the moment I was all, *Well, too bad, Geri. You lose the game that you should have never played in the first place.* Then I may or may not have called him an "effing creeper" when he kept texting afterward. And this time I didn't use "effing." I was furious with her, and, by extension, him. But now that I've literally walked a mile in her shoes, I can't say I feel the same way.

Now? I'm kind of a fan of Geri.

I sort of get why everyone's so into her.

I'll be honest. I'm having a lot more fun being Geri than I ever had as Reagan. Her friends are immensely entertaining and I love how nice they are to me. How great is it to walk into a room and have people excited to see me? I appreciate how her job makes everyone happy. Clients come in, all split-ended and unstyled, and bam! Forty-five minutes later, they're goddesses. Plus, singing in front of the audience at Brando's was a rush I'll always remember. Who knew she was talented?

(Okay, probably everyone but me.)

The best part is I'm connecting with Mary Mac and her kids in a way I never realized was possible . . . largely because I upped Geri's dosage.

I know, I know. This is so wrong.

And yet I feel like I'm onto something here and I'm not quite ready to inhabit my own life again. I've worked out the specifics in such a way that I'm able to feed/exercise/maintain my own body and life while Geri's physical self is asleep, so, really, I'm not doing anything unhealthy, per se, save for a possible tiny Thanwell addiction Plus, since we're on hiatus, Reagan's not exactly missed anywhere.

"Geri" is supposed to be "staying at Reagan's" out of convenience, but I keep being drawn back to the south side to hang out with Mary Mac's family. Yes, her kids are a little loud and a bit pushy, but they're also freaking hysterical. Teagan does an impersonation of me that had me rolling. (I think it was the day she kept calling herself "Doctor.")

When I'm not there, Mary Mac and I chat multiple times a day, while she ferries her brood to their practices and activities. I'm a little in awe of how organized she is. I found out her Christmas shopping was completed in October. *October.* That still blows my mind. Maybe her house is messy, but she's so on the ball in regard to all other aspects of her life, from her children to her volunteering to her marriage, that it doesn't matter. Sure, she always seems exhausted, but it's only because she puts in such effort.

I remember the amount of posturing and social climbing it took for me to rub shoulders with Wendy Winsberg's crowd. At no point had it occurred to me that some of the best people I'd ever meet are in my own family.

However, I hadn't yet realized any of the above when I was making my way up Clark after the Kassel brunch. The day had become decidedly cold since I'd headed to the restaurant, and I wasn't wearing enough layers. I must have been walking hunched over for warmth, so I didn't realize I'd body-slammed anyone until he helped me up.

And when I realized the kindly stranger was Sebastian, I truly did almost shart myself.

He looked great and he was so happy to see me that I couldn't help but reconsider the idea of us maybe, possibly reconnecting. That is, until he called me Geri and I realized I wasn't who he thought I was.

Long story short, that's how I found myself agreeing to dinner tonight at Frances' Deli.

Sebastian's already seated at a table by the window, wearing pressed gray flannel slacks and a shirt with French cuffs, which seems a bit formal for a relaxed deli-type meal. In fact, Frances' is so casual that it's one of the few places on the north side that's acceptable to my parents. On the rare occasions they've been in my neighborhood at lunch, this is where they insist on going. Dad's a fan of the Douglas Boulevard sandwich, which includes corned beef and chopped liver, whereas I'm normally a fan of ordering hot tea and swapping the Lipton's for a bag of the organic stuff I brought from home. Everything about this place is old school, from the pressed tin ceiling to the vintage wood paneling to the original marble-topped bar. To me, the space is dark and depressing, but there must be some appeal as they've been operating successfully since the 1930s.

"Glad you could come!" Sebastian says. He rises to kiss my/our cheek. Did he used to stand when I walked in the room? Can't recall.

Last week when Sebastian requested that we get together sometime to talk, I was a little curious about what he had to say to Geri, but not so much that I thought the conversation merited a meal.

Since then, though, I've made peace with all things Geri. I see now that any unpalatable behavior she exhibited stemmed directly from my actions. (Pretty sure I'd tell someone to go eff themselves, too, if they had a single thing to say about my weight.)

I'm learning that Geri's perpetually there for people, ready to listen, willing to help, all without a judgmental internal monologue. Maybe she's not a saint, but she's not the sinner I'd previously suspected, either.

Over the past few days, I've been trying to help her. I figure my inhabiting her is kind of like sending her to a day spa. I bought her some new, tasteful clothing, and I'm feeding her healthy foods and taking her on long walks. (I need to help compensate for the mass amounts of Mary Mac's cooking I've been eating, which, OMFG, that woman does unspeakable things with spareribs.)

I've also been working on a business plan for her potential salon. I found notes in her laptop, and Geri's ideas are perfectly solid, but she needs to present them in a professional prospectus if she wants to turn this into a viable venture. I'm in the process of doing that for her.

The thing is, I'm not entirely sure that getting over my incessant sibling rivalry is going to fix what's wrong with *me*. Having experienced being laid-back, friendly, and fun, not to mention relaxed about dietary constraints, I learned that I *am* uptight, I *am* dour, and I *am* kind of a pain in the ass about my diet. I'm also narrow-minded and my positive affirmations are nothing less than straight-up, overcompensating narcissism.

I'm neither victim nor martyr, so it's time I stopped acting like I am. No wonder I alienate others. No wonder I have virtually no friends. I've been allowing my anger and various proclivities to keep others at arm's length. I don't have close connections in my life, and at the end of the day, my job doesn't kiss me good night.

Speaking of employment, in all my time practicing and with all my training, I never closed out the day feeling exhilarated about what I do for a living. Sure, I've always reveled in the various benefits, like being recognized at Whole Foods and having George Stephanopoulos flirt with me, but the actual act of patiently listening to others' problems? Not really into it, if I'm being honest with myself.

I'm certainly not going to chuck it all for cosmetology school, but I do need to figure out what's next for me, and I suspect it's neither being a psychologist on television nor being a television psychologist.

Where does that leave me? I'm not yet sure.

But before I can figure out what's next in my life, I need some measure of closure, so last night I Facebooked Sebastian and suggested we meet after all. And here we are.

Sebastian grins at me. "You're radiant this evening."

I say, "No, I'm just windburned." I've been running by the lake this week and I've already shaved two minutes off of Geri's newfound ability to jog a mile. I'm very proud of her/us!

He scoots his chair closer to mine. "Don't sell yourself short, kid. Reagan didn't get all the looks in your family."

Oh, God, did he just wink?

I try to steer away from the subject of Geri. "Perhaps we should order."

"Nothing on the menu will be as delicious as you." He abruptly juts his chin in an effort to toss his hair out of his eyes. For some reason, he wears the front of his hair long, like he's starring in some 1990s Keanu Reeves surfing flick. Sir, I know surfers. Surfers have been friends of mine. You, sir, are no surfer.

The hair flip is his prelude-to-seduction move and it's only now occurring to me that it's comical. What's with the full-court-flirting press, anyway? Was Sebastian always smarmy? I feel like I'd have noticed if he was smarmy. I realize that Geri and I were never the best of friends, but we're sisters. Surely there's some code of ethics that prevents guys from hitting on their ex's sisters?

I challenge him. "What about your girlfriend?"

"What girlfriend is that?"

"The Hooters waitress?"

"Nonexistent. Pretty sure Reagan's still spying on my profile, so I made her up and posted on my Facebook so it'd get back to her." He reaches for my hand across the table, but I quickly busy myself with my napkin to hide my shock.

Now, that's patently unfair! I haven't been to his Facebook page in months, save for making our date last night, and that wasn't even as me.

I ask him, "To what end? Why make up a girlfriend?"

Sebastian flips his bangs out of his eyes again. Did I like his ridiculous hair when we were together? Because now I kind of think Morrissey called and wants his look back.

"Eh, I wanted to make sure she'd leave me alone. Figured if she thought there was someone new, particularly someone who was her intellectual inferior, she'd stop trying to compete and finally move on."

A waitress approaches and she peers down at me. "I'm sorry, do I know you?"

Are you freaking kidding me? Here? Now?

She says, "You were at the Original Pancake House a couple of weekends ago. I'm Brandi, remember?"

I have a newfound appreciation for people who are friendly, so I enthusiastically reply, "Oh, right, you're the actress!"

Brandi laughs. "Mostly I'm the waitress. I have a handful of shit jobs and I work nights and weekends so I can have my days free for auditions. You do what you gotta do, right? Anyway, you ready to order?"

I've barely said, "Seb, you go ahead. I'm not that hungry," when Geri's stomach lets out an audible growl.

"Don't go all Reagan on me," Sebastian insists. "Give her

a Zookie the Bookie sandwich and a matzo-ball soup. I'll have the same."

"Be back with your balls," Brandi replies, spinning on her heel toward the kitchen.

I hope she's a better actress than she is a waitress, and I mean that in the nicest possible sense.

"It's so refreshing to be with you. Reagan would have never done that," he says. I notice he keeps checking out his reflection in the window glass. Definitely Smarmy, coming close enough to Cheesy's border that its prime minister has issued orders to shoot on sight.

"What, have a sandwich with roast beef?" Because I eat roast beef all the time now. Mary Mac makes this homemade horseradish sauce that is slap-and-go-naked good. Yes, she gives her kids Chomp-tastic on occasion, but only as a supplement on the days she's too busy to pack seven lunches with a toddler on her hip.

He snorts. "More like speak to the waitress as though she were an equal. Actually treat her like a human being. That's what I find so appealing about you, Geri. You don't bring all the baggage. You know how hard it was to extricate myself from that crazy bitch's life?"

Okay, that was harsh.

"Hey, that's my *sister* you're talking about."

"Do you deny that she's a pretentious head case?"

I cross my arms over my chest. "I wasn't aware that options traders were also mental health diagnosticians."

He taps a couple of sugar packets into his iced tea and tosses the empties into the window well. "Look, she was always bossy and controlling and self-important, but she went full-on stalker after we broke up. She kept running past my house and calling and texting. I felt sorry for her. I was embarrassed for her. Clearly she couldn't get over me."

I'm trying hard to maintain Geri's happy-go-lucky facade, so I force a laugh. "Heh, yeah. But I'm curious—what was up with the booty calls? Like, why would you *sleep* with her if you didn't want to *be* with her?"

He flexes his pathetic chest muscles under his dress shirt. "I have needs."

My smile doesn't reach my eyes, but I'm determined to appear chipper because I'm finally, after all these months, homing in on the truth. "Do you have any idea what kind of mixed message your behavior sent? Why didn't *you* leave *her* alone? She'd be to the point where she was almost over you and then you'd call and say you missed her. You'd hook up and she'd think you were reconciling. She may have been"—I hesitate to say this—"a tad high maintenance before the breakup, but you shoulder plenty of blame after the fact. Plenty."

Sebastian folds his napkin and places it on the table. "Geri, why do you care? She's always been entitled. Since when does *Dr.* Reagan Bishop appreciate a single thing anyone's ever done for her? Remember when your dad found her house before it went on the market and then lent her the cash for the down payment? She never even thanked him, even after he gutted three bathrooms and a kitchen in his off time."

I swallow hard. I thanked him. Of course I thanked him.

I couldn't not have thanked him, because that would make me a monster.

Shit.

I immediately make a mental note to buy my father the best Christmas present ever. Do sixtysomething men like ponies?

But that's not the end of cut-rate Keanu's diatribe. "My aunt used to work with your mom in the mayor's office. Did you know Maggie pulled all those strings to get Reagan into Taylor Park? And that's not all. Then your mom used her influence to funnel clients Reagan's way when she opened her practice. Ten bucks says Reagan never knew she had help. Twenty bucks says Reagan definitely never thanked your mom for anything."

No, I was admitted to Taylor Park because of my grades . . . wasn't I? I was a terrific student. Granted, there were ten thousand applicants for a hundred openings, but I surely earned my spot myself. I guess it didn't hurt that Ma was employed by the mayor, but she'd never take advantage of a situation like that.

Or did I have a perpetual leg up and I didn't even realize it?

Shit, again!

A cruise. That's it. I'll send Ma and Dad on a cruise. I have tons of savings, so I can totally do this for them. A nice one, too, Mediterranean, maybe, and not on the line that's perpetually losing power and ruining everyone's vacation with sewage running through the halls.

"Reagan is not a decent person. At all. That's why I don't care how things shook out with us. And you, most of all? Jesus, Geri, you just take her abuse. You let her pile it on. She's never had your best interests in mind, so I don't understand why you're always defending her."

Geri was always defending me? I had an inkling, but this is confirmation.

He tosses his hair again. What was wrong with me? Was I so desperate to not be alone that this was somehow attractive to me? Also, his obsession with volleyball? Since when did

I care about volleyball? Boyd conquered the mighty Pacific with sheer beauty, grace, and athleticism, whereas Sebastian batted around a puffy white ball like an enormous LOLcat. So not the same thing. Why was I willing to subjugate what I liked to accommodate him?

"You always put her first. Remember when I met you guys at that party for the mayor? I was interested in you but you insisted Reagan and I would be better suited. You said she'd been on her own for a while and you wanted to see her with a nice guy. You made us dance together and you're the one who put her contact info in my phone when I specifically requested yours. When I called? Thought I was reaching you."

This is certainly news to me. Numbly, I nod.

"I initially went out with her to get closer to you. When that didn't work out, I rolled with it. Didn't have anything better to do. Figured I'd take our relationship to its logical conclusion and then I'd circle back to you. Oh, thanks, babe." Sebastian glances up through his bangs at Brandi as she serves us our soup.

She raises an eyebrow at me, clearly disappointed that I'm dining with this joker rather than Kassel and his goofy quotes. Sebastian takes a rather slurpy sip, and it's all I can do to not jam the spoon into his trachea. "I'm psyched you're here, though. Those times I asked you out and you were all, 'We can only ever be friends.' Knew you'd come around, babe. They always do."

My rage begins to percolate. "Can I ask you something, Sebastian?"

He takes another slurp. "Sure, babe."

"Why are we here?"

"Existentially?"

"No, why *this* restaurant? Of all the dining establishments in this city, why'd you take me here to this deli? You're always Facebooking selfies at beautiful-people places like Carnivale and Japonais and MK. Why'd you bring me here and seat us by the freezing-cold window?"

I'm pretty sure of the answer, but I won't have the closure I require until I hear him say it.

He flips his hair again. "Reagan goes to the gym up the street. Figured it'd serve her right if she walked by and spotted us out together."

Suddenly, I'm very glad to have ordered the soup.

Because it gives me something to dump on him.

When I get home, I'm still stinging from Sebastian's admissions, but seeing him stunned and humbled, soup dripping from every strand of smarmy hair on his smarmy head with Brandi slow-clapping in the background, I finally feel that chapter in my life is over.

Perhaps I didn't handle our breakup well, but he definitely exacerbated the situation. I wasn't aware he was capable of such treachery and I'm relieved to know I wasn't crazy to think he was toying with my emotions.

In retrospect, I understand that Geri was genuine in her support and she wasn't just singing my praises to elevate her own profile. Here she had the perfect opportunity to screw me over with Sebastian and she continued to conduct herself entirely aboveboard. Were our positions reversed, I'd have never returned the favor, and that is my failing.

Sure, she used to tease me about the *Battle of the Network Stars*, and she'd occasionally bite back at me, but I'm realizing her good-natured ribbing came from a place of love, not scorn.

In this past week and a half, I've worked to give Geri the push that she needs to live a more successful life, yet the changes I've made have been on my terms, not hers. And I've screwed up the one thing that would make her happy, and now it's incumbent on me to fix it.

But before I can make a plan, there's a knock at my door. Earlier, I heard Trevor and Bryce coming in and out, so it's probably them. They're going to be thrilled to find (me inhabiting) Geri, so I put on my brightest smile and I open the door. Only it's not the boys—it's Deva.

She takes one look at me and says, "Sweet Goddess, Reagan Bishop, what have you done?"

CHAPTER TWENTY-TWO

That's Just Nuts

"What do you mean? I'm Geri, of course," I say, trying to play it off. I lean against the doorjamb as though to block her entry. She's clad in head-to-toe Eskimo gear. Her coat consists of a number of skins crudely pieced together, and I'm almost positive I smell whale blubber. I'm half tempted to check the street to see if she's substituted a dogsled for her Lambo.

Deva's not buying it and she's as mad as I've ever seen her. Considering I've never actually witnessed her getting angry, this is significant. She shakes a large index finger at me and points at the amulet around my neck. "Don't get precious with me, Reagan Bishop. I'd recognize your aura anywhere. Explain yourself."

"How was Thailand?" I hedge.

"The *Philippines* were lovely and I see what you're trying

to do. Stop it, Reagan Bishop. Now, let me in and tell me what fraud you're perpetrating."

I step aside and she marches in. She pushes past me and goes straight to my bedroom, throwing open the door to expose Geri resting comfortably inside my shell. "Aha!"

"Shh! Don't wake her! She's going to come to soon enough and I don't want to have to explain this."

"Do you know how many laws you're breaking right now, Reagan Bishop?" Deva fumes.

That stumps me because I actually did some research and there are no laws, per se, dealing with inhabiting another person's corporeal shell. "Actually, no, I checked. Technically, I'm not violating any laws."

"Then you're breaking every karmic law! Body swapping just so you can torture your sister is unacceptable and—"

I interrupt, "But I'm *not* torturing her. I'm actually trying to improve her life. Please, sit down with me; I promise I'll enlighten you about everything."

Deva and I head to the kitchen, where I explain the whole sordid tale while I begin to brew some decaf.

"You've accomplished quite a lot in the past few weeks, and I applaud your attempts at personal growth," Deva grudgingly admits. "The eating thing was starting to be a problem— I'm not going to lie and say it wasn't annoying. And that's coming from someone who has a spirulina smoothie for breakfast. I'm curious as to how you're going to explain the big gaps in Geri's memory."

"I'll tell her she had a weird Asian flu followed by a bad reaction to a Thanwell."

Deva is incredulous. "You expect her to believe she lost almost two weeks of memory, despite having lived her regular life every day, Reagan Bishop? Would she not then consult a physician about this mythological flu? Or have testing done in regard to the Thanwell?"

"My plan was not without flaws," I admit.

"This is what happens when you use the amulets for evil, even if you did eventually come around. Perhaps it's time that you leave the metaphysics to me, Reagan Bishop."

"I don't disagree." The kettle whistles and I take it off the stove. Then I measure freshly ground beans into the French press and add the boiling water. "This needs to sit for two minutes," I explain.

I place the carafe on a tray along with a couple of mugs, spoons, some napkins, and a small pitcher of milk. "Do you want sweetener? I may have some maple sugar here somewhere," I say, scanning my cabinet.

"I come prepared," she replies, rooting around in her enormous carpetbag for a couple of squeeze tubes of agave. "This is not my first rodeo at your house, Reagan Bishop."

When the coffee's ready, I push down on the plunger and then pour us both a cup. Deva swirls in her sweetener while I add a splash of milk.

"How do you anticipate righting the Kassel situation?" Deva asks. "What if you've cost her her position on the show?"

"I repeat, my plan was not without flaws," I say. "But I'm going to fix this. All I need to do is see Kassel in person. He doesn't go to LA for Christmas for another day. I'll show up, I'll tell him about the bizarro behavior-influencing Asian flu, and all will be well. He liked her enough in the beginning to overlook one unfortunate brunch. Trust me, he's into her. All she needs to do is apologize for hurting his feelings with the creeper comment. I'll say she had terrible PMS."

Deva simply raises an eyebrow at me in response.

"Fine, I won't say *that*. But I'll take care of the situation tomorrow, then I'll hop back in my own body, and when Geri wakes up tomorrow night, I'll explain how we discussed all the stuff about her business plan while she was under Thanwell's influence. It'll all be fine. Trust me." I blow on my coffee and take a sip. Perfect!

"What you're claiming is that there will be no lasting costs, Reagan Bishop?" she asks with furrowed brows.

I scratch my arm and neck. Note to self: Buy new lotion. What works on me may not be moisturizing enough for her. "Why are you so skeptical? Believe me, I'm on this. All is well. I learned my lesson and it's no harm, no foul."

My throat tickles a little, so I take another sip of my coffee.

"It's my experience that my powers can have unintended consequences when not used for good."

My coffee must be too hot because suddenly my lips are tingling. I rub them vigorously. Plus, the dry winter air must be getting to me because my whole back itches right now.

Deva explains, "Last year, I assisted an old classmate with righting some karmic wrongs via bending the time/space continuum and—are you okay, Reagan Bishop? Your face looks a bit full."

I'm about to crack a joke about Geri's face always being full, but then I remember that I vowed not to say anything else hurtful about her, even in jest.

See?

New leaf, totally.

"Have you any allergies, Reagan Bishop?" Deva asks, narrowing her eyes. "Is there a problem with coffee or are you sensitive to milk?"

I try to reply and I find that I'm struggling to draw a

breath. How could this be an allergy? *I'm* not allergic to anything.

I take another deep breath and I feel like I'm trying to suck air through a cocktail straw. The room begins to spin and my heart races.

I glance wildly around the room, my gaze falling on the carton of almond milk still on the counter. The last thought to pass my mind before I black out is, "I guess it really was her ham sandwich."

"You tried to murder me."

"No, definitely not, I would never do that, Geri. Truly, I have a whole new appreciation for you."

I'm sitting in the stiff plastic chair next to Geri's bed, resting a comforting hand on her knee. Thanks to Deva's quick thinking (and amulet removal) (and carpetbag containing an EpiPen), the visit to the emergency room has been more of a caution and less of a necessity. They're keeping her overnight for observation, though. Apparently you do not just treat and release Maggie Bishop's kid, no matter how long ago she retired from city government.

Geri bats my hand away. "Do you have any idea how effed up it is to wake up in the hospital and find out some psycho has been working me like a life-sized puppet for almost two weeks? Have you any clue how *wrong* that is?"

"Hey, how come you didn't swear just then?" I asked.

"*What?*"

"You said *eff* instead of dropping your usual f-bomb. I was curious as to why."

Geri is livid and there are spots of high color on her cheeks. Although that could be the adrenaline.

"What is wrong with you, Reagan? Like, what is your

damage? You almost frigging kill me and then you're concerned about my *word choice*? So typical. You take a situation that is entirely your fault and find a way to use it to criticize me. It's frigging ridiculous."

"There, you did it again with the *frigging.* That doesn't discount my actions, and make no mistake, I owe you, yet I'm truly curious as to your sudden curse aversion. My God, you were like a stevedore before with all the graphic profanity."

Geri uses the remote control to raise the back of her bed so she's in a sitting position. "What does this have to do with fighting bulls?"

"I believe you're confusing that term with *matador.* A stevedore is a longshoreman. A dockworker."

Geri fumes, "This? Right here? Is why no one likes you."

I nod. "I know, right? And *you* were the one who taught me that. I owe you a tremendous debt of gratitude. If I hadn't stepped into your life, I'd have never discovered what was wrong with mine."

Geri flashes me a look of contempt. "I'm so glad I could be of service. Not. Look at you—you're still so smug. God. You almost kill me and you act like you've somehow done *me* a favor by turning it into being about you. Again. As always. Well, guess what? I don't *need* your help. I was doing fine on my own. You want to do me a favor? Then just get away from me, Reagan. Exit my life. Go live your miserable existence and leave me alone." She turns her back to me.

"I'm sorry, Geri. You likely don't believe me and I don't blame you. I haven't been terribly kind to you in the past. You deserved two big sisters who were interested and invested in your life. Instead, I fought you constantly and I took delight in showing you up. I tried to steal your limelight at every opportunity. That's shitty and I apologize. But in living as you,

I've discovered how amazing you are. You're a wonderful aunt and the best sister Mary Mac could ask for. You're fantastic to Ma and Dad. Your clients love you and your styles are second to none. And your voice? OMG, you sing like an angel. Well, maybe an angel after a booze and smoke bender, and I mean that in the best possible sense."

Geri says nothing in response, so I continue. "I wasn't a good person, but maybe if I'm allowed to be your big sister now, I could figure out how to be better going forward. I'm sorry and I love you."

She remains silent.

Finally, I rise and start to take my leave. "Okay, I'm going. But don't worry about the Kassel stuff. I'm heading to his place because I want to come clean in person. He needs to know because I imagine he'll want to see you before he leaves for LA. So . . . I'll see you later?"

I'm to the door when I hear her say, "Kylie was picking up some bad language. I wanted to swear less because of her."

"Kylie's a little sponge when it comes to words and information, isn't she? And she's absolutely lethal when it comes to playing Candy Land. Of course, Kacey Irelyn hates Candy Land but she'll play Barbies like no one's business. If your plotline is compelling enough—especially if there are teen-aged vampires—Teagan will faux-reluctantly join in as well."

Geri turns back around to face me. "Hey . . . did you really help me lose six pounds?"

"I'm sorry about that. I was wrong to try to change you. You're perfect the way you are."

Geri lets out a ragged exhale. "I might possibly be okay with a few less pounds of perfection."

"I'd have lost more if it weren't for Mary Mac's spare-ribs."

"The best, right?" We smile at each other. "I'm still furious with you, though. Maybe slightly less so. You're going to have to make amends to me, Gip. Like a penance."

This is progress.

"Tell me when and where."

"I'm not sure whether I should fire you or give you your own show."

Kassel was highly confused when I showed up at his condo and even more so when I began my convoluted explanation. But he was so delighted to hear he hadn't blown it with Geri that he was willing to listen to everything I had to say.

"How about I resign? My contract is up for renewal; how about I just don't sign it? I feel like I've gotten so far away from the practice of mental health that I feel like the world's biggest fraud and I can't keep perpetrating the lies."

Maybe this is my penance.

To give up this job.

I won't be famous and I won't be rich.

But maybe I'll be happier, and that's a fine place to start.

"I still don't understand why you would go to such lengths with the guests," Kassel says.

"Are you kidding? 'Big, big, I need it big! I need flattened cats! I need bingeing and purging!' I felt like I had no choice," I explain.

"So you're saying it's *my* fault?"

"No, ultimately these were my decisions based on my unequivocal need to succeed at everything I do. I should have just failed and moved on."

Kassel considers what I've said. "Maybe your resignation is fortuitous, because we're making some changes to the show."

"Like what?"

Kassel opens the briefcase sitting on the coffee table and begins to rifle through a stack of papers. "Looks like test audiences are tiring of the big, emotional climaxes. They don't want flattened cats; now they want more of a game-show element. More slime pits. They seem to connect with people being bashed with large, foam-covered reticulating arms. I'm meeting with the network while I'm out there with Walt to determine exactly what happens next. *I Need a Push* may end up a literal statement."

"You're going to make guests eat bugs, aren't you?"

He gestures toward the mantel. "My six Emmys point to yes."

"What do you suggest I do with the guests like the equestrian and the guy who was afraid to fly? Do I contact them? Do I offer my services free of charge?"

Kassel shrugs. "Listen, Peace Corps, they understood that what we were doing was for entertainment purposes. Haven't you ever read the fine print in the credits? They received both personal and home makeovers, quite a bit of compensation, and in some cases, Ford F-150s. Plus, DBS is paying for follow-up therapy to anyone who wants it. *I Need a Push* was never about mental health; it was about putting on a show. Mission accomplished."

"Then why do I feel like this is such a loose thread?"

"Maybe you *feel* too much, Peace Corps. Besides, I've been in touch with a few of the guests. Sandy the equestrian's back in the training ring and Clark from the helicopter episode flew commercially for the first time over Thanksgiving. He wrote to thank me. Sent me a selfie holding up an airline soda and a bag of nuts. He was sweatin' like a son of a bitch, but he was there with his seat back and tray table in the upright position. I guess thinking they'd succeeded was tantamount to actual success."

"You're kidding. That's so gratifying to hear."

"'Member the systems analyst? Bernie's determined to try to hit a Blackhawks game with me. Nice guy, but I wonder if he's gay. Kept looking at my junk at the Bears game. Not gonna lie—it was a little weird. Oh, wait—that was *you*. Huh. Still weird."

I can't help but blush at the memory, even though any interest I might have had in Kassel has since dissipated. I really hope he and Geri get it right because I like the idea of sharing the children's table with him at our next major family holiday.

That is, if anyone in my family's still talking to me.

"If you're done with *Push*, what's next for you, Peace Corps?"

"Therapy."

"Going back to private practice?"

"No, I mean as an actual patient."

"Well, I understand your compulsion to succeed on the job, but wearing your sibling around like a winter coat? That's . . ." He trails off.

"Twisted?"

He smiles. "Yeah. You're one twisted sister."

CHAPTER TWENTY-THREE

Groundswell

I'm alone in my apartment when there's a knock at the door.

"Yo-ho-ho!" I hear from the hallway.

I open the door and Bryce and Trevor shuffle in wearing Santa hats and carrying presents. "Hey, boys! What are you both still doing in town? I thought you'd be on your way to Philly by now."

Trevor says, "Driving to Nana's in St. Louis tomorrow and Bryce is coming with. My family's gonna be there."

"You're not heading home for Christmas?" I ask.

Bryce shakes his head, causing his Santa hat to slide to the side. "I was already there for Hanukkah. I'm a member of the tribe, son! Festival of lights! Eight crazy nights! Shalom, playa!"

"After St. Louis, we're doing Aspen for New Year's," Trevor adds.

"I likes my powder fresh," Bryce confirms.

"Nice. I thought you'd left because you guys haven't been home, so now I have a chance to give you these." I hand them two wrapped packages. Bryce rips open the paper to reveal premeasured, ready-to-hang curtains.

I explain, "The rods are already up, so these will just slide on."

"These drapes, dog?" Bryce asks. "'Cause that is *off the chain*! Ready to get my privacy on, son! You wants to see my bone chones, you gots to pay a dolla!" He high-fives both Trevor and me. This was actually the more utilitarian gift of the two, so I'm delighted at their enthusiasm.

Trevor opens his gift to find a large casserole pan. "That requires some explanation," I tell him. "Anytime you want me to fill this with a casserole, you bring it up here, okay?"

"You could make us something anytime we want?" Trevor asks, incredulously. "Like, dinner? Like, even once a week?"

I nod. I wanted to do something nice for the boys, but I also have quite a bit of time on my hands right now, so I figured the best gift I could give would be that of myself.

Trevor looks from the pan to me back to the pan, almost overwhelmed with the bounty of it all. "Will you use cream of mushroom soup and spaghettis and canned tuna?"

"If that's what you want."

There is cheering and chest bumping and a good bit of dancing. Who knew "spaghettis" could cause such a reaction?

Bryce nudges Trevor. "Hey, playa, give her ours."

Proudly, Trevor hands me his gift. I gingerly open the newspaper-wrapped present, without once questioning if they actually read the paper first. I saw my new therapist for the first time today and we discussed how my constant judgment of others has been an unhealthy pattern.

I open the box to find a sturdy mug boasting a picture of Trevor with his thumbs up and the caption "World's Best Landlord." Bryce hands me his, too, and I find the same thing inside, only this one has a photo of Bryce.

I'm surprised at how touched I am by their gesture. I love that they put thought into their gifts and how they're going to make me laugh every single time I drink a hot beverage.

Bryce explains, "Now you gots a set for your friends and shit."

Although I'm not entirely sure if anyone whom I don't pay is speaking to me right now, I assume at some point there will be people in my life again and I will have them over for coffee.

Everyone in the family is waiting to follow Geri's lead since she's the injured party. My Christmas dinner plans are on hold until I can determine how I'll be received. Of course they all heard what happened. You can't keep masquerading as your sister/sending your little sister into anaphylactic shock a secret, at least not in the Bishop household. And Deva said she needed space but promised to revisit our friendship when she's back from Aspen.

"Wait, are you seeing Deva in Aspen?" I ask them.

"Stayin' in the guest room, playa!" Bryce exclaims.

"She's getting 'World's Best Hostess' mugs," Trevor admits.

I tell him, "She'll cherish them," without a hint of insincerity.

I bid the boys good-bye and return to my task at hand. My new therapist believes I need to process the events that led me here, so she's given me an assignment. But before I can even begin, there's a knock at the door again.

I'm laughing as I open up. "You guys want a casserole already?" But it's not Bryce and Trevor standing there; it's Geri and Mary Mac.

"We're coming in," Mary Mac announces. She's carrying a grocery bag that clinks as she moves. She wanders back to my kitchen while Geri stands in front of me with her arms crossed.

She eyes me for a full minute. "I've decided to forgive you," she tells me. "But you have to do one thing for me."

"You're seriously going to forgive me?" I ask, voice wavering. "This truly is a Christmas miracle! Anything! You tell me anything and I'll do it!"

"Let me style your damn hair already. This Wonder Woman thing you have going on? I'm over it. Get a chair and meet me in your bathroom."

I peel off my sweater and pull on a T-shirt; then I grab the chair from my desk and drag it into the master bath. In the time it takes me to change, Mary Mac's put something delicious smelling in the oven, while banging around preparing appetizers.

Geri's already in the bathroom with her scissors, lotions, and potions, as well as two glasses of wine. She hands one to me.

"Bitch," she says.

"I know," I admit, eyes cast down.

"No, silly, Bitch wine. I told you, I'm good. I thought about everything and I'm over it. You and I are starting again. We're officially Kool and the Gang." She begins to run her hands through my mane and asks, "What are you thinking? I have a few ideas in mind, but I want to hear what'd make you happy."

"What about long layers?" I ask.

"Sounds good," she replies, holding her scissors and gathering my hair into a low ponytail.

Then, before I even realize what's happening, she lops off one solid foot at the elastic band.

"What are you doing?" I shriek.

Oh, my God!

My hair! My gorgeous hair!

"Do you know how long I've been growing this? What, I mean, how, I mean *what the f—*"

"Huh," Geri says, holding up my tail for inspection. The long strands glint under the harsh light of the bathroom. "What do you know? I guess I *was* still mad at you." As I'm about to shout like no one has shouted before, I catch a glimpse of her grinning in the mirror. "We're going to be okay, you and me."

If losing my hair means being on solid ground with my family, then this is a small price to pay indeed. "Then . . . I guess it's worth it," I finally reply.

Geri tucks my ponytail into a plastic bag and shoves it in her purse. "I'm keeping this, though."

"To the victor go the spoils," I reply.

She nods. "Besides," Geri says, "you're gonna look like sex on a stick when I'm done with you, and you'll never miss all this bulk." She then proceeds to give me Julianne Hough's rough-cut bob and, for good measure, weaves in a few coppery-colored highlights, taking me from "stern librarian" to "total beach babe." I can't stop touching my hair and admiring how freely it swings. I still look like me, only a better version.

"I'll be damned if I'm not actually sex on a stick now," I say.

"Never doubt me," Geri says.

"Doubt you?" I cry. "Damn, I'm ready to invest in you. Seriously, if you need a cash infusion for your business, you talk to me. I have decent savings and I really believe you can make something of your own salon."

"Let's talk about that in the new year," Geri says. "Now we eat."

We exit to the living room, where Mary Mac's set up a buffet of all her best dishes. I begin to salivate the second I catch a whiff of her spareribs.

"What are you doing for New Year's Eve?" Mary Mac asks.

"Um . . . no plans," I reply.

She nods. "Well, you have plans now. You're going to stay with my children while Mickey and I spend the night at the Palmer House. Bring earplugs, you'll need them."

I begin to fill my plate. "Any other surprises you two have planned?"

They exchange a glance and then say, "No," in unison, like there's something they don't want me to know.

I sense they still don't trust me.

But they do love me.

So there's that.

Christmas passes without incident (unless you count Aunt Helen's Jell-O salad as an incident), and I make it through New Year's Eve with flying colors. However, the stress of the last six months—or my blatant refusal to get a flu shot—must have finally taken its toll, because I spent the first two weeks of the new year flat on my back, and not in the sexy way.

Really, it was more of a couch-bed, in-and-out-of-consciousness, catch-up-on-the-*Housewives* way, only this time I had Mary Mac to bring me matzo-ball soup.

(Do not even start me on what that woman does to matzo-ball soup. Bottle it, sell it, share it with the world, in the name of all that is good and holy.)

I don't fully have my strength up until the third week of

the month, so I'm only now truly beginning to work on my project for my therapist. I need a change of scenery from my apartment, so I head to Whole Foods and grab a table overlooking the river in the upstairs dining loft. No one recognizes me now with my new cut and color, and that's actually a welcome change. I'm done being semi-famous.

I stir honey into my tea and then open my laptop. My therapist advised that I write down everything that's transpired, so I start at the beginning.

Do I know you? I type, and then I can't help but smile.

Maybe it's only a single line so far, but it's the first step in a new and improved life.

I'm not sure what's going to happen next for me, and that's truly refreshing. I've had every moment of every day plotted out since I was sixteen. I always feared the loss of control, but I realize now that my greatest failing was in not loosening up.

The well-appointed woman peers at me over her Whole Foods shopping cart, brimming with free-range chicken, organic fruit, and glass-bottled Kombucha.

I may not be proud of everything I've done after I finish writing this story, but I absolutely believe it's the necessary, most cathartic next step. Geri insists I should try to get published, but maybe I should write more than the first two lines before I shop for an agent.

I close my eyes and try to remember what happened that first day when someone jostles my table.

"Here's what I've figured out—Geri's going to stay at your place and she promises she'll keep up with Trevor and Bryce's casseroles while we're away. Oh, and I finally found your passport in your underwear drawer. Which is a major bonus, because it's not exactly like you can board an international flight without one."

My eyes fly open. "I'm sorry, I think you—" Then I realize I recognize not only the names of all parties involved, and the voice, but also the face.

The most handsome face I've ever seen, with kind robin's egg blue eyes and tawny hair and the most magnificent tan.

"Boyd?"

My heart immediately begins to hammer out of my chest. "Boyd, what are you doing here?"

He points at his tray laden with salad bar items. "Meeting you for lunch? I'm a little early, but I finished at the travel agency so I figured you might like the company." He glances down again. "Shoot, I meant to grab a Kombucha. Be right back, Ray."

Then Boyd kisses me on the crown of my head before he saunters away from our table and lopes down the stairs to the beverage coolers. I immediately grab my phone and dial Geri, but it goes to voice mail and the same happens with Deva.

I need answers and I need them fast, so I type Boyd's full name into a search engine. The first hit is a news article about how the Rip Curl surf company in Queensland, Australia, has signed professional surfer Boyd to represent their brand and he's due down there for a press conference.

I guess he's not just a bartender anymore.

But how did he end up here?

With me?

Making travel plans?

I mean, Boyd doesn't need to be anything but a bartender—I realize that now. And I believe that once I finish figuring myself out, I'd have gone back for him. Yet somehow, someone decided to speed up my own personal timeline.

But who and how and why?

An employee rushes past so quickly rolling a garbage can that it creates a breeze on the back of my neck.

Oh, my *ponytail*.

Geri must have taken my ponytail to Deva and perpetrated one of the more complicated methods of swapping with me. I wondered why Deva had been avoiding me. I'd thought we were cool when we were in the emergency room with Geri, but then she was all weird a day later, claiming she needed space.

Deva didn't require "space"; she simply couldn't keep a secret.

When I count my blessings, Deva's at the top of the list. She's the first woman friend who ever liked me in spite of all my terrible qualities. She saw the potential of the person I could be and she stuck with me. I so look forward to showing her exactly how good a friend I can be.

Astral projection would account for all the time I was out for the past few weeks when I thought I was sick. But why would anyone want to body swap with *me*?

I quickly group text both Geri and Deva: Did you do this??

Deva replies first:

Pack your nun-screen, Regal Beagle—Austria is hat!

And from Geri . . . my sister *and* my friend, who is wise in ways I never thought possible:

Sometimes we all need a push.

ACKNOWLEDGMENTS

For all my readers, I'm forever in your debt. Thank you for continued support, especially those of you who've been there since the first iteration of Jennsylvania. Please know how hard you rock. Every time I see your happy faces at an event, I can't get over how lucky I am to have this job. You are truly the best!

A million thanks go to my editor, Tracy Bernstein, for continuing to push me. I'm better at what I do because of your guidance. As always, heartfelt thanks go to Kara Welsh and Claire Zion for letting me do my thing and never once saying, "Time travel? Body swapping? Are you sure?" Ham-handed high fives from Deva and me. For Craig Burke and Melissa Broder, thank you for your tireless efforts! Sales, Marketing, and Production, you are my Dream Team, and Mimi Bark, just when I think you can't possibly do a more fantastic cover, BAM. Here you go again.

For Scott Miller, Super Agent, you, you're very good. (And thanks for keeping everyone calm when I broke the news about my new three-wheeled bike.) For Tiffany Ward and Jon Cassir of CAA, I send the kindest regards.

ACKNOWLEDGMENTS

I'd be nowhere without my family of choice—Joanna, Atlanta Julia, Stacey, Gina, Karyn, and Tracey. The world is better—and so much more fun—because of y'all. (See, Julia? I totally speak Southern.)

Huge thanks for my literary sisters Beth Harbison and Sarah Pekkanen for your advice and guidance, and for the Perpetual Awesome that is Emily Giffin, Jennifer Weiner, and Lisa Lampanelli. And big kisses to early readers Benjamin Kissell, Lisa De Pasquale, and Alyson Ray. XOXO!

For Christine Weiler, M.A., L.P.C., thank you for all your insight into Cognitive and Behavioral Therapy. Any mistakes in this book are mine. (Which clearly would be the case anyway, but I still wanted to get that on record.)

Finally, for Fletch, for everything, but especially for not giving me *too* much grief over the three-wheeled bike. Love you.

And I also love my ginormous cherry red adult tricycle.

(But that's part of my charm, yes?)